An
Honest
Lie

Open Heart
Publishing

ISBN:978-0-578-06925-8

i

Salvador Dali ~ One day it will have to be officially admitted that what we have christened reality is an even greater illusion than the world of dreams.

Friedrich von Schlegel ~ The most insignificant authors have at least this similarity to the Author of the Heavens and the Earth: that after a days work is done, they have a habit of saying to themselves, "And behold, what he made was good."

Mary Caroline Richards ~ Let no one be deluded that a knowledge of the path can substitute for putting one foot in front of the other.

Kelly Jacobi

Cover/Illustrations

Eric Trant

Alumnus

Terry Sanville

iii

Rob Rosen

Raleigh Dugal

Patrick
Scalisi

Jessica Stilling

Claire Ibarra

C. B. Calsing

Alumnus

v

Jess Dunn

Bob Clark
Alumnus

William Walton

Dennis
Thompson

Cynthia
Witherspoon

Staff

Debrin Case
Publisher

M.E. Johnson
Sr. Editor

Davin Kimble
Jr. Editor

Erin M. Russell
Jr. Editor/ retired

Table of Contents

Every year "**An Honest Lie**" showcases new authors who are vying for the opportunity to earn a book contract with **Open Heart Publishing**, and that is where your assistance is required.

By visting the voting portal you can vote for them via the ongoing poll, which counts for one vote, or if you are serious about helping your favorite author win this opportunity you could increase their chances by either purchasing a copy of the book or other associated merchandise.

Visit the voting portal today at
Http://ahlvol2vote.debrincase.com

So vote today, vote often, and encourage others to vote for your favorite authors.

One Small Step

Eric Trant

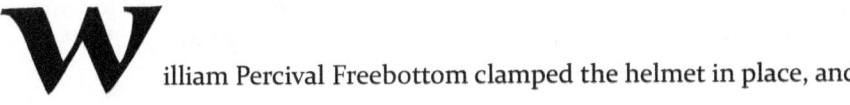

William Percival Freebottom clamped the helmet in place, and then began the process of snapping the thick leather gloves onto the end of his thick leather sleeves. He was almost ready.

"We have company tonight, Percy," his wife said to him. "Can't you wait until tomorrow night?"

From behind the half-dome of glass, Percy shook his head back and forth. "Not tonight, Martha. Tonight's a full moon on the winter solstice. I think maybe there's something in the season that makes my walks easier."

Martha waved her hands at him. She always waved her hands at him, adding a roll of her eyes. Percy loved his wife, his beautiful Martha Marie, the only woman in this solar system who'd tolerate such an outrageous man.

Her deep, Martian green eyes rolled up to the ceiling and then blinked at Percy. Martha flicked her wrist again, shooing him. "All right, all right. Fine, baby. I'll finish the bratwursts, and Lucy and Jeff and I can play three-handed until you're done. Just don't be long, okay."

"An hour this time. No more than an hour, I promise."

But Martha was already down the hall, headed back to the table to entertain their friends. Percy doubted she'd heard much of his promise through the dull enclosure of his helmet.

They'd been playing Euchre when Percy had excused himself. He'd put the brats on the burner to boil, added half a bottle of Shiner Bock beer to the mix, and then drank the remaining half as he walked to his bedroom and began the complicated task of suiting up alone for his space walk. Usually Martha helped him, but tonight she'd shooed him off and said, "Do it yourself, baby." She blew him a kiss and smiled and took another drink from her wine and shuffled the cards.

Martha didn't mean to disregard Percy, not really. On the nights when they were alone, on those other magical full moon evenings, Martha would help Percy shrug on the NASA space suit, pull on the boots, fit the helmet and the gloves into place and help him check the gauges and, most importantly, charge the oxygen tank.

During the rest of the month, the space suit stood on a mannequin rack in the corner of their bedroom, next to a tall blue oxygen canister. How many other women would put up with him? Not many, Percy thought. Not many at all.

Percy walked down the hallway. The heavy boots clumped on the wooden floor. He angled himself through the kitchen, pausing to lean over the brats. He couldn't smell them now that he was suited up. The oxygen had already purged the suit, and the most over-powering smell was that of leather and plastic tubing, a dry sort of odor that reminded Percy of a shoe store. But the bratwursts looked good. They were boiling up nicely. The steam fogged the half-dome space helmet.

Percy backed away from the stove, careful to keep his backpack from hitting any of the kitchen wares.

"Hi, Jeff, Lucy." Percy lifted his hand in an awkward wave.

Jeff and Lucy waved up at Percy from the breakfast table, each holding a handful of playing cards. Jeff said, "Don't leave me in here too long with these girls, partner! They'll tear me up."

"You look fabulous," Lucy said, "That's a real suit, right?"

Percy nodded. What other woman but Martha would let Percy buy an outright, fully-fitted NASA space suit? The suit was real, all right.

"May I touch it?" Lucy said.

"Sure." Percy held out his hand and Lucy felt the glove, squeezed the thick fingertips, and ran a finger up his sleeve.

"Is that leather?" she asked.

"Yes, ma'am. Cows are the toughest thing from here to the moon." Percy raised his voice so they could hear him above the muting of the helmet's airlock. A few specs of spittle decorated the bottom half of his visor.

"Neat," Lucy said.

"You're gonna have to let me suit up one day," Jeff said. "That looks cool as heck."

"We can snap you in later, if you want. But for now, I gotta get going. I'll come back in once I'm finished. Wish me luck!"

"Good luck!" they all said.

"Be careful, baby," Martha said. "I'll come check on you in about an hour."

4

"Love you," Percy said to her.

Martha leaned back in her chair and opened the patio door for Percy. Percy walked through the door, and she closed it behind him.

Percy could hear them laughing, toasting, drinking their wine and their beer as they dealt out the rest of the Euchre hand. Their voices were dampened by the door and the helmet.

"Your husband's insane!" Percy heard Lucy say.

They laughed. Percy didn't have to look back to see Martha nodding her head in agreement and laughing with them. "He's my Percy-baby." That's what Martha said, even though Percy couldn't hear her say it. The walls and the helmet were too thick for her soft voice to penetrate, but that's what she'd said all right. That's what she always said, and then she'd run her fingers through her hair, tighten her pony tail, and keep dealing the cards.

I'm her Percy-baby.

Percy's back yard spanned a dozen acres in every direction. Two trucks were parked out front, beside a Toyota Camry, in front of a raised porch. Trees spotted the acres, and farther back ran the treeline and the creek. All around him stretched barbed wire, barns, penned hogs, and lazy cattle dozing the full moon away.

All above him stretched the brilliant galaxy, God's polka-dot network of connect-the-dot puzzles. The nearest celestial object, of course, was the moon. Percy often wondered if man would ever have ventured into space if not for the moon. What good would it have done? Why go into the black nothingness, only to come back?

But God put the moon there for man to wonder at, to ponder in the long nights before television, to tease man into exploring space. The moon was the first dot in God's connect-the-dot universe.

Percy dragged his lawn chair into the middle of the yard. The lawn chair was one of those lay-down sorts, the kind women used for sunbathing. Nobody sunbathed in this chair. The only use it got was moon bathing once per month, on the night of the fullest moon, with Percy and his NASA-issued space suit.

Percy checked the chair's position against the moon, gauging how the moon would pass over the next two hours. Tonight the moon was full, bright and inviting, not a cloud in the sky. The night stretched from horizon to horizon in all directions.

Percy lowered himself into the chair, careful not to tip it over and spill himself onto the grass.

"Oh, yeah," he said. "Tonight's a good night. Tonight's a real good night."

The first time Percy flew into space was when he was a child. He hadn't meant to, but it had happened nonetheless. So many brilliant things in this world are accidents.

Percy lay on the trampoline in his back yard, alone in his sleeping bag, staring up at the moon. He was eight. The dogs huddled beneath the trampoline, and in the distance, Percy heard the coyotes howling at the full moon.

It was winter solstice, the longest night of the year, and the temperature was well below freezing, almost in the teens. Percy huddled inside his sleeping bag and watched his breath form a cloud above his head.

The moon looked close enough to touch. The stars were brilliant white specks on black. A haloed rainbow framed the moon.

Percy stared from inside his sleeping bag. He imagined he could touch the moon, that it was here, on his fingertips, beneath him and not above him, and that he was falling toward outer space. Percy felt himself fall a few feet, and then he bolted upright on the trampoline.

He looked around. He hadn't moved, but the sensation of falling had certainly registered in Percy's eight year-old brain. He had felt the fall.

Percy pulled the sleeping bag tighter around him. The crisp air chafed his nose and throat. The coyotes sounded closer, but they always sounded closer the longer he listened. So far, the dogs beneath Percy had not stirred.

Percy lay back down and looked up at the moon again, and let himself slip into that same state of disbelief, where the moon was below him, where gravity was upside-down and instead of pulling him, gravity pushed him. He imagined the world leaning sideways and pouring him into space. Percy was a fish inside a glass off water, tilting toward the moon, falling, feeling the push of gravity on his back.

And he fell. Percy fell and fell and fell. He fell upward and the moon grew larger. Percy heard the rush of air past his ears as he was thrust downward, or upward, however he thought of it, but thrust toward the moon, toward God's first dot.

Percy kept his eyes on the moon with pinpoint vision. He found a dark spot and focused there, watching it grow larger as he fell through the sky, through the stratosphere, and into the outer reaches of Earth's atmosphere. Percy pulled the sleeping bag tighter around him as the air thinned. He felt the heat sucked out of him, and his nose and cheeks ached with a deep and immediate frost. Percy's eyes burned from lack of blinking.

Then, he realized he couldn't breathe. The air had thinned to a nothingness. Percy's head grew heavy. Thick blackness began to close in on Percy, and that's when he panicked. He lost sight of the moon, began to thrash, and he felt the sudden and irresistible tug of gravity on his back.

Percy fell again, but this time toward the Earth, toward the dirt and the center of our spinning rock. He fell away from the moon, feeling the rush of air reverse itself and whip against his back. After a few seconds of free-fall, Percy's lungs found oxygen, and his head began to chase away the deoxygenated darkness. He fell and fell, until finally he was back on the trampoline, wrapped in his sleeping bag, looking up at the moon.

His mother scolded him for staying out so long that his nose nearly got frostbite. His father laughed and said, "That's just Percy."

The dogs beneath the trampoline never stirred.

Percy turned forty this year. His beautiful wife Martha had grown more beautiful with age. The fact that she supported Percy's monthly habit thickened his affection for her, in the same way constant stirring thickened sauce. Month after month she helped Percy seat himself in his lawn chair, stirring his heart.

Tonight, though, Percy lowered himself alone into the lawn chair. No Martha out here. She was inside, laughing and drinking and dealing cards with their friends. Tonight she wouldn't watch over him while he tried yet again to fling himself off the Earth.

Percy lay there, looking up at the night moon. "There must be something about the gravitational pull," he said, whispering. The words dissolved against the glass visor.

"Like the lunar tides, the gravity, the pull. There's a wave of energy, I can feel it. I just have to find it again and ride it up. It's a slide on a playground, off we go."

Percy shifted his weight, getting comfortable in the lawn chair. He cracked his back, which was tight with age, and with hauling box after box of

Martha's Christmas gear down from the attic.

"I can feel it. I just have to catch it."

Percy settled in, clearing his mind the way he always did. He breathed deep, closed his eyes for a few breaths, and then opened them and stared at the moon, unblinking.

"Coyotes," he whispered, repeating his monthly mantra. His breath sucked out of the helmet and cycled itself through the ventilation system. "Trampoline. Dogs beneath. Full moon. Rainbow moon. Winter Solstice. Falling. Men have been doing this for thousands of years, falling to the moon, lassoing the moon, pulling it to them, but they never made it. They died in their sleep. They died in space, the way I almost died. Suffocated. Frozen. People called them lunatics. Lunatic. I am a lunatic, a man made crazy by the moon."

The moon possessed the same rainbow halo as it had on the night he'd drifted off his trampoline all those years ago. Percy wasn't sure if the discolorations around the moon had anything to do with the event he'd discovered, but he was certain that the timing had not been random. It couldn't be random. There must be something to the way the moon and the Earth interacted in their mutual orbits.

Percy's mind pondered the scientific aspects of flying to the moon, trying to ignore modern science and see something larger and more powerful than simple physics, and he didn't feel any movement at first, but the moon began to grow larger in his eyes. His peripheral vision caught only dark night sky, no longer picking up the angles of the garage and the barn; just nothing but blackness on either side of Percy.

He heard more than felt the whipping of the wind against the space suit.

The night sky was clear. No clouds marked Percy's passing. The wind whipping against the suit could have been a breeze. He could have been stationary, laying in the lawn chair facing upward. The world around Percy didn't seem to move, or suck him forward or thrust him ahead. He ignored the disorientation that resulted from lack of landmarks and instead found the dark spot on the moon he'd seen all those years ago.

Percy marked the moon's size against the lower ring of his helmet visor, and using his peripheral vision noted that the moon was in fact growing larger, slow as a minute hand, until the edge of the moon touched and then crossed the lower edge of his helmet.

Percy stared at the moon. He slid toward it. He felt his heart rate increase, but controlled his breathing. He couldn't panic this time. He wouldn't. This might happen only once every few decades. He might be dead the next time the moon and the Earth aligned just so.

Percy noticed the wind stopped whipping against the suit and that he seemed to be approaching the moon at a much faster rate than he had a moment before. Even through the thick suit, he felt the cold pinch of space grip him.

He should have been weightless, but he didn't feel weightless. Percy wasn't sure what should happen in weightlessness, whether his lungs or stomach would somehow feel lighter, but he didn't feel much different than he had laying in the lawn chair.

Percy picked out a dark spot on the moon and focused his mind and eyes on that single patch of black. It was near the top of the moon, up where the lunar poles were located; a place where nobody on Earth could possibly see.

He monitored the approaching moon, figuring how soon he'd reach his destination. He kept his eye and mind on the moon, on the dark spot, and ticked off the seconds as he raced toward it. One Mississippi, two Mississippi, three Mississippi...

When Percy reached sixty, a quick calculation suggested the moon might be close to an hour away, maybe more.

Percy marked the moon's location against the reference of his lower visor, and whispered the seconds again, verifying his count. One Mississippi, two Mississippi, three Mississippi...

He reached the same calculation. The moon was definitely an hour away, maybe more.

"And I have two hours of oxygen," Percy said. The overwhelming silence of space answered him. All he heard was his own breathing, and the gentle chuff of the suit's ventilation system.

Unless he measured the moon against his visor, Percy had no sensation of movement. He could have been floating there, stalled, stopped and lost in the empty darkness and burning up what little oxygen he'd carried with him.

Percy risked a glance at the large watch on his left arm. It had ticked off twenty minutes. "One-hundred minutes left, give or take. Hopefully it's give."

Percy Freebottom's first words on the moon were these: "Dark as a witch's pit, ain't it."

He'd arrived on the dark side of the moon, atop the lunar pole, and he wasn't sure how long he had before sunrise, or if the sun even rose from this angle. For all the time he'd spent trying to get to the moon, he'd spent surprisingly little time actually studying the moon. What mankind already knew about the moon didn't seem relevant to Percy. He'd discovered something science had overlooked, and so why bother with what science already thought they knew.

But the science clicked in his head anyway, unrelenting. He spoke into his visor, echoing the words back to his ears against the plugged silence of the black-and-gray otherworld surrounding him. "You know, a compass doesn't work on Earth's poles, so maybe there's something about the lunar poles that makes them special. Maybe that's it, like the Northern Lights, the Auroras or whatever they're called. Or a solar wind, perhaps. Who knows, but, well..."

Percy kicked the moon's powdered surface. He couldn't see beyond what his headlamp illuminated, but the ground looked as if it had been covered by volcanic ash. A plume rose above the toe of his boot and in slow motion blossomed and spread and settled back to the ground. He knelt and dug his finger through the ash, or soot, or dust, or whatever scientists called this stuff. Powdered mineralites, perhaps.

With slotted boot prints, Percy stomped out the shape of a heart in the sand. He decided "sand" was as good a term as any. That's what they called it when he was a kid, Moon Sand. He stepped off the size of the heart to be about twice his height, knelt inside it, and dragged his finger through the moon sand, writing, "Percy loves Martha." The darkness swallowed it whole when he walked away.

He tried not to think of Martha, but he did. He wondered if she had already come out to check on him. He wondered if his body was still in the chair, severed from this consciousness, or if he'd literally been transported to the moon, body and suit and all. What would Lucy and Jeff say about the lunatic Percy, and would it even matter?

"Hard to celebrate your own death," Percy whispered. "I doubt Neil would've stepped on the moon, if he'd known he wouldn't see a thing, and the sight would kill him. I doubt if any of them would have come up here."

He'd watched the first hour slide past him on his watch. After the first glance at his watch, Percy realized he had reached some sort of point-of-no-return. Maybe he'd crossed a threshold, or peak, and had been on some sort of energetic downslope. Even if he'd had oxygen enough for twenty years, he wasn't sure he'd be able to get back to Earth.

"Not now," he said. "Not ever. It's a one-way trip for Percy baby."

From here, Percy couldn't even see the Earth, and likewise, the Earth couldn't see him. The irony wasn't lost on him, and despite what he knew was coming, he had to laugh. The Americas had been populated for thousands of years before Columbus discovered them. The Vikings had sailed there centuries before Columbus. Yet when Columbus landed and planted a flag, he got credit for discovering an unknown continent.

Now Percy was the lunar version of the Native American, the Inca and the Maya and the Viking warriors. He was the first here, the first to discover a shipless means of space travel, and later, if anyone ever identified and named the phenomena that brought Percy to the moon, they'd name it after themselves, and Percy would be nowhere in the credits.

"Yeah, well, we'll see about that," Percy said to his visor.

Percy drew something else in the moon sand, stomping it out in huge letters with his boots, the words so large that when he finished and surveyed his work, the headlamp barely illuminated beyond the final word. He added an exclamation point the size of a school bus.

Finished, he lay there next to the exclamation point, his back against the moon as he stared into the silence and waited for his oxygen to deplete. The stars and the infinite darkness between them had never looked so crisp, so sharp. To his left and right, and above and below him was the pitch emptiness of the dark side of the moon. Every few seconds, his oxygen tank chuffed, "Hmph."

Percy switched off the space suit's headlamp. "Save the battery pack," something said in his head. "Save it for what?" something answered.

In the end, it didn't matter. As Percy lay in the darkness, watching the stars stare at him, he felt the sensation of movement, though there was no reference for him to gauge its passing. He pushed his elbows back and no longer felt the moon beneath him.

Inside the helmet, Percy could just turn his head enough to see that the moon and his giant letters that were now far, far behind him, fast becoming a pinch of dust with the Earth and Martha fading to a bright light, and then blinking into nothingness. Whatever interstellar wind he'd caught this time was tornadic compared to the gentle breeze he'd ridden up from Earth.

Max burst into Tong's office, looked right, looked left, as if he were checking for someone else inside the eight-by-eight cubicle, and then slammed the office door closed and threw down a set of the latest mini SAR snapshots. "What the heck, Tong. Look at this!"

"Calm down," Tong said. He'd been reading the latest news on China Daily, getting the Asian scoop on Obama's Cairo speech to the Muslims. Tong had learned it was best not to trust any media to cover its own leaders, and so he made a habit of cross-referencing not only US news sources, one against the other, but he also checked China Daily and Xinhua, making sure he could balance one slant against the other. Somewhere in his internet bookmarks, Tong had a couple of Islamic websites he would check later, after he'd addressed whatever it was Max Fuchs felt was so urgent.

"Sit," Tong said. He motioned for Max to sit in one of the office chairs. Except for a small window next to the door, the office was an enclosed box, with no view to the outside world. "What is it, Max?"

Max didn't sit. Instead, he ran his fingers through his thinning blonde hair and then stabbed his finger into the stack of pictures on Tong's desk.

"Look!" Max dug out one of the pictures and held it up for Tong to see. "Look at this, Tong! What the heck! This is a blowup of the latest Rozhdestvensky K- scan."

The picture was a clear black and white image, labeled with the source, scale, date, and location.

Today's date--June 4, 2009, in Gregorian units--was written next to the words, SAR Lunar Pole N Rozhdestvensky K 12281, and a scale in meters. SAR stood for Synthetic Aperture Radar, and it was one of NASA's tools on India's Chandraayan-1 satellite, which had been circling the moon for several months, mapping the lunar surface, especially the lunar poles. Nobody on Earth had seen the lunar poles. The simple fact was that mankind needed a different perspective to see the moon's poles. The lunar poles were not visible from the ground.

NASA had piggy-backed some of her instruments onto the Chandraayan-1, along with tools from Bulgaria and Germany and, of course, India. The SAR would graph the poles of the moon, while NASA's M3--Moon Mineralogy Mapper--would analyze the more common and visible regions, such as Apollo-11's landing zone.

Tong took the picture out of Max's hand. He noticed Max's fingers were shaking.

"Do you see it?" Max said. "There, in the lower left." Maxwell Fuchs moved behind Tong's chair and leaned over his shoulder, pointing with his shaky finger. "There. Right there."

Tong saw it all right. He rubbed his eyes, squinted, and then held the picture up closer. "Writing?"

"Yes, writing, and boot prints all over the place where no landing has ever been recorded. We blew up the tread. They're NASA issue all right, but no sign of a landing zone. The prints start and stop and that's it. The guy poofed! How does an astronaut poof, Tong!"

"Someone landed and we missed it?"

Max responded with a wild-eyed shake of his head. He raked his fingers through his hair again and tapped the picture in Tong's fingers. "Nobody landed, Tong, that's what I'm saying, are you listening? They walked on the moon without landing on the moon. As for who did it, read it. It says it right there. It's stomped out with our boots, big as the side of our building."

Tong shook the picture as if the words would somehow fall off and land on the desk. The words defied all logic and stayed put, and he read them aloud. "It says, Percy Freebottom was here! Who in the hell is Percy Freebottom?"

Weight

Terry Sanville

She heard the engine's rumble and looked through the peephole in her front door. A red vehicle pulled into the driveway behind her father's rusted pickup. Retreating along a narrow passage of stacked newspapers, she wiggled around boxes on the service porch and pushed outside into a backyard of amorphous mounds nearly hidden under blackberry vines. Stepping over piles of cardboard and lumber, she worked her way along the house's outer wall and peered through a crack in the side-yard gate.

A tall silver-haired man in a blue uniform climbed down from the truck. He tugged at his neat mustache, crossed her porch, and gave the front door a rap. After no response, he strode toward her hiding place. She turned to flee, but he yanked open the gate before she could escape.

He stepped back.

"Ah ... good afternoon, ma'am." He tipped his hat. "I'm Inspector Whitford with the San Bernardino Fire Department. Are you," he glanced at his clipboard, "Sandra Walters?"

She nodded and pulled her cardigan closed over her blouse, her heart thudding.

"We've received a complaint from one of your neighbors that there's rats in the junk piled in your backyard."

"I ... I haven't seen any rats," Sandra murmured, "and none of what I have is junk."

"Do you mind if I take a look? I'd also like to look inside."

"No ... I mean yes. I ... I wasn't expecting anyone."

"I understand."

His voice sounded like soothing notes from a well-played cello. She studied his face furtively, liking the sculpted nose and black eyes.

"Would some other time be better?" he continued. "I could come back, say at the end of the week, and ..."

"No! I don't want anyone snooping around my place. I'm not hurting anyone."

"Ms. Walters, I'm sorry, but we may have a serious fire hazard here and ..."

Sandra spun and ran through the yard. She turned down a flight of steps and pushed on a door with flaking paint. It opened a few inches, and she slid inside the musty basement. Dropping to her knees, she crawled through a tunneled maze of cardboard boxes, and then climbed the interior stairway. In the front room, she ducked into her sleeping space, a cave formed by an armchair, sofa, and her mother's piano. Columns of sheet music and plastic bags full of junk nearly surrounded the concert grand.

She breathed deeply and sneezed from the dust. Heavy footsteps thumped on the front porch and the flap of her mail slot rattled. A folded piece of paper fluttered to the floor. She hurried to scoop it up and scanned the official form. *They're coming in five days*, she thought. *No way I can clear a space ...*

In the break room, Inspector Whitford filled his coffee mug, then moved along a corridor in Headquarters Fire Station. As he passed an open door, a voice hailed him.

"Hey Eddie, have you taken care of that complaint on 46th? The neighbor keeps bugging me about it."

"I just left an inspection notice, Commander. The woman wouldn't let me inside... but I got a good look at the yard. The place is messed up."

"How bad?"

"Big time. We'll need to get Mental Health involved, and probably a contractor."

"Have you talked with the violator?"

"Yes. She's seems okay, in her forties, it looks like she takes good care of herself."

The Commander grinned. "I didn't ask if you're gonna date her. Does she understand why we need access? Is she a nut job?"

"Yes and probably. She claims that none of her stuff is junk, but I saw plenty. I bet the house is packed solid."

"What did the neighbors say?"

"Haven't talked with them yet, and it'll take me till Friday to get a warrant."

"You know the drill. Invite the police if you think she could get violent."

"Will do, Commander."

Whitford returned to his cubicle, called up the case number on his computer, and transcribed his field notes. He thought about his last hoarding case, a retired schoolteacher whose tract house had been crammed with rusted space heaters, gallon-sized pickle jars, and office papers. In the garage, they' had discovered a safe and used a cutting torch to open it, only to find it filled with old ammunition. *Jeez, we almost lit up the neighborhood with small arms fire.* Whitford grinned to himself. *I should take it slow with the Walters woman. Give her a couple of days and have another chat before the inspection. Getting her to trust me is going to be the real trick.*

As the light outside waned, Sandra crawled from her cave and entered the bathroom, the only space her mother had insisted she keep clear. She stared at herself in the mirror, her chestnut hair twisted into a bun on top of her head, her face smooth and makeup-free. Running a hand down a cheek, she turned the shower on full and slipped out of her jeans and blouse and into the stall, scrubbing hard with a washcloth and a bar of Ivory. The room filled with steam. She cracked the side window and toweled off. On the wall next to the mirror hung a framed poster of a child in an old- fashioned washtub with the words: "Cleanliness is next to Godliness. But I say it's next to impossible."

Sandra moved to the front room and sorted through stacks of clean clothes, changing her mind twice before making a final selection. After dressing, she scooted around the piano, sat on the bench, and selected a Mozart concerto from a stack of sheet music. The yellowed keys felt slippery under her fingers as she sight-read the piece. She thought about her mother giving piano lessons that time after her father died, when friends became as scarce as clear space in their home. Every Tuesday, her

19

mother would select a piece of complex music and give it to Sandra to learn. She had one week to play it cleanly or she'd be roundly criticized.

Mama he's been gone ten years and I'm still doing her bidding, she thought as she'd frowned. *I have' got to find more music, got to surprise myself with something challenging.* As she played, she thought about the tall inspector. *I know he'll want to come inside ... I could hide ... they might never find me.*

At the end of her practice, she donned a hooded sweatshirt, grabbed a bag of dirty laundry, and retrieved her shopping cart. She moved quietly along dark streets until reaching the boulevard with its ragtag collection of laundromats, second hand stores and minimarts. At Mel's Used Books, she pushed inside.

"I've been waiting for you," the clerk said. "I just got two boxes of music from an estate sale."

Sandra smiled. "How much?"

"Ten bucks for the lot."

"You know I can't afford that."

"But this stuff's primo, in great shape. And some of it is old, published in Austria."

"I don't care where it's from. I'll give you five dollars."

"Can't go that low. I can sell it in the shop for ..."

"Yes, maybe in twenty years. Nobody buys used sheet music, except poor students."

The clerk stared at the cardboard boxes behind the counter and shook his head. "Yeah, okay. You got a deal. I don't have room to store it anyway."

"There's always room for music."

Sandra loaded the boxes into her cart, not looking at their contents. On her way home, she stopped at the Circle K to buy day-old sandwiches, and then washed a load of clothes at the Laundromat. Back at the house, she stacked the cartons in what used to be the kitchen and fingered the yellow pages, mostly Strauss waltzes and polkas, Christmas carol books, and a beginner's manual for ukulele. *I'll get more tomorrow ... it's been almost a week since I checked the thrift stores. But Christ, the fire guys are coming.*

Inspector Whitford parked in front of the house next to Sandra's, stepped from his car, crossed a clipped front lawn and wide porch, and tapped on the front door of the single-story bungalow. Getting no response, he banged with a closed fist. The door swung open and a blonde woman carrying a toddler glared at him through the screen.

"Yes, what do you want?" She eyed his badge.

"I'm Inspector Whitford with the San Bernardino Fire Department. Are you Lillian Burns?"

"Yes, I'm Lilly."

"You filed a complaint with our department about your neighbor and ..."

"Jeez, I thought you guys would never come."

"I'm sorry, we've been really busy. But I've already been next door and talked with your –"

"That's more than I've been able to do," Lilly said, frowning. "We've lived here four years and I've never spoken with ... with whatever her name is."

"It's Sandra Walters."

"Ah. Well, if you've seen Sandra's backyard you know why I'm complaining. I can't have a rat-infested trash heap next door to where my little one plays."

"Yes, I understand. What can you tell me about your neighbor?"

"Not much. She stays inside during the day. At night she drags her cart stuffed with crap back and forth from God knows where. I see lights inside her place."

"And you've never talked with her?"

"Nope."

"I'm sorry it's taken us so long to respond. I've scheduled an inspection this Friday and I'm going to try talking with her right now. But it may take some time to resolve her issues."

"Yeah, I figured that." Lilly frowned. "From the looks of her property, it took years to get that bad. Can't you guys red tag it or something and kick her out?"

"Yes, but we try and work with residents to – " A ripple of piano notes sounded and he turned toward the Walters house. "Is that her playing?"

Lilly smiled for the first time. "It sure is. Every afternoon we get classical, jazz, pop. She's really good. I'd like to go over and listen but I'm afraid to get near the place."

"I understand. I have your phone number, and will let you know what's happening with our abatement process."

She ducked into the house, struggling to control her squirming child. Eddie sucked in a deep breath, crossed the parallel driveways, and clomped onto Sandra's porch.

Sandra fingered a difficult passage of the Mozart concerto. Someone tapped on the front door. She stopped playing and closed the piano lid, holding her breath. Another knock came, this one rattling the frame.

"Who's there?" she called. Her voice sounded hoarse.

"Ms. Walters, it's Inspector Whitford again from the Fire Department. Can I speak with you?"

She moved toward the door. "You can't come in. I told you before."

"That's all right, Ms. Walters. Could you come out onto the porch and we can talk?"

"Now's not a good time. Just go away."

"Ms. Walters, ah, Sandra, I'd like to talk with you before I come back Friday with my whole crew. Did you get my inspection notice?"

"Your what?"

"The notice I dropped in your mail slot a couple days ago."

"Well, yes. I still don't want ..."

"I understand, but can you come outside so we can talk? It'll make Friday's inspection go easier."

"Oh, all right. I'll be there in a minute." She backed away from the door and squeezed her fingers, trying to decide. She considered hiding, but the force of the inspector's presence on her porch frightened her. *Maybe if I talk with him he'll go away ...*

She stepped into the bathroom on her way to the door, and she tucked wayward strands of hair behind her ears. She then walked to the back door, stepping outside and working her way through the side yard., she opened the gate and joined the inspector on the front porch. He sat on one of two rusting metal chairs, part of a patio set her father had bought when she was in junior high.

As she approached, he stood, towering over her. "Sandra, thanks for talking with me. I didn't mean to interrupt your piano playing."

"Yes, well, you did. What do you want?"

"I want to talk with you about this Friday."

They sat on the cold seats. She pulled her sweater tight around her body. "So what if I don't want you on my property?"

"I'm sorry, but I will have a warrant issued by a judge that will let me inspect your yard and residence."

She shivered. *I knew this day would come. Maybe I should just burn the place. That should make the Fire Department happy.*

"You mentioned your crew, who are you talking about?" she asked.

"I'll bring two or three other inspectors and somebody from County Social Services."

"Why the County?"

"Well, ah, sometimes people who collect lots of things have psychological issues that ..."

"You think I'm crazy."

"No, not at all. We're only concerned for your safety and that of your neighbors."

"I don't want a bunch of people coming into my house and disturbing my things."

"Ms. Walters, I'm afraid that might have to happen. And it would be easier for everyone if you would help us."

Sandra stared at her hands. "What if ... if your "crew," as you call them, stay outside but only you come inside?"

The inspector grinned. "I've got a better idea. What if you invite me in right now? I'm already off shift and can inspect your place quickly, get it over with so we can move on to the next step."

Sandra clutched herself and rocked slowly back and forth. "What ... what do you mean, the next step?"

"Myself and Social Services would work with you to take care of your excess, ah, 'belongings'. Wouldn't it be nice to have your yard clear? Maybe even the house?"

"Yes, I suppose. But I'm not going to throw away ..."

"No, of course not," he said hastily.

Sandra leaned back in her chair, remembering how she'd played on a backyard swing set with two little girlfriends. Then her father had begun to dump building materials in the yard, a truckload every weekend. Before long, the neighborhood kids had stopped coming over. Her mother had tried to keep the house clear. But, by high school, Sandra had created a warren of tunnels in the basement beneath interlocking boxes filled with her father's tools, plumbing supplies, and used bricks.

Coming back from her daydream, she found the inspector staring at her, quiet, waiting. She trembled, felt her body go hot then cold.

"What say we go inside and you can show me your home?"

Sandra nodded and led the way through the side gate and past the basement steps. "I'd take you in that way, but you're too big to squeeze through. Your wife must feed you well."

"She's feeding some poor guy, but not me. I've been divorced five years. What about you? Do you live here alone?"

She stopped and glared at him.

"It's all right, you can trust me," he said.

"I'm not sure about ... I don't know many people that I can trust."

"Well, I hope I can become one of them," the inspector said and smiled.

In the backyard he pulled a digital camera from his pocket and quickly clicked off a dozen shots. "Boy, in another couple years those vines will cover it all."

"I know. It got to be so much, I didn't know what to do."

Taking her arm, the inspector guided her up the back steps, his hand warm, gentle. A shiver rippled down Sandra's spine. She led him through the back door and service porch into the kitchen where she clicked on an overhead light.

"You still use any of these?" he asked, motioning to the stove, refrigerator and dishwasher, all covered with boxes and packed bags.

"No. After mother died, I disconnected all of it. I buy my meals at the Circle K and restaurants."

"That can get expensive."

"My father's estate left me enough."

"Well, you're lucky these appliances are electric. But stacking all these combustibles on top of them makes us fire guys nervous. Plus, if this is your primary entrance and exit from the dwelling, a lot of this must be cleared away."

"But it's important papers, music and such, things I might need if I decide to teach piano."

"Yes, you play wonderfully. But if you have people in your home, you'll need to provide for safe passage."

"So you're saying, I'll have to get rid of all this?" She motioned with a trembling hand.

"Don't worry, I'll help you decide on what to keep and what to throw out. I've worked with others doing the same thing."

"I've ... I've always had a hard time deciding."

"I'm sure we can do it. Let's move on."

The inspector placed a hand on the small of her back and guided her forward into the front room. He whistled softly at the shoulder-high columns of sheet music that nearly surrounded the piano.

"That's a Steinway, isn't it?" he asked. "My grandfather owned one. Said it was the only piano worth playing." The inspector clicked away with his camera.

"It was my mother's," Sandra said, smiling shyly. "She was a music teacher."

"Is that where you sleep?" He pointed to the foam pad, blanket and pillow in her cave.

"Yes. I ... I feel safe with the piano as my roof. All these things make me feel safe. I don't know if I could live without them."

"Excuse me for asking, but have you ever been married? A spouse or a companion can also make you feel safe."

Sandra shook her head. "I ... I dated for a while, but ..."

"Well, you're certainly attractive enough. With this house cleared out, you could have friends over, maybe find someone to share your life with."

"You sound just like my mother," Sandra said. "She always had high hopes."

"Nothing wrong with that." The inspector grinned. "Would you like to play me something?" He pointed to the piano. "I love just about any kind of music."

"No, I can't. I only play for myself."

"Okay then, let's check the basement. Are there lights down there?"

"No."

"That's all right, I've got a flashlight. Lead the way."

Sandra removed her sweater and placed it on a stack of similar garments. She slipped easily between the heaps of clothing and stacked household items that crowded the stairway. The inspector joined her at the bottom after a precarious descent. His flashlight beam bounced around the huge room stuffed with boxes of all sizes. The place smelled of old grease and mildew.

"What's with all these tunnels?" he whispered in awe.

"I store my parents' things here. I can get to anything I want through the tunnels."

"I'm sure you can, but the fuel load of all this stuff... and what if you were in there and the tunnel collapsed. Maybe we can decide on a better place to store these things."

"You want me to clear all this out?"

"It would be a start."

"But I've arranged it so carefully. I don't want to change ..."

"We can talk about it later," he said, sounding impatient.

Without warning, she ducked into one of the tunnels. "Follow me, I'll show you." She heard him grunting as he followed her deep into the maze, shoving past the tight spots. "No, this way," she called after he took a wrong turn.

At a wider section in the passage she stopped and waited for him to catch up. "I ... I wanted to show you this." She pointed to the top of the tunnel, at the interlocking boxes that formed the ceiling. "They're perfectly set. There's no danger of anything collapsing."

He stopped and, reaching up, tentatively pushed at a box. "I don't know,

Sandra. One good jolt from an earthquake and this whole mess could come down on you."

He's acting just like I thought he would. What I see as secure, he sees as dangerous.. She pulled her knees to her chest and rocked back and forth. They're going to take it all away ... I can feel it ... they'll never understand the comfort of chaos.

The flashlight beam danced wildly as the inspector moved toward her. She scooted to one side to make room. He crawled next to her on hands and knees. Turning to sit, he lost his balance and fell sideways. The bottom tier of boxes moved. A loud rumble and a crash was heard, followed by the sound of more things falling. With a shout, he pulled her down and covered her body with his own. His heaviness grew immense, forcing the air from her lungs, not letting her breathe. He said nothing. His breath hissed, then stopped. Sandra felt safe, this perfect stranger and her own past pressing her full length. In the darkness she savored their weight.

The Megalomaniac

By Rob Rosen

Mrs. Greene," the doctor said to me as he gently sat me down and stared unnervingly into my eyes, "has your husband been experiencing any strange symptoms? Any unusual character traits as of late?"

I paused before answering. Two years had gone by, actually, since the start of it all. Two years that may as well have been twenty. Two years, two million dollars, and two lives irrevocably altered – not to mention two matching Porsches in our driveway and the two-carat ring on my finger. And really, the changes had been positive for the most part, so in all honesty, I didn't think anything was seriously wrong.

This whole thing began on an odd Monday morning. My husband, Bill, woke with a start, ran to the shower, and hurriedly got dressed, all the while whistling a happy tune. Now this, on the surface of things, seemed innocent enough, but hindsight is 20/20, and my vision would blur considerably over the course of the next twenty-four months.

You see, Bill was never a morning person, and when I say never, I mean *never*. Getting him up and out the door was akin to rolling a log over a searing hot beach. Oh sure, you could do it, but it practically broke your back, and by the time you were done, you were a sweaty, stinking mess. Mondays were like rolling two logs over the entirety of the Sahara.

So on that morning when the alarm went off only once with no ensuing snoozes, instead of the usual five or six, I should have sensed something was amiss. But I, gloriously oblivious, turned over and went right back to sleep. Ignorance truly can be bliss, as it turns out.

And, that's how it all started. It was a small thing, a happy thing, really, but it was still a thing. One day your life is rolling merrily and blandly along and the next day there's a glitch, a bump, *a thing*. My thing, and many of the others that followed, were bonuses, tucked merrily into the plus column of my life; so rather than complain, which would have been silly, considering I was able to sleep-in an extra half hour, I ignored the peculiarity of my husband's behavior and pleasantly drifted back to La-La Land.

By the time I again woke up that fateful morning, my husband had already left for the office. Our schedules had always been different, with my departure for work often following his, but this time was different. Bill was not only long gone, but he also left me breakfast; and not cold cereal or toasted bagels either, mind you. No, he made me an omelet and home fries, which were waiting for me in the oven when I went downstairs. There were also fresh-cut flowers in a crystal vase on the table and a nice little love note next to that.

"What the hell?" I whispered, checking the nearby wall calendar. "Not my birthday, not our anniversary, not even Groundhog's Day. He must be having an affair."

I'd seen just such a thing on Oprah: *Cheating Husbands and the Tricks They Pull*. Wait, it might have been Jerry Springer. In any case, though exceedingly nice, it was all just a tad bit fishy, if you know what I mean. Still, the aroma of a warm breakfast instantly obliterated any lingering fish odors, and I wiped those nasty misgivings gleefully out of my mind as I poured ketchup over the potatoes and fixed myself a nice, hot cup of java.

That night, however, was more of the same. I arrived home to find my husband, who was usually plastered to the TV by that point, fixing us a four-course meal. He'd also cleaned the living room and the kitchen, and neatly folded the clothes I'd washed the night before.

"Who is she?" I asked, almost in tears.

"Who's who?" Bill responded, innocently, as he marinated the steaks and buttered the corn.

Bill's nostrils usually flared when he was lying, and he'd stutter, neither of which he was doing at that moment, so I dropped it. Besides, I'd had a long day and was happy for the turn of events, however benevolently strange they may have seemed. Granted, the hot bath Bill had drawn for me, replete with floating rose petals, was equally odd, but far be it from me to look a gift horse in the mouth, especially a horse that smelled so wonderful.

Half an hour later, we sat down to dinner. "So how was your day?" I asked, after I downed half of my perfectly cooked steak.

"I quit my job," he responded, light as air. I nearly choked on my meal, but Bill kept right on eating as if he had said something as inconsequential as, "he'd changed the air in the tires."

"You did what?" I managed, after a few sips of water.

"I quit. I told them they weren't paying me what I was worth, that it would take two people to do my job, and that no one could ever do what I do better than me. Basically, I told them the truth."

"The truth as you see it." My heart was racing as visions of home foreclosures and car repossessions rattled around my addled brain.

"The truth as it is," he replied, as cool as the cucumber that rested snugly in my salad.

"And what did they say?" I set my knife down for fear of what I might do with it.

"What could they say? They gave me a raise and a promotion right there on the spot." At last he stopped eating just long enough to look up at me and smile. "You're now looking at the new Vice President of Finance. Oh, and it pays thirty thousand more a year. Do you think this house is too small?"

Actually, I did, but that was beside the point. I had two options open to me: I could berate him for taking the chance of being without a job, ergo an income, or I could congratulate him and finish my meal. Naturally, I chose the latter. Why rock a boat, I figured, that had clearly sprung a leak.

And so, for the next three months, my husband woke to the first buzzer, hummed a happy tune, and fixed us both breakfast. On top of that, as if that alone wasn't enough, he bought us completely new wardrobes and a year's membership at the gym and tanning salon. My husband, who I'd known for ten years, had grown uncharacteristically vain, seemingly overnight.

But to tell the truth, I kind of liked the change. We looked fabulous in our new outfits, lost some much-needed weight, and glowed as if we'd just stepped off a boat from Tahiti. People stared at us whenever we walked by. Neighbors who had never given us the time of day before stopped and chatted. And most importantly, from a social standpoint, we were forever being invited to dinners and events by the muckamucks in Bill's company. We were, in short, big shots.

Now, though the picture I paint appears pretty on the surface, all was not exactly sunshine and roses. The money was nice, sure, and so were the perks associated with Bill's new status, but Bill himself had also undergone a serious personality change. You see, the reason Bill started getting up on time each morning was to primp and preen. Up until then, my husband would shave and shower, dump a glob of gel in his hair, and be done with it.

By the time the promotion came, and then the snazzy new clothes, he was spending an hour in the bathroom. Instantly, our medicine cabinet was brimming with moisturizers, hair care products, wrinkle creams, eye gels, neck firmers, and a whole assortment of products I'd never even heard of before, at least not for men. Bill's eyebrows alone made mine look like overgrown bushes. In other words, he was all of a sudden quite full of himself.

"What gives, hon?" I asked, one morning, as I watched him painstakingly ready himself for the day ahead.

He looked at me as if I was the crazy one, but answered, "Just striving to be the best man I can be. It's kind-of like putting the finishing touches on Michelangelo's David." He smiled, winked, and went back to his routine.

Fine. It was a strange comment, but I thought he was joshing me. I knew men went through mid-life crises, only Bill's was apparently hitting earlier than expected. And honestly, he looked super. My husband, who had always been nice looking, was now downright stunning. The problem wasn't that I knew it; the problem was that he knew it. If we passed a mirror anywhere, he'd stop and look at himself and then comment on his good looks. Same thing for windows he walked by, spoons he held in his hand, and anything with a reflective surface. Narcissus, in other words, had nothing on my husband.

But did this worry me? Not too, too much. I was happy that Bill was happy. And Bill was happy, let me tell you. He beamed with self-confidence. It practically oozed from his very pores. And it was, believe it or not, somewhat sexy. My husband fully and wholeheartedly believed in his abilities, and so I believed in them too. I unquestioningly supported him in all his endeavors, as I thought a caring, loving partner should. Plus, if the truth must come out, I was starting to accept his boasts as facts. In my mind, and certainly his own, my husband was the most handsome, most successful, smartest man around. If that made me look good as well, then it was icing on the proverbial cake. And for some, especially us, the icing was the best part of the meal.

Within a year, my husband was once again promoted, this time to President of Financing. Again he was given a big fat raise, and again he asserted his eminence. His reputation grew and grew, and so did his ego – okay, both our egos. The wife of a successful businessman, I figured, was equally successful. So I let his frequent bragging roll off my back. If he was cocky, he was rightfully so. If I was cocky, then we were like two peas in a pod. And speaking of pods, ours was rapidly growing.

Our smallish house was quickly replaced by one twice its size. Our two old compact cars were traded-in for the aforementioned Porsches. And our wardrobes, which once fit snugly into a single closet and a chest of drawers, now occupied an entire room of their own.

"A great man needs great clothes," my husband would say, all the while supplementing his cache.

"A great many of them, too," I would add, as my own wardrobe increased exponentially.

All of this might have been enough. We had a fabulous home, expensive possessions, and a super life together. We were living dream lives.

But what's good for the gander isn't always good for the goose, *or enough*, to be precise. My husband wanted more, much more. He also believed, beyond any shadow of doubt, that he deserved it. He let one and all in on this little secret. From country club to country club and from one dinner party to the next, Bill spouted his accomplishments and abilities to anyone who would listen. Oh, and they listened, all right. They listened closely and they acted quickly.

"Power," my husband said, shortly after accepting his party's offer to run for the state senate seat that had been unexpectedly left vacant, "is now the one thing I lack. And you, my love, will make a stupendous senator's wife."

I trembled at the thought of it; and not out of fear, but out of lust. There's no aphrodisiac like power, and the desire for it shined in both our eyes.

Bill held his job and his salary on an advisory level, for the time being. His company was quick to realize the benefit of having a state senator so closely associated with it, and they gladly gave him as much time away from the office as he needed. I, on the other hand, eagerly left my company and headed out on the road to campaign for my husband. We quickly became the poster children for all that was good and right with the American way: you work hard, you play fair, and you succeed beyond anyone's imaginings.

Strangely, Bill's ever-growing ego served him well. The public loved a confident man, it seemed; throw in his good looks, charm, and million-dollar smile, and we were a sure thing. And that's just what we were. Bill walked away from the election with an overwhelming margin of victory. I was beside myself with joy. Bill, on the other hand, was not so jubilant.

"It's only a state senator," he practically whined as he plucked his eyebrows in the aptly named vanity mirror.

"That's like saying you only won the state lottery," I replied, hanging my Chanel suit up.

"No, one is luck, the other is earned. I plan on earning what's rightfully mine. Mark my words, two years from now it will be United States Congressman, and after that, who knows what."

I knew what came after that, but held my tongue. I chalked it up to deserved exuberance. Besides, I figured, look how far he'd come in such a short amount of time. The sky really was the limit when it came to Bill, or at least that's what it seemed. Just what Bill's limits were I was soon to find out.

After the election, I saw less and less of my husband, except on television, where his sound bytes and dazzling image appeared regularly. Bill toiled for endless hours to make a name for himself. Work became his all-encompassing passion. The only occasions at which I spent any considerable amount of time with him anymore were charity events and fundraisers. My face, by then, had a permafrozen smile on it from all the publicity shots we took. And still I was my husband's most ardent supporter – well, second most ardent; Bill himself was numero uno. Therein, of course, was the seed of his inevitable collapse.

His deriders, of which there was a growing number, called him a maniacal windbag, a blowhard, and an egocentric, power-hungry autocrat. All this was true. It was a hard thing to deny. But what was also undeniable was that Bill was effective at his job. The personal qualities and work-related accomplishments he bragged about were all accurate. He did work harder than anyone else did. He was the smartest, handsomest, and ablest man in the Senate. To say that those opposing him were jealous was surely a gross understatement. Of course, on the opposite end of that teetering seesaw was yours truly. I was always there to stand up for him, to espouse his talents, and to give him the support he so richly deserved.

And that's why I was the first one they called from the hospital. Was I expecting this? Perhaps. After all, the human body can only take so much abuse before it starts to shut down. Surprisingly, it wasn't his body, as it turned out, that was doing the shutting.

Mrs. Greene," the doctor said to me, "has your husband been experiencing any strange symptoms or any unusual character traits as of late?"

I snapped back to the present. "As of late? Not exactly. I don't think he's been himself for quite some time. Why? What's wrong with him?" My heart sank as I read the doctor's name on his jacket, Dr. Marvin Hoffman – Department of Psychiatry.

"Your husband was found in his office today staring at himself in the mirror. He was non-responsive to his staff and kept repeating over and over, 'I am President Greene. I am President Greene'. They brought him directly here."

"So there's nothing physically wrong with my husband?"

"Physically, no. He's the picture of perfect health. Mentally is another story entirely. After examining your husband for the last several hours, I believe he's suffering from megalomania. It's a psycho-pathological condition characterized by delusional fantasies of wealth, power, or omnipotence. In short, he's a self-liar to the nth degree."

Oh boy. That sure made a hell of a lot of sense. The shrink had just described my husband to a tee. "Will he be alright? Is it treatable?" I asked, once I regained my composure.

"Yes, like a bipolar disorder or schizophrenia, it can be treated with medications. Eventually he'll be right as rain, just like he used to be," he said reassuringly, and then stood up. "Your husband is free to go, Mrs. Greene. I strongly suggest you have him see a private psychiatrist as soon as possible so he can begin his treatment and be on the road to recovery. Here's a prescription in the meantime."

I shook his hand, took the piece of paper, and went to collect my husband, who smiled warmly at me upon my entrance into his room.

"So what did the doctor say?" he asked, with a kiss and a hug. "Am I going to be okay?

I looked at my bronzed, handsome husband, with his expensive suit and flawlessly coiffed hair, then looked down at my own stunning outfit and sparkling diamond ring, and with a smile and a wink, I replied, "You're gonna be just fine, Bill. The doctor said you'll have to take it a bit easier from now on. After all, this country needs a strong man like you. So if we're going to make it to the White House, as planned, you'll need to conserve some of that boundless energy of yours."

"You're going to make a perfect first lady," he said as we walked outside, arm in arm. The prescription in my hand, naturally, went straight into the garbage can.

Origin

Raleigh Dugal

Ezra was named after a poet whose last name he could never

remember. The school librarian said the guy was a real upstart and had been in mental institutions, but he and Murray thought that was a total crock. Murray was six days older, five inches taller, and so it seemed to Ezra, about a billion times cooler. They met every day on their way to and from the bus stop to cut through the cemetery that they weren't supposed to cut through.

"I'm telling you, they got to be dead," Murray said. He pounded a fist in his palm to make the point. His first name was Matt, but there were three other Matts in fourth grade, so everyone called him Murray. Even Ms. Cohn, who Ezra and Murray both thought was stupid. She had kept them inside at recess for "passing notes." Really, they were doodles of dinosaurs eating cavemen, but she called it passing notes. When they had been caught passing this "note," everyone in the class went "*wooooo!*" the way TV shows did when people kissed.

"All of them have dead parents," Murray said.

Ezra tightly clutched his fists, something he did when he was thinking hard. Once in math class he snapped a pencil and it had landed in Ms. Cohn's coffee.

"Batman, Spiderman," Murray ticked them off on spindly fingers. "Hell, Spiderman's parents *and* his Uncle Ben are dead."

"Superman had parents," Ezra countered.

"Are you kidding? Cripes, his whole planet is dead. He's the last of his kind."

Before Ezra could reply, Murray jumped into the middle of the nearer, eastbound traffic lane. He heard the faint hiss of an approaching vehicle rebounding off the guardrail twenty yards away.

Ezra held his tongue. He hadn't realized they'd reached the stone arch at the bend on Siegel Lane, the rear entrance to the cemetery that jutted out along Route 105. The old back road was narrow and winding, and drivers tended to speed around the straightaway that lined the cemetery after the sharp bend. Ezra and Murray's parents used to encourage them to cut through the cemetery until some older kids got arrested for knocking over graves.

The archway loomed over Ezra. An ancient-looking statue was perched at the top, hunched and faceless with the stubs of broken wings jutting out of its back. He always wondered if it had been an angel or a gargoyle. They (really just Murray) had been running their experiment every couple of days for the past month. They couldn't do it too often or they'd get caught, but it was part of the ongoing argument. Since runners ran a lot to get faster, Ezra argued they could get super speed like the Flash just by practicing. Murray disagreed, but he figured if anything was right about Ezra's argument, they'd have to train under super conditions. Like these.

Looking at Murray rooted in the middle of the pavement made Ezra uncomfortable. He wore an awkward look on his face, as if he were feigning worry, like this was no big deal, but since it was no big deal to him it wouldn't be a big deal to anybody else, so he had to have a dangerous attitude. Ezra swore he could see his calves twitch beneath his denim pants.

"Not yet," Ezra said.

"I know dammit ," Murray hissed. The branches along the edge of the road were rustling in the breeze, but the roaring motor of the approaching vehicle drowned them out.

Like they'd learned in science class, this was the "control." They had a second part to the experiment to see if the two of them actually developed super speed, which they had yet to try.

"What about the Punisher?" Ezra asked. His mother wouldn't let him read the Punisher because he wore a big skull and used guns.

"I guess you're kind of right, but his wife and kids got whacked by the mob," Murray said from the side of his mouth, keeping his eye on the corner while cocking his thumb and forefinger like a gun. "They saw some murder they weren't supposed to. Not much better." Murray's dad owned the hobby shop in the center of town, so he could read whatever comics he wanted.

A pickup wheeled around the corner, the driver's arm slung casually out the side window. The cars always shocked Ezra when they finally appeared, roaring like hungry animals.

"Now!" Ezra screamed.

He streaked through the gate, dirt clods kicking up behind his heels as he darted around tombstones. The brakes of the truck wailed but he didn't look back, knowing Murray would be panting behind him when they reached the old Name Elm at the heart of the cemetery.

Murray leaned against an old, white tombstone with an illegible inscription. The only thing on it Ezra could read was the date, December 25th. Close by, the elm rose up out of the ground, squat and fat, its limbs spread wide as though it were trying to escape its own gloom.

"Daredevil?" he asked hopefully.

"Dead," Murray answered between breaths.

"So you're saying there's no way I could be a superhero unless my parents die?"

Murray straightened, stretching out his back. "It's just part of the mix. Something bad has usually got to happen to *you*, too."

"Worse than dead parents?"

Murray jumped and grabbed a low branch, then swung upward, branch by branch, until he was almost at the top of the tree.

"Not worse, just bad. Like how the Hulk got blown up in a gamma bomb or Wolverine lost all his memories. It's called your origin."

Ezra shrugged his backpack off and jumped at the branch. The tips of his fingers brushed the bark.

"Need a hand?" Murray asked. He'd pulled out his pocket knife and begun carving his initials into the tree, right next to Megan Crossman's. Putting your name next to a girl's on the tree meant you liked them. If they saw it they'd either be mortified and scratch it out or pass you a note in class full of hearts and stars and bubbly squiggles.

"Nah," Ezra said, pulling out his house key, which he never really used because his father was always home, to scratch his own initials onto the trunk. The girls all put theirs in the higher branches so the boys would have to work to get to them. Even the top of the tree, now dimpled with buds, was littered with names. Down on the trunk were mostly curses. Ezra carved E.D. next to a word he wasn't allowed to say.

"Now, Iron Man," Murray continued, casually lowering himself by his heels and swinging like an acrobat, "He was a real smart guy. Of course his parents got killed in a car accident. Then a bomb exploded next to him and screwed his heart all up," Murray said, clutching his chest dramatically. Ezra absently mimicked him.

"So he built a suit, not red and yellow, the first one was gray, to save his heart. But he gave it powers, too," Murray finished, flipping from the branch and landing with a flourish.

"Powers," Ezra repeated.

"Yeah, sure," Murray said, unwrapping a Snickers bar and breaking it in half. "Like his repulsor rays."

The taller boy stuck out his palms like a traffic cop, striking the same pose Iron Man did when he employed the deadly weapons. Then he tossed half the Snickers bar to Ezra. The two munched on peanuts and nougat with relish, each wondering whose mother would call them from the porch first.

"Are you sure Batman wasn't Robin's dad?"

Robin was a stretch for a superhero, but it was a shot.

"Don't be a numbskull. His parents were The Flying Graysons, in the circus and all, with the trapeze and stuff."

"So *they* made it," Ezra said proudly.

"Nope," Murray laughed. "They fell and broke their necks. I'm telling you, they're all dead."

Suddenly a mother hooted from a porch. Murray scuttled out of the tree, spider-like, and Ezra sped off, kicking up clods of dirt. Neither of them realized it wasn't one of their own.

The scent of the glue hit Ezra the second he opened the door, a thick tangy scent that reminded him of passing around construction-paper hearts on Valentine's Day in kindergarten. "I'm home," he called, then called again, and one more time while kicking off his shoes. He heard the shower running and knew he'd have to go into the bathroom, his dad wouldn't hear him from out in the kitchen. That's where he was playing with the glue.

Whump! He heard from the bathroom, then a swear word, then another *whump!* Ezra knocked on the door. His father opened it quickly and peered down at him through thick, steam-covered spectacles.

44

"I'm glad you're home," Ezra's father said, and dragged him excitedly through the doorway. His denim shirt was soaked, stuck fast to his chest, and his wide-wale corduroys were frazzled like the fur of a wet dog. His long gray hair hung down around his shoulders in wet clumps.

"Look," his father said, pulling back the orange curtain just enough to stick his head into the shower. He kept talking but his voice was muffled by the sound of the water and the curtain. Ezra sighed and pulled a small pebble from his pocket and dropped it into the bucket of glue. At first it floated on top, but the white ooze steadily sucked it under to the bottom. Ezra's father nudged him and Ezra stuck his head into the shower beneath his father's.

Inside, the wall was plastered with facecloths of all different colors, each spread out in a different shape. Dozens more lay at the bottom of the stall, soaking up the running water.

"I glued those today," his father chattered. "Problem is, I use the wet ones and they stick so I can see how they'll land." Ezra's father bent, grabbed a cloth, and *whump!* flung it against the wall, where it stuck in the rough shape of a butterfly. He held his chin between his thumb and forefinger. "That's perfect, see? But now I need to do it all over again with the glue."

"So?" Ezra asked.

"So then it doesn't come out the same."

"Let me try," Ezra asked, reaching for a cloth halfheartedly because he knew better. His father's hairy hand landed on his head.

"I'm going to submit this to Milwaukee. I can't screw it up," he said. A long time ago, before Ezra had been born, his dad sold some weird sculptures to a galleries and museums for a lot of money. One was still on display in New York, he'd gone to see it twice. That one was a broken rake next to a scattered pile of leaves, only they weren't real leaves, they were made of dead people's hair. He'd never seen the other one because it was in Minnesota. For as long as he could remember his dad was trying to come up with the next big sculpture, trying to get all his art friends to like him again, the ones that only came around every couple of months and smelled like cigarettes and always asked him weird questions about what he was learning in school. They had a big shed in the back yard with a padlock on it that nobody went into except Ezra's father. He spent most of his time out there, even in the winter, and whenever he finally came inside he was covered with the sharp smell of paint or some other chemicals.

45

"Of course, the shower will be running in the exhibit," his father said, hands on hips, examining the scene. "How could we underscore the frightening measure of stasis without the constant motion of the water?" His head wagged, sorry for anyone unable to grasp the concept.

Realization dawned for Ezra. "Um, how are you going to get the cloths into another shower?"

"I'll cut the whole thing out of the wall with the bandsaw," he announced proudly. He waved his arm up and down and went *Bzzzzzz*, like he was holding a saw.

"How will Annette get ready for work?"

"We'll put a new one in, you and me, like a project."

"*Bzzzzzz!*" Ezra said, waving his hand in the air. "Can I help take it out?"

"As long as you don't touch these," his father said, tugging lightly on a blue cloth. It slid along the tile and plopped wetly at the bottom of the tub. "Shit." He stepped back into the shower, fully clothed.

"Too bad, that one kinda looked like a dinosaur."

While he watched his father wipe the droplets from his glasses, he wondered what the world would be like if he were dead, if he were completely gone. Ezra couldn't imagine it.

For dinner, Ezra's mother made a fish, head and tail and all, gazing up at them like a fourth dinner guest. She fried it in an iron skillet on the stove and flipped it the way they flipped pancakes in cartoons. Ezra's father sat quietly through most of the meal, anxious over the shapes of facecloths. His mother complained about the mango chutney she'd made with the fish.

She was a lot younger than his father, young enough to make people look at them weird on the street. She wore long skirts and fresh flowers in her hair and smelled vaguely like cedar clippings in a hamster cage. His parents thought he didn't know, but Ezra had heard them fighting once and found out that his dad had been his mother's teacher in high school.

"You ought to draw comic books," Ezra said to his dad, pulling a bone from between his teeth. His father snorted, momentarily coming out of his trance.

"Ezra," he laughed lightly, but saw the look of hurt on his son's face and quieted. For Ezra, comic books were art that was alive. They told a story and were bursting with action and color and life. They made real things seem fake and fake things seem real, which was what Ezra thought his dad was always getting at when he talked about art.

"You'd make tons of money, and people would get to see your stuff *all* the time," he pleaded.

His father opened his mouth again, then stopped to smile to himself, shaking his head the same way he had when looking over a piece of his art.

"Someday you'll realize the exciting things in life aren't as overstated as a comic book," he said, not without affection. "Something will inspire you, and the world won't keep you from taking hold of it."

Ezra changed the subject. "Can you pass the salt?" he asked. When he got his hands on it he poured it all over the fish. "How come we never have fish sticks?" he complained.

"Because they're processed and have lots things in them you wouldn't normally find in fish," his father said, eyes glued back to his own plate.

"Did my real parents die? Am I an orphan?" Ezra asked hopefully.

"Do you *think* you're an orphan?" his mother returned in a calculated tone, as if the conversation were about to teach him a lesson, the way his teacher spoke when somebody answered wrong.

"How should I know? Anything could've happened."

"You've seen the baby pictures with all of us together."

"Superman had baby pictures too. He had all types of baby pictures, and his whole planet's dead. He was the last of his kind," Ezra cried, doing his best to sound reasonable.

His parents traded tender, patronizing glances that annoyed him. His father smiled, sighed, and resumed brooding, as if he could brood on cue, the way that kid at school could make himself vomit. He learned the word *brood* from his mother when he'd stayed mad at her for days after she forbade him to play in the cemetery. "Stop brooding," she'd said, and explained the word when he looked puzzled. He knew it meant other things, too: *The mother hen protected her brood from the fox.*

"Were you hoping you were Superman?" his mother asked sweetly.

47

"That's stupid," Ezra growled.

"It's okay, everyone wishes they were someone else sometimes," she cooed, caressing his shoulder across the table, arm extended over the solemn fish head. At that moment his father thrust himself up from the table, spraying chutney everywhere, and sprinted into the bathroom. *Whump! Whump! Whump!* came the sounds from the bathroom, offset by short, ecstatic gasps from his father.

"That new kid Billy Ingols is adopted, that's all," Ezra said. His mother nodded sagely, but a smile played at the edges of her pretty young lips, and Ezra knew how stupid she must have thought he really was.

"I'm not stupid," he said resolutely.

"Of course you aren't. You're my son."

She crossed to the other side of the table, ruffled his hair and took his plate to the counter. The clinks of the plates and silverware in the sink mingled with the pound of his father's facecloths into a strange, musical din. Ezra felt a pang as his throat closed. Tears stung his eyes. What if they were both gone, he thought. Since Murray had given him his first issue of Spiderman, he'd wanted to be a superhero. But in order for that to happen, his parents would have to die in a car accident, or get mugged on the street. He couldn't even comprehend life without them.

"You should get some rest soon," his mother called over the dishes and the staccato thumps from the bathroom. "I have an early appointment tomorrow, so you'll have to make yourself breakfast."

In the middle of the night Ezra woke and really had to take a whiz. He crawled downstairs, sleepily reached inside the bathroom, and flipped the light switch. Nothing happened. He retrieved a flashlight from the junk drawer in the kitchen and returned. With the aid of the flashlight, he could see that the stall was gone, or at least the functional half. Straight metal pipes gleamed in the dusky flashlight beam. The bathroom light was smashed, along with some of the plaster on the ceiling.

"What the hell," Ezra muttered quietly under his breath. His father had must have cut out the stall in the middle of the night with the bandsaw without waiting, because he'd had his great inspiration. His boot prints tracked through the fiberglass dust all over the floor. Ezra knew they'd lead straight out to the shed where his father had locked himself in.

Ezra peed and flushed the toilet. The pipes rumbled and sounds came from deep inside the walls, down in the darkness.

His eyes widened. Ezra leaned forward and peered down, between the studs of the naked wall. Far below, he spotted a wild knot of pipes and wires and vents lit faintly by the glow of the furnace, hypnotized.

Suddenly he slipped on the wet floor, falling forward. Flailing, he clutched the hot water pipe running up from the basement with his right hand. Before he could even scream, he jerked his hand away and dropped the flashlight. Palm throbbing, Ezra bent to pick it up but found, strangely, he couldn't move his hand at all.

Shaking, Ezra edged his face closer to his hand. A dull ache had begun to work itself across the back of his fingers and down to his elbow. By the dim light of the cellar, Ezra saw deep red streaks.

The point of a large nail protruded from the wall, into the back of his hand, and out of his palm. He'd slammed into it pulling away from the pipe. A fresh stream of his blood trickled slowly downward, wrapping around the metal like a candy cane, dribbling down into the basement. Through the thin space between the walls, Ezra saw his blood drip onto the furnace, into the knot of metal and pipes and wires and switches. A singed, coppery scent floated back up, and he grew dizzy.

Under other circumstances, Ezra might have screamed, like when he'd been hit in the neck by a pitch, or cried, like when Max the bully pushed him off the swing. He didn't do either now because he was transfixed, because he was inspired. Like his dad.

"Your dad is definitely weird," Murray conceded the next morning. Ezra had just told him about the shower stall, fidgeting nervously, wondering if he should clue his friend in to his plan or if the bigger boy might try to stop him. His hand was wrapped in gauze and he'd told Murray he'd hurt it helping his mother slice vegetables. The grass had been all matted where his father had dragged the stall out to the shed, and he'd stayed in there all morning. Ezra hadn't had to explain a thing except to Murray.

The two of them trudged along the iron fence that encircled the cemetery, trampling the shoots of crocuses popping up from the ground. The mornings were still cold, even under the new blanket of spring. The archway loomed larger and larger in the distance.

"That's not the big deal. I'm going to try the experiment today," Ezra said nervously.

49

"Don't worry, I'll help you out. You always help me."

Ezra kept twirling Iron Man's origin in his mind. That was his strategy. "This has to work. We can't kill our parents or anything."

"Christ, no!" Murray yelled. "That's just the opposite! You'd be a villain!"

"Well yeah, I knew that would make me a bad guy," Ezra said.

"Only the worst villains do something like that," Murray said, "Like Carnage."

They stopped at the arch and stood silently beneath the shapeless statue, waiting with their ears pricked up. The minutes dragged and Ezra worried the bus would come along before a car. Murray kicked a stone from one toe to the other while Ezra watched it go back and forth. For a small moment he couldn't keep Iron Man in focus, and doubt filled his mind.

"What if this doesn't work?" he asked softly.

"Shhh," Murray said, one finger to his lips, the other pointed at the sky. The faint rush of traffic rebounded off the curved guardrail. This time, he was the one by the side of the road.

Ezra didn't think Murray had heard him, but then the bigger boy's face grew very serious, and he started talking. "Dad says things never just work, but even though the world's mostly garbage and everything's against us, that doesn't mean we can't *make* it work," he said. Murray's dad was divorced, so they talked together like adults sometimes, like they were best friends. Ezra had seen it hundreds of times in the shop.

"I thought this was stupid at first, but maybe you were on to something," Murray said.

Beaming, Ezra stepped into the road, fists clenched around his backpack's straps. Instead of stopping in the eastbound lane, he moved all the way over to the westbound one, the second phase of the experiment.

"Don't be crazy, get in the other lane," Murray hissed. Ezra didn't move. The rushing echo from the guardrail grew louder and mixed with the rustling of the trees into a single noise. "It's not going to prove anything if you do it, you haven't honed your powers yet at all!"

The second phase was to dart back through the cemetery gate when the car appeared, crossing both of the lanes instead of one in the same perilous few seconds.

"Take off the backpack! It'll slow you down!"

Ezra lowered his head and clenched his fists tighter than ever, even though it hurt. Blood oozed through the gauze around his palm. Just to be safe, he'd stuffed an Iron Man comic in his backpack, dog-eared to a flashback of the hero's first appearance. Murray ran up and down the side of the road, like a dog shut in by an electric fence. He flapped his arms wildly, but Ezra would not look away from his destiny, his inspiration, afraid if he flinched he would run too early, or that Murray might come and snatch him out of harm's way.

An old, wood-paneled station wagon glided around the corner, smooth and hard, like magic.

"*Now!*" Murray screamed. "*Now now now!*"

The car never slowed, the driver perhaps thinking Ezra was rooted on the far side of the road, maybe waiting for a bus.

Ezra didn't dart until Murray had screamed *now* six or seven times, all blended together in one pained howl. A Styrofoam cup flew out the car's window, painting the last few feet of pavement between Ezra and the wagon with a coffee-stripe of panic. The horn blared uselessly and a dog barked somewhere. Man, animal, and machine cried out together as the driver finally slammed the brakes. They screeched loudly.

Ezra hoped the comic in his half-zipped backpack would fly madly into the air, pin-wheeling before fluttering poetically onto his motionless, jelly-like body, human bones smashed all to powder. The grill of the station wagon bore down on him, a boy who was certain in these final moments that he would be rebuilt as a powerful robot.

His memory could be completely lost. Humanity might shun him. He could never see his parents again. He would be a brooding hero-robot, longing for the richness of his former human life while preserving the sanctity of others. His bones would be made from helicopter blades and his heart would pump gasoline.

Whump!

Suddenly Ezra was flying, soaring high above the ground, above Murray, above the entire town.

He could see the tombstones and mausoleums and the top of the Name Tree, all backlit by the bright orange of the freshly risen sun.

Then everything winked out, changed the color of oiled metal, and he felt like a dark machine humming in the middle of a field on a starless night.

The Registry of Lost Socks

By Patrick Scalisi

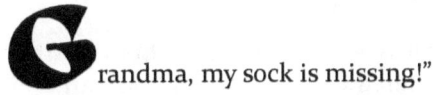**G**randma, my sock is missing!"

The cry came like a muffled entreaty as Peggy withdrew her head from the dryer. She looked around the sparse laundry room, taking in the worn linoleum floor and dated appliances before deciding that the garment in question was indeed missing. Then she rummaged through the basket again, sifting through her jeans, tops and underwear in a vain and ultimately fruitless search.

That sock was one of her favorites, too!

Peggy willed an image of it in her mind, hoping it might conjure the delinquent stocking out of thin air. The pair had been a present from her grandmother, the fabric woven in a pink argyle design that stretched halfway up Peggy's spindly shins. Peggy normally hated long socks — equating them with her school uniform and, simultaneously, discomfort — but the pink argyle ones were different. The bands were very stretchy, which meant they didn't cut off the circulation to her toes or even leave red marks at the end of the day. In the winter, Peggy wore them to bed, and they kept her feet warm all night long.

Now the socks were missing.

Peggy forced a contemptuous grimace and marched upstairs, her ten-year-old feet thumping harder than necessary on the floor. Her frown relaxed when she didn't find Grandma in the kitchen, and nearly disappeared when Peggy realized her grandmother wasn't on the second floor, either. That meant Grandma was either on the third floor of her massive old house or she was in the attic.

Peggy peered around the corner that led to the third-floor landing. Sunlight streamed from the rooms directly across from the top of the staircase, and plush carpet crunched underfoot. Peggy tiptoed up the stairs, much different from her furious footstamps of only a few moments ago. She looked into the bathroom, then the spare bedroom, then the studio. Grandma was nowhere to be found. That meant...

The attic.

The word sent physical shivers down the length of Peggy's small body, making the hair stand up on her gangly arms and her feet rise and fall in the invisible rhythm of dread. She hated the attic. H-A-T-E-D it. There was no scarier place in the whole house.

Grandma's home was big enough as it was — three stories — but the attic added another whole floor: a level cluttered with canyons of boxes and mountains of old dressing wardrobes, a veritable city of junk, valuables and everything in between.

And home to those...*those things*.

No one else believed that something lived in Grandma's attic, but Peggy had seen the creature (or creatures) once when she was five. This had left her with a profound fear of the attic that would probably last a lifetime.

Peggy put one foot on the bottom step of the attic stairs and withdrew it quickly, as if she had stepped into a scalding hot bathtub. Instead of venturing any farther, she cupped her hands together and shouted for her grandmother.

There was the sound of footsteps on the floor above her, and Peggy knew Grandma was coming. Moments later, the old woman appeare56d at the top of the stairs, framed in the doorway like the ancient Oracle come down from Delphi.

"Hello, honey," Grandma said, "I didn't hear you calling."

Grandma made her way down the stairs at a spry shuffle. She was still healthy for her seventy-eight years, with only a touch of arthritis in her left ankle, which she had broken as a young woman, and a full head of curly gray hair. The latter was styled by her hairdresser every other week, a ritual that ensured no curl was ever out of place.

"Grandma, I lost one of my socks," Peggy said when the old woman reached the bottom of the stairs.

"Did you look in the dryer?" Grandma asked.

"Yes," Peggy said, with an emphatic shake of her auburn hair, "And in the washer and on the floor and in my basket. It's missing!"

"Oh dear," Grandma said, "well, let's take a look."

They went back to the laundry room together and scoured the area from one end to the other. Peggy knelt on her hands and knees to check under the appliances while Grandma looked in the corners and behind the bottles of detergent. They met again moments later in the center of the room.

"Nothing," Grandma said.

"Nothing," Peggy agreed.

"You'll have to check with the Registry of Lost Socks," Grandma said.

Peggy scrunched her nose. "There's no such thing!"

"There certainly is!" Grandma retorted. "I haven't had the occasion to visit the Registry in a long time. Every now and then, I let them keep the socks that go missing."

"If you let them keep your socks, why did they take one of mine?" Peggy insisted.

"Well," Grandma said, "these things happen. There are mix-ups, socks taken that aren't supposed to be. You'll have to go plead your case if you want your sock back."

"How do I do that?" Peggy asked.

Grandma waved one of her wrinkled arms. "Come with me, and I'll show you."

The old woman trundled past Peggy and up the stairs to the second floor landing.

Peggy thought she knew every inch of her grandmother's house, having spent many afternoons exploring all the nooks and crannies (except, of course, the attic). She knew there was little chance that she would have missed this so-called Registry of Lost Socks.

When Grandma reached the second floor landing, she walked over to the laundry chute and stood by it. A small door (about two-feet square) had been set into the wall. Peggy knew that when dirty clothes were dropped into the chute, they fell neatly down it into a pile in the laundry room. She herself had used it many times, and with much enjoyment. After all, how many houses these days still had such an antiquated feature?

Peggy didn't have to walk fast to keep up with Grandma's shuffling gait. As Peggy joined her grandmother on the landing, the girl asked, "How far is it? Will we have to drive to get there?"

"Heavens, no," Grandma replied, "in fact, you're nearly there." She pointed to the laundry chute.

"Grandma!" Peggy exclaimed with undisguised seriousness. "I can play *with* the laundry chute but not *in* the laundry chute." These words were nearly an exact echo of the instructions Grandma had fervently repeated on many occasions. "You told me so."

The old woman cocked her head to one side, as if listening to music that no one else could hear. "Indeed I did," she said "and that's good advice, but this is the only way to get to the Registry of Lost Socks."

Grandma turned to the chute door, balled her hand into a gnarled fist and knocked. She knocked three times, then once, then three times again, then twice. She waited a minute, then touched a certain spot on the wall as delicately as her old fingers would allow. Peggy watched in awe as the wall swung outward.

"How did ..."

"Ah, ah," Grandma interrupted, "no more questions. Now's the time for listening. Do you remember the knock I just did?"

Peggy nodded emphatically. "Three, one, three, two," she recited.

"Very good!" Grandma said, "Now, I want you to go inside this door— it's dark, but not too scary — and crawl to the very end of the tunnel. When you get there, repeat the knock *exactly* as you heard it just now."

Peggy started toward the door. Then she stopped and turned to her grandmother with eyes narrowed and brows nearly touching. "Is this a joke," she asked, "Or a game?"

Grandma put her hands on Peggy's shoulders. "The only way to find out is through that door. Now, off you go."

Peggy turned back to the hidden passage and frowned. She was scared that the darkness would be a complete veil of black, was even afraid that creatures from the attic might be living in the dark spaces behind the landing. Instead, the walls of the tunnel seemed to glow with a faint iridescence that revealed a dusty but otherwise empty floor.

"You're sure it's safe?" Peggy asked as she looked over her shoulder.

"Absolutely."

Peggy turned and began crawling.

The tunnel should have slanted down, as it did to deliver dirty laundry to the basement, but was instead flat. Peggy looked back once and realized that the door she had come through had disappeared. Panic seized her for a moment, but after several deep breaths, she continued onward at a faster crawl, hoping the other end of the tunnel was near.

58

Her wish was granted. In seconds, Peggy's hands touched a solid wall. She began searching for some kind of knob, then remembered what Grandma had told her. Peggy repeated the designated knock: three, one, three, two. When there was no answer, she pushed violently against the wall, which gave way more easily than she expected. Peggy tumbled head over heels and landed in a pile of fluffy towels.

The mound of cotton nearly enveloped her, the smell of laundry detergent and fabric softener filling her nostrils. Peggy lifted her head like a periscope and looked around. She was in her grandmother's laundry room, but the room was different than she remembered. Café lights hung from the ceiling where once there had been florescent strips. The linoleum was gone too, replaced with real tiles arranged in an art deco design. Where the washer and dryer once stood, there were now two doors with frosted-glass windows. One read WASHER, and the other DRYER.

"Can I help you, miss?"

Peggy jumped out of the pile of towels and lost her footing. She landed on her back with a thud, and stared up at the wooden hat stand that was moving toward her. Somehow, the stand had taken on an animated (almost human) quality. It moved on three short tripod legs with more flexibility than real wood had any right to exhibit. The long shaft of the stand seemed to serve as its body, and the four racks as its arms. The hat stand stopped a few feet short of Peggy and bent toward the girl at what might have been its waist.

"Can I help you, miss," the hat stand repeated.

Peggy yelped and shuffled backward in a type of reverse crab-crawl.

"No need to be alarmed, miss," the hat stand continued,

"your grandmother told us you were coming."

Peggy stopped crawling. Her arms gave way and she flopped onto her back. "Grandma?" she asked. "Where am I?"

"My dear, you are at the Registry of Lost Socks. Agnes — that is, your grandmother — told us you were coming to issue a complaint."

"That's... that's right," Peggy managed as she sat upright.

"Very good, miss," the hat stand said, standing back up and adding, "My name is Basil Tophat. If you would be so kind as to sign the visitor register, we can begin investigating your claim."

59

Peggy nodded. The hat stand began shuffling toward the table where Grandma usually kept her detergent. The bottles of bleach and fabric softener had been replaced with a large, leather-bound book and a feather quill complete with inkwell. Basil Tophat stood next to the ledger and waved one of his arms toward the quill pen. Peggy obediently made her way over and signed her name in the book. The task was more difficult than she expected; the ink kept forming unsightly blotches that made her signature nearly illegible.

"Very good, Miss—" Basil looked down at the ledger "—Miss Margaret Hawthorne."

"Oh, no one calls me that," Peggy said. She was starting to like the strange, polite hat stand. "You can call me Peggy."

"Very well, Peggy," Basil replied. He reached for another large tome with two of his four arms and turned expertly to a specific page. "Now, if you would please describe the missing article to me."

"Um...well, it's a sock," Peggy began. "A pink, argyle sock. It comes just below my knee and it's stretchy, but not too tight."

"Stretchy, but not too tight," Basil repeated as he flipped through the large tome. The hat stand was using all four of his arms to scan and turn the pages, stopping occasionally at an item of interest before moving on.

"I don't — oh, oh my!" the hat stand said.

"What?" Peggy exclaimed. "What's wrong?"

Basil replied, "I'm sorry, dear, but you'll have to speak to Mister Dryer about this particular case."

The hat stand closed the tome with a definitive THUD and replaced it on the shelf. Then he led Peggy over to the door marked DRYER.

"This is Mister Dryer's office," Basil explained. "He will give you further details."

Then the hat stand shuffled back to his spot next to the table and left Peggy standing near the door. She reached out and touched the handle, only to find it covered in condensation. Peggy gripped the slippery knob, turned it with difficulty, opened the door and stepped inside.

Steam filled the office. Somewhere from the back of the room came the sound of rapid, phlegmatic coughs. Peggy followed these distressing noises until she was face-to-face with her grandmother's old-fashioned dryer.

It was the dryer that was making both the sound and the steam, each cough rocking the dryer's door open to emit more white clouds.

"Are you all right?" Peggy asked. After her encounter with Basil Tophat, she did not find it unusual that the dryer might be able to speak.

"Just a — just a moment," the dryer said between breaths. The appliance broke into a new fit of coughing and then fell silent.

Not sure what to do, Peggy said, "Mister Dryer, my name is Peggy Haw—"

"Yes, I know who you are," Dryer said rudely. "You're the one responsible for this forsaken cough!"

Peggy felt as if she'd been physically slapped. "Me?" she cried. "No way!"

"Don't try to deny it!" Dryer continued. "That sock of yours is stuck in my hose!"

Peggy's anger disappeared when Dryer mentioned the missing stocking. "My sock," she asked. "stuck in your hose?"

"That's what I said, isn't it?" Dryer replied irritably. "And if you want it back, you're going to have to help me."

"Fine," Peggy said. "I'll help you, but only if I can get my sock back."

"Children these days," Dryer grumbled, half to himself. Then, in a louder voice, he said, "Yes, that's the arrangement. Must you repeat everything I say?"

Peggy crossed her arms but didn't argue. Instead, she asked, "What do I have to do?"

"Finally, an intelligent question." Dryer broke into a brief fit of coughing, then continued, "You need to get the special brush your grandmother keeps, the one with the ticklish bristles for cleaning my hose."

"I'll go right now." Peggy turned to leave but couldn't see the door because of the steam. Then she turned back to Dryer and asked, "Where is it?"

"The attic."

Peggy froze when Dryer spoke the word. She felt her insides turn to ice cream and frozen mush that stopped her even from breathing.

"The attic..." she finally managed.

"Criminy! Here we go again with the repeating!" This reprimand sent Dryer into another coughing fit. When it was over, he added, "Yes, the attic. Your grandmother keeps it up there because she doesn't have the occasion to use it. Heaven knows she should. Then we could avoid disasters like this."

"But, there's something … alive up there," Peggy pleaded.

"You're right,there is." Dryer paused dramatically. "Dust bunnies."

This revelation took Peggy aback, so much so that she almost started giggling. A squeak escaped her lips before she clamped both hands over her mouth. After a moment, she said, in barely a whisper, "That doesn't sound so bad…"

"Doesn't sound so bad!" More coughing from Dryer. "You've been up there! You know how the Dust Bunnies make people feel! They're a mischievous clan, hiding in the shadows, always on the move — like nomads. Do you know what that word means?"

Peggy nodded.

"They're very territorial," Dryer continued. "If they sense intruders, they'll attack with all the dust at their disposal, enough even to make a certain little girl with healthy lungs go into a fit of coughing that would burn her chest and water her eyes."

Peggy found that she was afraid all over again. If she couldn't go to the attic, she couldn't get the brush. And without the brush, she would never see her sock again.

"I'll do it," she said, trying to sound braver than she felt.

"I'm so glad," Dryer said with a hint of sarcasm, "and because you've decided to go, we'll give you some help. BASIL! GET IN HERE!"

Basil Tophat waded into the office, his four arms waving ineffectually at the steam. "Yes, Mister Dryer?"

"Peggy here will be venturing into the attic," Dryer said. "Get her what she needs."

"Yes, Mister Dryer."

Basil bent at the waist again and shuffled out the door. He returned moments later, holding a pair of unusual objects in two of his arms.

"Took you long enough!" Dryer said. "Show her what we've got."

The hat stand didn't seem perturbed by Dryer's comment. He ignored the reprimand and held out one of his laden arms.

"This," Basil began, "is a handkerchief. Your grandmother got it in China when she was with the U.S.O. That's how she met your grandfather, during World War II. Did you know that?

"This is no ordinary handkerchief," Basil continued. "It was made by a Chinese magician from silk harvested under the light of the full moon. If you wrap it around your nose and mouth, it will keep you safe from anything those cretin Dust Bunnies can throw at you."

Peggy took the handkerchief and turned it over in her hands. She had never felt anything so smooth. Her fingers glided over the silk as if it were coated with ice. The strands had been woven into concentric diamond patterns and dyed the most vivid shades of red, purple and orange that Peggy had ever seen. When she was done examining it, she folded the handkerchief into a triangle and tied it around the back of her neck.

Peggy shook her head. She didn't think about her grandfather often; he had died when Peggy was very young. Even so, his photos adorned Grandma's house, including one of Grandpa in his smart Navy uniform. Peggy could tell he was a handsome man.

"Let's move it along," Dryer said, impatience making his words nearly spill over one another. "Enough with the reminiscing and the history lesson. Basil, isn't there something else?"

"Yes," said the hat stand.

He proffered his other arm, which held a metallic spray can emblazoned with the words DUST MUST: THE MUST FOR DUSTING.

"Furniture polish?" Peggy asked.

"It's the only weapon we have against the Dust Bunnies," Basil replied. "You see, they're allergic to it."

"At the very least," Dryer added, "you'll give 'em a taste of their own medicine! Now, Basil will show you out. The brush is in the northwest corner of the attic, above the studio. Don't come back without it!"

Basil was shuffling Peggy out of the office before she could respond. She felt the hat stand's four arms on her shoulders, then found herself back in the main laundry room.

"Don't take it personally, Peggy," Basil said when the door had closed behind them. "Dryer is always grumpy when he's congested. The sooner you get that brush, the sooner you can have your sock back and the sooner he'll be in a better mood."

The hat stand pointed two of his arms toward the laundry room door.

"Now, you'd best be on your way," Basil continued. "No need to exit through the secret passage again; it's more of a rite for first-time visitors."

"It was a bit scary," Peggy admitted.

"And if you couldn't do it, you would have never found us. But no worries," Basil said and twirled one of his arms with a flourish, "for now you can exit through the main laundry room door. Do that and head straight for the attic."

Peggy nodded. She couldn't think of anything else to say to forestall her journey, so she gripped the can of Dust Must and started toward the door. Once outside, she expected Grandma's house to be as subtly changed as the laundry room had been, but everything appeared normal.

It was almost sunset, and the last light of day painted everything in tones of golden sepia. Peggy started toward the stairs when she heard a noise coming from her grandfather's study — a room her grandmother hardly visited except to clean. Peggy ventured toward the open door and noticed a young man sitting unconcernedly at the desk.

"Who are you?" Peggy cried. "How did you get in here?"

The man didn't respond. He was referencing something in a book while scribbling notes on a piece of paper. Then he closed the book and replaced it on the shelf behind the desk.

"Hey!" Peggy shouted, angry now that a stranger was inside the house. "I'm talking to you!"

The man turned toward Peggy, but seemingly stared through her to the opposite wall. When Peggy saw the man's face in full, a gasp of shock caught in her throat. She recognized the man now from a photograph her grandmother kept of a young Navy officer. It was her grandfather.

Peggy spun around the room, realization spreading out like ripples in a pond. The furniture in the office was different than she remembered, as well as the décor. Where a landscape painting had once hung over the couch, there was now a map of the Pacific Ocean with characters in a language Peggy had never seen; where there were once pictures of children and grandchildren on the desk, there was now some kind of bronze sword.

Peggy fled up the short flight of stairs that led to the kitchen. This, too, had changed. The microwave was gone, and so was the coffee maker. The appliances that were there seemed ancient (like something out of an old movie) and a young woman was standing at the sink, rinsing lettuce in a steel colander.

The initial shock had passed, and Peggy recognized the woman as a young version of her grandmother. Agnes finished with the lettuce, set it on a wooden chopping block and wiped both hands on her apron. Then she turned toward the towering refrigerator without noticing the presence of her future granddaughter.

"They can't see me," Peggy said to herself.

Still nervous about venturing into the attic, Peggy decided to take the most circuitous route possible. She passed through the dining room, where Peggy saw her grandparents (now slightly older) sharing a meal with a younger version of her own parents. They were either still dating or newly married, and both wore fashions that had gone out of style years ago. In the parlor, Peggy saw her grandparents sitting before a massive, old TV; in the guest bedroom, she saw her mother cleaning with a feather duster and a vacuum that resembled a cylindrical robot; and in the studio, she saw her grandfather playing guitar. None of the people ever stopped to look at Peggy, it was as if she were a ghost intruding upon the living.

Finally, Peggy stood before the attic door. The sun was sinking lower now, nearly obscured by the trees surrounding the house. In a few moments, it would be nighttime. Peggy pulled the handkerchief over her nose and tightened the knot around her neck. Then she gripped the can of Dust Must harder than ever before, threw open the door and made for the attic at a maniacal run.

The Dust Bunnies were upon her immediately, launching their gray, puffy bodies from atop the surrounding boxes and pulling at Peggy's hair and clothes. Peggy screamed, the sound muffled by the handkerchief. She brought the bottle of furniture polish to bear and began spraying at random. The creatures fell back, some sneezing in fits that caused their bodies to explode in puffs of dusty particles.

With a way clear, Peggy began to navigate toward what she thought would be the northwest corner of the attic. The Dust Bunnies seemed to disappear at once, and Peggy hoped that her initial attack had frightened the creatures enough to leave her alone. Unhindered for the moment, she began a frantic search that led her through one valley of junk after another, concluding finally at a dead end of boxes higher than her head.

As Peggy began to backtrack to find the correct path, she was confronted again by a fresh attack from the Dust Bunnies. The creatures reappeared in the same amount of time it had taken them to disperse, this time clinging to Peggy's shoes. She aimed two bursts of aerosol that scattered the Bunnies, then tried another row in the maze of her grandmother's attic.

As time went on, the Dust Bunnies became less bold, attacking only when Peggy seemed to be on the right track or when she rounded a corner. Checking to see that the handkerchief was still firmly in place, Peggy continued her search as quickly as possible, making steady progress toward her goal.

Finally, she rounded an old highchair and crib that were wrapped in plastic, and spied the object of her search. Even as the brush caught her eye, she knew her task was hopeless. The Dust Bunnies had marshaled their strength for a final assault, their gray bodies covering the length of the brush handle and intertwining among the bristles. They spotted her at once and launched themselves into a colorless mass of dust. Peggy raised the can of Dust Must and depressed the trigger, only to hear a hollow gurgle escape the spray applicator.

There was no time to flee and no place to hide. Peggy dropped the can and turned her head away from the cloud. She brought her arms up in defense, feeling the dry, cottony bodies brush uncomfortably against her skin.

Despite that fact that the creatures nearly enveloped her head, Peggy's handkerchief performed its task admirably. The Dust Bunnies seemed to realize that their attack was practically ineffective — even though Peggy's eyes had turned red and watery. She shuffled toward the wall where she thought the brush should be and groped blindly with one hand. At last, her fingers closed on the plastic shaft.

For a second, the Dust Bunnies crowded up Peggy's arm as far as the elbow. Then the girl brought the brush up in a quick warding motion and the creatures on her arm fell to the floor. As this happened, Peggy used the brush to sweep the Bunnies into small piles, then crushed them underfoot. Doing this, she began making her way back toward the attic door, always keeping her eye on the vertical rectangle of light that led to the stairs.

Her progress was painstakingly slow. Without the can of Dust Must, Peggy had to attack the creatures every three steps. For their part, the Bunnies seemed determined to keep in their possession the weapon that would mean the demise of so many of their kind. It was only after what seemed like hours that Peggy was finally back at the door.

Peggy swung the brush in one final arc to ward off any remaining Dust Bunnies and slipped out the attic. Once outside, she braced her back against the wall and closed the attic door with her foot, watching as a few final Bunnies escaped from the attic. These she crushed tidily between her hands to prevent them intruding farther into the house. Then Peggy sat on the top stair and waited for the breath to return to her body.

When she had recovered enough strength, Peggy ventured down the attic stairs on wobbly legs. She felt as if she had run a mile or was extremely nervous — or both. With one hand on the banister and another on the brush, she started back toward the second-floor landing.

It was full night now, and the house was mostly dark. She half expected to meet her grandmother, or at least some of the ghosts, on her way back to the laundry room, but all the rooms were empty. The memories that had lived in the spare bedroom, in the parlor, in the kitchen and in the dining room had all faded back into the ether where dreams live. Peggy doubted she would ever see them again, except in her own mind.

Basil Tophat greeted her at the entrance to the laundry room, waving his four arms in excitement when he saw the brush. He didn't even wait for Peggy to fall into step behind him; he started at once toward Dryer's office, shouting all the time, "She has it! She has it!"

Finally, Peggy stood in front of Dryer once more.

"I had my doubts about you," Dryer said with less gruffness than before. "You turned as white as your grandmother's linen when I mentioned the attic."

"Getting the brush wasn't easy," Peggy admitted, surprised that her voice worked at all. "The Dust Bunnies —"

"— won't bother you again," Dryer interrupted. "I think they've discovered that you're a force to be reckoned with."

"But I ran out of furniture polish," Peggy said. "And I can't wear this handkerchief all the time."

"Bah!" Dryer shouted. "They're cowards. They'll be hard pressed to unlearn the lesson you taught them today. Now, let's get to work! No doubt you'll find some of them clogging up my pipe when you clean it out. Basil, get another can of Dust Must!"

Basil left, and Dryer opened a hatch on the top of his head that Peggy had failed to notice earlier.

"Sneak that brush in there," Dryer instructed. "Don't worry. You won't hurt me. Pull out whatever you find."

Peggy began working the brush inside the hatch just as Basil returned with a new can of Dust Must. He waited nearby as Peggy inserted the brush deep inside the hatch, and then began withdrawing it slowly.

At first, nothing came out. Peggy's arm was clean, along with the first inch of the brush handle. Then a few Dust Bunnies escaped the hatch, which Basil dispatched with two quick sprays from the aerosol can. Some inert dust came out as Peggy continued to withdraw the brush, then came a hair tie, a ribbon with a pendant tied to one end, and a blackened handkerchief that once might have been white. As the tip of the brush emerged from the hatch, Peggy saw her pink argyle sock affixed to the bristles at the very end and a squeak of glee escaped her compressed lips.

Dryer took a deep breath and let out a long, dusty sigh.

"That's better," he said, his voice slightly changed now that he wasn't congested. "We both have what we wanted, eh? Tell Agnes she would do well to use that brush more often." Dryer paused as if contemplating something. After a moment, he said, "Never mind that, I'll tell her myself the next time she's down here."

"But Grandma said she doesn't visit very often," Peggy said.

"That's true," Basil replied. "But I think she'll come to say hello when you show her this."

Basil held up the bit of ribbon that Peggy had rescued from Dryer's hatch. Now that she saw it clearly, she realized it was some kind of award, and that the pendant tied to the end was fashioned in the shape of a heart.

"It's what she's been looking for," Basil continued, "your grandfather's Purple Heart. He got it in the war and it's been missing for some years now, and Agnes thought it might be somewhere in the attic."

"And Dryer had it all along!" Peggy exclaimed.

"Well, if she used that brush once in a while, she might have found it sooner!" Dryer said, his bad mood resurfacing.

Basil leaned down to Peggy's ear. "Ignore him," the hat stand whispered. "Why don't you go give this to your grandmother?"

Peggy cradled the ribbon in her hand, excitement swelling in her chest. That her grandfather had been honored in the war made her extremely proud. That she had won her own battle today made her prouder still. When her elation reached its boiling point, Peggy gripped the medal and her sock in one hand and rushed toward the laundry room door. There, she stopped, turned and waved to Basil. "Thank you!" she cried.

The hat stand waved back with all four arms.

Peggy took to the stairs two at a time, calling for Grandma the whole way. She found the old woman preparing supper in the kitchen (much like the scene Peggy had witnessed earlier).

"Grandma!" Peggy cried. "I'm back from the Registry of Lost Socks! Look what I found!"

Grandma wiped her hands and examined the thing that Peggy clutched gingerly in both hands. A gasp escaped her lips.

"But — how — wherever did you find this?" Grandma asked.

"Mister Dryer had it," Peggy replied, "along with my sock." She held up the pink stocking as evidence.

"How on earth did Dryer get hold of this?" Grandma continued. "I've been looking everywhere! I wanted to put it in the parlor next to your grandfather's picture." Grandma's eyes sparked now with recollection, or tears, or both. "He was very brave, you know, your grandfather. He got this for saving another man's life. They were both hurt, and they were both discharged. I didn't complain, though, because your grandfather was back with me before the war was over."

"I'm so glad I found it," Peggy said. "Dryer said you should visit more often."

"I'll have to take him up on that offer," Grandma replied. "Now, help me find a nice place for this on the mantle."

Grandma began moving toward the parlor with Peggy close behind.

"Did I ever tell you how we met," Grandma asked over her shoulder "your grandfather and me?"

"Nope," Peggy replied.

"Well," Grandma said. "It's a lovely story. And it begins with me getting locked out of the U.S.O. barracks. Your grandfather was kind enough to bring me to the Consul of Misplaced Keys. Would you know they have an office in China..."

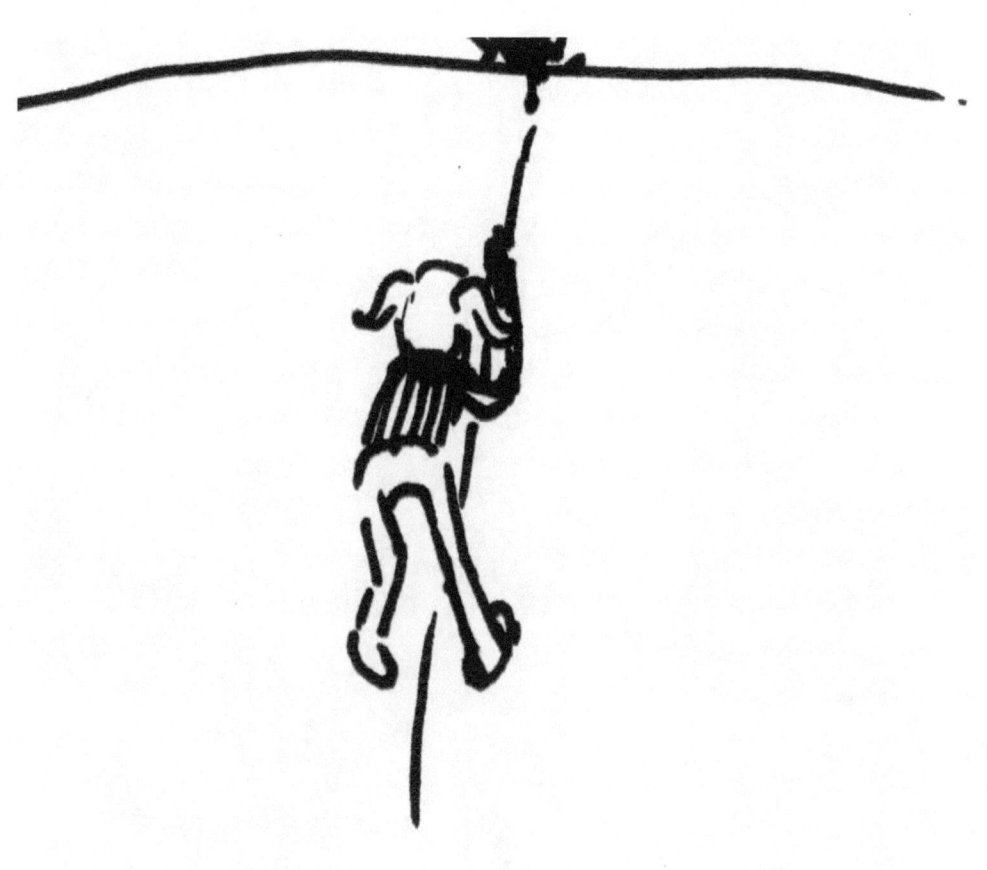

The Other Side of the Wall

By M.E. Johnson

Imposingly tall and forbidding, it was a wall of sturdy stone that had

stood for ages and would stand for ages more. It marked the boundaries of the property while serving as sentry, denying passage to both those outside and inside. It was also a backdrop for the lush gardens of the property and the Victorian mansion that seemed plucked right out of time.

It was an impressive wall indeed, and might have boasted being bigger and better than everything else, except for the one other thing on the property that was taller, the massive oak tree that had surely stood where it was since the beginning of time. It was the only one of its kind on the property, in the side garden near the gate.

There was only one occupant on the property now. There had been two, but one had voluntarily left, and would never return. She had, of course, told him otherwise.

She hadn't really lied. She had just omitted a few key things, only telling him that she would be away for a while. She didn't say how long a "while" would be, but it apparently wasn't any time soon. He had already spent so many seasons waiting for it to happen that he eventually he had just quit waiting.

That had all happened a forgetfully long time ago. He barely remembered his mother now. Strangely enough, he didn't miss her. You might suppose he would, but he didn't. What he did miss were the answers she always had for his questions. "How old is that tree?" "What do squirrels eat?" "What is on the other side of the wall?"

A few days before she left, he had noticed strange metal objects mounted all around the house and grounds. They hadn't been there the day before. He went to her and asked what they were. She replied that they were magic eyes that would keep watch over him while she was gone. It was a plausible enough answer for him, and somewhat comforting to know she would still be watching over him, so he believed it and gave it not one more minute of thought.

While she was with him, she schooled him in many things, things that would prove more important to his life than math or science or reading and writing. She taught him to never go beyond the wall. She had been telling him that all his life, in fact. He'd asked why many times, but the answer was always the same. There was nothing over there to interest him. Eventually he just quit asking.

Here, in the expansive gardens there was plenty of room to roam and run and hide and play. He had invented many games. There was much to discover inside the house, too. In fact, his curiosity took him all over the grounds, inside and outside. It had taken him to the highest pinnacle on the house, what he thought was surely the highest place in his little world. But it wasn't. The wall was still taller than the house. And the tree was still taller than the wall.

Many nights passed in which he contemplated climbing up that tree and peering over that wall. He had studied it from the ground looking up, from the windows in the mansion looking out, and even from atop the house looking down. Some of tree's arms grew close to the wall. Using the tree, he thought, he might be able to get on top of the wall, and if he could do that, he would be able to look over it and see what was beyond.

Tonight though, he was determined to do more than just contemplate. He was ready for action. Tonight, he was going to try climbing up into the arms of that tree. I say "try" because he had never climbed a tree before.

It was a long anticipated thing, and he couldn't wait to get started. But first though, he needed to appease the hunger that filled his belly. It was early and he had just risen from his slumber. (Mother had always taught him to rise at sunset and sleep at sunrise, and this was what he always did. She said it was better for him).

So as he did every evening, he went to the place in the wall where the gate was and retrieved the box of food that was there. Mother had always said that someone delivered it. She had also said that someone came by to tend the gardens and clean the house. But, he'd never actually seen any of these people. He knew they came because little things were different each night. Blooms that were there yesterday were gone today. New plants appeared where dead plants had been. The mud he had tracked all over the house was nowhere to be seen.

Mother had explained it once, saying that a "Foundation" took care of those things. They had gardeners and house keepers to tend the property, and made sure his food was delivered too. It made no sense at all to him. He didn't know, or care to know, what a "Foundation" was, let alone a gardener or housekeeper. Food was always by the gate. His bed was always warm. Play was only a reach away. Day followed night, weeks followed weeks, seasons followed seasons, and so on and so on and so on.

He was an insignificant cog in the grinding wheel of life, and didn't realize it. He'd neither made his mark on the world outside, nor had it marked him. The trees and the grass might grow taller. The stones in the wall might grow older. And he might grow older and taller, but it was all still relatively insignificant.

He finished his meal as night ate the last bit of daylight, then proceeded to stand beneath the giant oak, gazing up at its mighty branches. He might have stood there for an hour or two contemplating climbing. This was not an act to take lightly. Doing it meant disobeying his mother.

When he felt he was finally ready and certain in his resolve to do this deed, he took a deep breath, took the first step, and then the next, and on up he went. It was an incredibly easy and thrilling climb up into those branches, hearing its pops and crackles, smelling its sweet sap, brushing through its leaves, watching the ground dwindle further and further away, until he thought he must be climbing straight to Heaven, it looked so high.

He stopped once to take a good look around, saw that the wall was easily within his reach, but that he was also nowhere near the top of it yet, and that was the goal, reach the top of it so he could look over it and see what lay beyond.

So he climbed some more, checking his progress frequently. When at last he got high enough to at least see the top of the wall, he paused for a moment. He saw stars in the night sky beyond and that piqued his curiosity. He had seen the same thing when he had climbed onto the roof of the house. And now, he wondered what else might be the same over there, over the wall. It was truly deep thinking for him.

Eventually, he came back to the here and now and resumed his upward trek. When he got high enough to finally reach the top of the wall, he sidled over to it, and in a single easy step, was up on top of the wall. He stood there on unsteady feet, relishing the moment, seeing the stars up above, and feeling the breeze that blew past. Then, he started getting dizzy, so he sat down and dangled his feet over the wall. Below him were streets and buildings and people. He had never seen these before and had no concept of their names, or that they should even have a name, so therefore they didn't need a name. But for the sake of the story, let's just call them streets and buildings and people and things.

And there was more than just the sights to delight his mind. There were smells, many of them never experienced before. Some he could identify, some he could not. Some smelled good, like food. Some didn't smell good at all.

He sat up there transfixed by the world below him. The streets and yards were vacant of people now, as most were tucked safely inside their homes for the night. But there was still much to see, smell, and hear. He watched a couple of dogs roaming around. Cats howled not far away. He readily recognized the eager chirping of summer-time crickets, another thing that was the same on both sides of the wall. He stayed transfixed that way until sunrise, when sleepiness and hunger finally brought him down out of the tree.

His mind reeled with the evening's sights, smells, and sounds. They consumed him as he consumed his food. They consumed him afterward, and beyond that to when he went to bed, so much so that he hardly got any sleep at all.

He awoke the next evening to renewed curiosity. His food tasted bland and plain, made so by the overwhelming memory of the good food smell from the other side of the wall. He hungered to have that taste in his mouth.

As you may expect, he was soon back up that tree and sitting on the wall. Sights, smells, and sounds transfixed him again and he sat still as stone for a long time. Then the thought occurred to him that he would like to be down there on the ground, among those sights. He would like to find the source of that wonderful smell of food, but how? There were no trees and no adjacent buildings on the other side of the wall to use in climbing down. There was only an empty street at the bottom of the very tall wall.

He sat there for the rest of the night, pondering this new dilemma. When morning came he climbed back down again, and still puzzling over it, ate his food and went to bed.

He awoke the next night to find his covers all thrashed about upon the bed. The sight spurred an idea, and he sat there for a time trying to figure out how to make it work. He envisioned a long line of covers. Somehow, he knew he had to tie them together, and he did, in various ways. Sometimes they worked, sometimes they didn't. But after much trial and error, he finally got it right.

When, to him, it was finished to perfection, he gleefully gathered up his make-shift rope and hauled it up the tree. It took him some time to figure out how to secure one end, but at last, he got that too.

It was then that it occurred to him that he hadn't eaten yet. It didn't matter. All he cared about right now was the tug of curiosity. He tossed the rope over the wall and watched to see how far down it would go. It didn't go far at all, so he hauled it back up and spent the rest of the night hunting down things to lengthen it with.

In fact, it took him several more nights. It was a big house and things were stored all over the place. At one point, he'd become convinced that he'd found all he was going to find, having stripped all the beds and cabinets. Then he found the massive trunk buried beneath the debris in the attic. It held a treasure trove of sheets and linens and fabrics so long that they had to be rolled. Tonight, he would finally have a long enough rope to reach to the ground below the wall. At least he hoped it would be long enough.

It never did occur to him that he could use the gate. He'd never seen it used before, and so naturally just assumed it was as solid of a barrier as the rest of the wall. So, he paid it no attention at all.

When he finally had all his fabrics tied together, he hoisted this new section of rope up the tree and secured it to the rest. He was getting rather skilled at rope making by now.

His moment had finally come. He tossed the rope over, watched it ripple and cascade as it gently unfurled down. It didn't quite reach the ground, but it looked close enough to him.

He was about to climb down when the enormity of it all came crashing down upon him. He was about to do something his mother had said he should never do. What would happen if he now disobeyed her? Would something bad happen on the other side? Would he be injured or hurt? Or would he just have to face her displeasure, an even worse prospect, when she returned? He had never acted against his mother's wishes before. He had always done as she asked. It was important that he please her (she had told him so herself).

Then it occurred to him that he had already climbed the tree once, against her wishes, and no harm had befallen him. So logically, it must be okay to climb over the wall now, too.

He never once pondered whether he would be able to get back up his make-shift rope, or that he would even need to. He had no idea that the world inside the walls was actually his sanctuary. He naively believed that life on both sides would be as calm and gentle as on his side, which it wasn't.

Time ticked away again, but he was too lost in these new thoughts to even notice. Then the smell came again, stronger, more potent. It made his mouth salivate. Not drool, just salivate. It brought him back to the here and now, to the decision to use his make-shift rope or not. That smell smelled awfully good, and he was awfully hungry (He had, once again, bolted out of bed and climbed up the tree before eating, and was now regretting it). So he gripped the rope, put one leg over the side, and then the other, and then let the rope take him down to its end. There were a couple of times where the rope seemed to lengthen by itself, making him think his knots would unravel, but to his surprise, they bunched up tighter instead.

As he descended, he stopped to survey the scene below him from each new vantage point. He could hear people talking and shouting not far away. He kept looking for a glimpse of them, and of course, for the source of that smell as well. He knew those voices meant others like him because he understood many of their words. But he couldn't imagine what they looked like. The only other being he had ever seen or known before was his mother. Did they all look like her?

Before he knew it, he had reached the pavement and no longer needed to hang onto the rope. He was down. He looked around, unsure of what to do next. There were no people in sight, just empty streets and dark buildings. He didn't even see the raccoons or the possums, or any of the other creatures of the night. He did see a stray dog that ran from building to building sniffing at everything along its way, but his mind didn't register it at first. It wasn't until the dog was out of sight that it did. The dog had followed a smell. Maybe he could do the same thing, follow his nose to that wonderful smell.

In a moment, he was on his way, crossing the road, peering at what lay behind and between the buildings. There wasn't much between the buildings, just the ground and blank walls. However, what lay behind the buildings, he discovered, was mesmerizing; another street and more buildings, some with lights on, some with voices drifting out. He had come to one such spot and stopped to survey his surroundings. There was a building ahead with many colorful lights. Happy sounds came from it. And something else came from it too, the source of that wonderful smell of food.

He crept over to the house, down the length of its side, and to its end, where he stopped abruptly. A small noise of surprise and delight escaped his lips. The sights, sounds, and smells before him were unlike anything he could have ever imagined. There were colorful balls of light hanging from the tree branches. He heard music, but couldn't identify it. And there were people. Yes, people. More than he had ever seen before, of all shapes and sizes. (And none of them looked like his mother). They were all sitting round a table, eating food. And it was, unmistakeably, this food that he had smelled. The urge to taste it was intense. He could think of nothing more than walking over to that table and tasting some, right now.

So, he stepped forward, into the light bathing the back yard at the home of the people eating that tasty smelling food.

First one, and then another of the people looked over at him, then all the people at the table erupted from it amid screams and shouts of terror. And they were all looking directly at him.

Was there something behind him? He whirled around and looked every which way, but nowhere did he see anything that would be cause for their reaction.

Lights were coming on in other houses now too, and then with a startling clamor, more shouting people began coming out of the houses. He heard, "Get your gun!" But what was a gun? "What is it?" screamed another. "Yes, what is it?" his mind echoed.

People were fleeing in terror everywhere he turned, either back to the safety of closed doors, or off in a direction away from him.

The activity alarmed him. He searched in every direction for the source of their terror, but as before, he could see nothing that would cause it. What should he do? Should he run, but which way? Should he even do anything at all? What was this invisible menace? Was it coming after him too? Nowhere could he see anything of threat, and that made him afraid even more.

More people came out, some carrying sticks pointed in his direction. He whirled around to see what they were pointing at. It had to be something behind him, because there was nothing frightening in front of him. But there was nothing there other than more people looking at him, screaming, and running away. He saw a young girl peek out at him from the corner of a nearby house. But there was nothing threatening about her either.

Whatever it was that was scaring everyone was truly clever. No matter how hard he tried, he couldn't see it anywhere. He wondered what it would be like to be that invisible. It must not be fun, or people wouldn't scream and run.

Something went zinging past his head, sizzling a bit of skin off his ear before burying itself in the ground. Pain erupted in his ear. Another zinging thing went past, and another, digging into the ground with terrific force. He didn't know what they were, but he did know he didn't want any more of them hitting him.

He tried to avoid them as he ran away, but no matter where he went, they followed. Eventually, they dwindled down to only a few, missing him by greater and greater distances. But new noises were popping up all around, each of them getting louder, stronger, and closer. One was unlike the screams of the people. It was a scream that had a pitch that rose and fell, rose and fell, and rose and fell. It was horrible. Perhaps that sound came from the invisible thing the people were running from. The thought sent more fear shuddering through him. It literally hurt his ears to hear that wail. And as it got closer, so the pain got greater.

He now desired to be away from this place of screaming. Why hadn't he obeyed his mother? He would now be safely and happily playing in the house or on the grounds if he had just done as she had said.

It was all converging on him and it was more than he could take. He no longer cared about that wonderful smell that had lured him over the wall. What he cared about now was getting away from that terrible wailing thing and keeping away from the flying things that buried themselves in the ground.

He started moving among the shadows, slinking away as silently as snow. He wasn't even sure which direction he was going, back to the wall, or away from it. It didn't matter. He just wanted to be away from this awfulness. Maybe if the thing didn't see or hear him, he'd be safe. After a while, it seemed to be working, so he stopped to rest, and to decide what to do next.

Just then, one of those sizzling things flew straight into his arm, went all the way through, and burrowed into the ground. Pain exploded in his arm, so bad it was that he screamed out loud.

That brought a cascade of shouts from the people who had caught up with him. They hadn't stopped after all. So, was the invisible scary thing behind them too, now? It was all getting most confusing.

More sizzling things came flying past. One grazed his leg, sending new pain spreading throughout his body. He took off running.

He passed another house, and then caught a glimpse of the wall, just beyond. And there was his rope as well. Relief washed over him. Sanctuary was only a short distance ahead. He ran for it, his mind racing just as swiftly as his legs. How had he managed to evade it? How had he not seen it? And worse, if he still couldn't see it, how would he know when it was gone?

He made it to the wall with no time to spare. Although it seemed he had momentarily lost the thing (and the people chasing it,) he knew they weren't far behind. Grabbing the rope, he shimmied up it as if it were an extension of his own body.

He knew something wasn't right long before he reached the top. The rope was too taut, and there was something dark at the top of the wall, where his rope spilled over the side. Was it the scary thing? Did it wait for him at the top of the rope? Panic stopped him cold.

Then a voice came floating down to him, urging him to hurry. It had a soft lilt that reminded him of his mother. Perhaps that's why he instantly obeyed and scurried up the last few feet of the rope. At the top, he was surprised, and a bit relieved to find that the dark shape wasn't the scary thing. At least it didn't look like a scary thing. It was a young girl of about 10 years. Well, 10 years as we would count it. He actually didn't pay any attention to her age, or gender at all. What mattered to him was that this girl was at the top of his rope. He had no idea how she had gotten there, or why, and she didn't give him time to think about it. She grabbed his shoulder and pulled him up, gave him a "shush" to be quiet, then hastily pulled the make-shift rope back up into the tree.

She then gestured to him that they should climb down, and without waiting for him to acknowledge, proceeded on ahead of him.

He followed her down the tree, marveling at her agility and skill, and wondering who/what she was and why she was here.

When they reached the ground, there were a million questions running through both their minds. They chattered back and forth as children often do, and before long they got to know each other. He lived here. She lived at the house with the colorful lights and food that smelled good. She had seen him there and had followed him here, having beat him by several moments. After all, she had the advantage. She knew the neighborhood.

She was as inquisitive as he was, and every bit as playful. You might think that was the reason she stayed so long that night, but it wasn't, of course. At least, it wasn't the only reason. In her eyes, he was the injured bird that needed her superior nursing skills, something any young girl would jump at the chance to do. That night she cleaned up his wounds and bound them with torn pieces of linen from the make-shift rope. She fluffed up his bed, and shared some of his food with him, too. It was evident that he was in a good deal of pain. But as there was nothing the girl could do for him, she settled on cradling him up in her arms and gently rocking him as she told him one of her favorite bedtime stories.

When he awoke the next evening, it was to find all his wounds dressed with clean neat bandages. The pain was gone, too. He wondered about it only briefly and then dismissed it as unimportant. He was used to waking to find things changed or different. And it wasn't the first time he had awakened to bandages either.

They quickly fell into a routine. Shortly after dark he would climb the tree, let down the rope for her to climb up, and then wait for her arrival. She, on the other hand, would let herself into the yard through the gate. He never saw her because he was always busy watching for her to approach the rope. So to him, she always just appeared. It was like playing peek-a-boo.

Sometimes she would bring him tidbits from home, a piece of chicken, an apple or two, the meatballs from her plate of spaghetti, or a pocket full of stale popcorn. Sometimes she brought candy, his favorite of all. She even once brought him some of that good smelling food he had sought the night he climbed over the wall. That was a treat beyond delight.

They would always make time to play, too. They would race up and down the tree in daring-do challenges. He found all of her challenges so delightful that he was soon teasing her back. She apparently loved it as much as he did, because they played it so often.

Then one night she brought a book, and story time became official. And so it went, night after night after night. After a while, he began to notice that her eyes looked puffy and tired. Black circles framed them. She yawned a lot, and was prone to falling asleep. But, being the simple creature he was, he gave it no consequence.

Then the night came when she told him she couldn't come again for a while. Her parents had noticed her eyes too, and had correctly guessed that she was sneaking out of the house at night. The thought had mortified them. They had heard the recent gossip about a strange creature that had been terrorizing the neighborhood. In fact, gossip now had him devouring helpless neighborhood pets. Children would be next.

So, they grounded her and made sure that future outings would be noticed immediately. In fact, she would probably be punished the moment she returned home.

Before she left, she gave him a huge hug and made him promise to not try to follow her or anything stupid like that. She would be back in a few days, after things at home settled down.

He tried to not show his dismay, but by now she knew him well enough that he couldn't fool her. Even so, he did as she wished and promised he would wait for her return.

While she was gone, time passed slowly, ever so slowly. Everything was boring. He even tried some of the games he used to delight in. They were no longer any fun at all. There was no one to play with; no one to chase up and down the tree; no one whose giggle made him laugh. There were no new stories. It was terrible. The books she had left with him no longer kept his interest. All he could think of was how soon she would return. In a way, it was like when his mother had left, and at the same time, it was different. One thing for sure, this time he noticed the emptiness, the boredom, the aloneness. He felt them all keenly.

Weeks came and went and still the girl did not return. He sat in the tree every night, watching for her. He began having thoughts about going over the wall again. But he had promised the girl he wouldn't, and he felt he should keep his word, although he knew he would eventually break it.

It was a quandary that kept his mind busy for some time. Eventually he came to the firm decision that he was just going to have to go look for her. So, the next night, after a meal from the box at the gate, he put his plan into action. He climbed the tree, tossed the rope over, and went down it to the street. He knew exactly where to go. He had secretly followed her home many times.

In no time at all he was hunkering beneath her window. It was closed and locked with curtains drawn shut. He knew she was inside asleep in her bed. So, he waited outside her window, hoping she would wake and notice he was there. But she didn't, not that night nor any of the nights after that.

He waited patiently for all of them, then finally, one night, decided this would no longer do. It was more than just her presence he desired. He wanted her companionship as well. So, he plucked up his courage and rapped on the window.

Nothing happened. So, he rapped harder, and longer, and within moments lights were turned on and voices were heard. Then the curtains flew back from the girl's window, and there she was, on the other side of the glass. She saw him immediately and threw open her window to let him in, then motioned for him to hide under her bed. She had closed the window back and had just slid back under her covers when the door to her room opened and in marched her father. She pretended to sleep as he checked the room and window, and then left.

Out of bed she flew, picking a pair of blue jeans from off the floor and putting them on as she had motioned for him to come out from under the bed. Throwing the window back open, she stuck her head out to see if the coast was clear, then made him follow her out.

They sneaked out into the night just in time, for just moments later, her father left the house, carrying his gun. Before he could finish checking his yard for signs of intrusion, several neighborhood men had joined him, some of them also with guns. They all huddled together to plan their hunt, with the girl's father heading the pack. He had a good idea where to look next. He had seen the make-shift rope and suspicioned that something, or someone, from the other side of the wall was terrorizing their neighborhood. So, with the bluster of ego fueling his actions, he proudly led the way for what was now a hunting party.

The girl reached the gate first, having initially led him straight to it. It was, after all, the place she always entered from. But no matter how hard she tried to convince him to pass through it, he just wasn't having any of it. Instead he gave up arguing with her about it, grabbed her by the arm, and dragged her around to the make-shift rope hanging over the wall, waiting for its user's return. He signaled to her to climb up, and after a moment she did. He followed, urging her on as they went. Something was giving him a sense of urgency, a sense of impending doom, and he didn't like it. It made him want to hurry.

Just as they neared the top of the wall, the hunting party came into view. Everyone turned and saw each other at the same instant, and after that, it was a race; he and the girl racing to the top of the rope; the hunting party racing to catch them. It was a flurry of activity. The hunters were shouting

84

to one another those things that hunters should never shout, "There it is!" "It's got my daughter! Stop it! Stop it!" "I have it right in my sights!" "Then shoot it!" "No! Don't shoot it." "Yes, shoot it! Hurry!" "No! Don't shoot. You'll hit my girl too!" And then it was too late to say anything more. A gun went off, sending death in a straight line that aimed for his heart, entering through his muscular back to pierce his heart, then exiting straight out of him to bore into the girl, piercing her heart an instant later. No sooner had that bullet pierced his back than he came to the shocking realization that the monster he had feared and could not see didn't exist. It didn't exist because in fact, there was no 'monster'. There never had been one. He had been the 'monster' all along.

It was that epiphany that stopped his heart, not the bullet passing through on its way to kill the girl. It was a cold epiphany, flitting along in his thoughts until the moment was right. He didn't have time to wonder about this epiphany, to absorb it into consciousness, or hold it out for examination. He had it, and then he was dead.

His arms had been reaching for the shoulders of the girl when he died, and that's where they were when the bullet killed her, holding onto her shoulders. She was in the moment of taking that single step from the top of the wall to the branch of the tree when death singed its way through her heart. She died so swiftly that it was too late to halt that final step, and her body, instead of being supported by a sturdy foot on the tree branch started to fall, down through the tree to the ground, taking his body with it.

When they landed at the bottom their hands had clasped together (or at least so it appeared). Maybe it was a final connection between friends, and maybe that's just how they happened to be positioned when they landed. Either way, it would soon make an impact on all.

From the other side of the wall came an anguished voice that wailed the inevitable cry of a parent who has just lost a child. There was a moment of stunned silence, and then the hunting party was off to find their way in to the other side of that wall. The death of the monster had to be confirmed. Bodies needed to be collected. Everyone, of course, wanted to be involved.

With the mass of people rushing the gate in the side yard near the tree, no one really noticed the indistinct woman who blended herself into the mass. They paid her no attention as she slipped in through the gate, and over to the tree.

It was as she had hoped it wouldn't be. He was there, lying on the ground, his body obviously broken in many places, his eyes glazed in a permanent question, his chest expelled of all breath of air, looking as lifeless as a discarded rag doll. It had not been a good decision to leave him living alone. But that had not been her decision. Time after time she had told them that the subject wasn't ready yet, and time after time they grew too impatient to wait. And it was a shame about the girl.

Maybe they would listen now.

She drifted away from the crowd as sirens sounded in the distance. The crowd was growing loud as well, lots of shouting and arguing and pleading and gossiping, and a good bit of wailing. No one would notice her absence and she could quietly slip inside the house.

Once there, she looked around, memories flooding her mind. She thought of him as she remembered the games they had played together, his curiosity for everything in his world, and the surprises that had given him such delight. Most painful of all were the memories of when he had come to her for solace, comfort, and companionship. She had bonded too well with him, and that was why she had been taken off the project.

She had much to do. In time, there would be a new subject to work with, a new trial to run, and hopefully, better parameters to work within. She might even get used to sleeping during the day once again.

Girl Walks Into a Bar

By Jessica Stilling

S tories happen quickly. There's a beginning, middle and end and then out of nowhere the story is finished. A guy walks into a bar, pulls out a semi automatic, shoots the bartender in the head and leaves. End of story. Except now the guy is walking around somewhere and there's a funeral on the other side of town and a grieving widow and now the bartender's son has decided to move to California to get out of the drudgery that was his father's life. But stories are concrete, they don't move on, we don't see that, the rest. They end.

He was sitting on the couch with the baby. The baby was nine months old and crawling all over the back of the red leather seat. So the guy turns his head for a second (and how many times have we heard that, I just looked the other way, just for a second and little Timmy or Johnny or Susie was gone). But life is full of clichés and stories aren't, and he was looking back at his wife fixing up the table for dinner, or the television where some elaborate commercial was showing another guy, a fake guy with blond hair and a perfectly chiseled jaw, driving a fast car with a fast woman, or down at the floor, he was just looking down because his eyes were tired. The baby slipped, fell off the couch, got stuck between the leather and the wall and snapped his neck. Just like that, there was a scream, a tight, constraining baby scream. The parents were panicked by that scream and then it went silent. And it was the silence, that silence which was deafening and terrifying, that caused the blood pumping inside their bodies to stop, freeze up, constrict.

Cue major freak out, cue wife crying, cue drive in the ambulance and wife trying to tear the guy's shirt off in the ER waiting room. Cue doctor coming out; cue her shaking her head, twenty-six-year-old med student with a look on her face like they don't pay her enough to do this. They don't pay anyone enough for this, honey. Cue the guy's wife trying to tear his shirt off again. Cue the guy wondering why everything is ending. He's in a red sweatshirt; there are grass stains on his white tennis shoes. The guy's wife's hair is blond and she has blue eyes, but no one can see them because she's just too hysterical. Another doctor comes out and we cut.

We don't have to see any more. We don't have to linger. Maybe we'll gossip about it around the dinner table, a few friends talking about a distant friend, the friend of a friend of a friend, you know the deal, shaking our heads, 'that's so sad, but it's not me so how sad can it be?' Maybe we'll hear about it on the news, a story nestled between something about the President and something about a local grocery store going out of business. But we don't have to see it all, we can tell the story without feeling a thing. It is possible. I just did it.

Girl walks into a bar. I'm already there, sitting with a double of scotch, raw whiskey, heavy whiskey. I've had four already and there is stubble on my face, not much, I'm not growing a beard. I'll shave tomorrow morning, maybe. My dirty blond hair is cut short and I am a lawyer. Despite all the scruff I am a busy New York professional in half a three-piece suit with some Chivas in my hand. I am full of clichés these days.

It's a Manhattan bar, but not too flashy. I'm on the Upper West Side, Seventy-Ninth and Amsterdam, no Village hotspots for me, no bouncers and lines at the door. I grew out of that in college. There's a shiny wood grain bar with brass edges and the shelves in back, and the top shelves (that saying had to come from somewhere) are beautiful creations full of expensive stuff. I bought a vodka and cranberry juice once for a lady and it cost fifteen dollars. There are tables in the back, mostly full of couples, and an old man sits at the edge of the bar in a suit kind of like mine, only I don't think he's just come from the office. I think he simply throws on a suit and goes out drinking every night. I've seen him here before. I've been here before. Maybe I'll be that guy someday. Every bar has them, the crazy old man with nothing better to do. The bartender doesn't talk to him. The bartender doesn't talk to me, or anybody.

Girl walks into a bar and it's raining outside. It is dark and raining and there is a full moon and by the way, it is always midnight. Bars close at four in New York City even on weeknights. That's what sets us apart.

She's wearing red, a tasteful red dress which covers her arms, her knees, no plunging neckline, with black heels. I try to tell if she has any hose on, but I don't see any. Her hair is red and brown, a deep, dark auburn, and she's wearing a big floppy hat like those you see in the movies when people are at the beach. Except, it's November and no one's been to the beach in New York in a while.

The girl sits down two seats from me and I look at her.

"You got a name?" she asks me, and I feel like she should be lighting up a cigarette. You can't do that in New York City bars anymore. You can't do that at clubs or restaurants. Soon you won't be able to do that in your own home.

"Ryan," I answer. Everyone's name is Ryan. I'm from a whole generation of Ryans and Davids, Jasons and Michaels. Everyone had the same name in my elementary school, the girls too, Jennifers, Amandas, Lindsays and Amys. It wasn't like now where little Flower sits next to little Apple in school, and I can honestly say I don't know which is worse.

"Hi, I'm Rebecca," she says, looking out at the bartender. He doesn't have to say anything and she orders a martini, gin, shaken. Good girl.

"How are you, Ryan?" Rebecca asks. I take this opportunity to move a stool closer.

"I'm fine, fine," I reply.

"I feel like shit," she counters.

"Good for you," I answer. "Did something happen?"

"My husband just died."

"Did you know him well?" I ask, a little confused. Is she talking about her estranged husband, has he been in a coma for the last five years so now it really doesn't matter?

"Yes," she answers and the bartender hands her the martini. She takes a sip, a dainty sip, though she might have taken a gulp there is that much force behind her swallow.

"No, really?" I ask, grabbing my own whiskey and taking a mouthful. I take another and the bartender picks up my glass. He'll be coming back soon with more. Sure, the bartender doesn't talk to anyone, but he knows how to do his job.

"Stop it," she replies coldly.

"Was he in a coma, did you know him well?" I can't stop, it's like a train wreck. But it's not fair, this woman has brought this on herself, coming in with that dress on, sitting at a bar as if she's ready to light a cigarette and talking about a dead husband as if she were mentioning the Yankees down four to seven in the sixth.

"He was my husband, I knew him," she replies. "He was walking across Madison Avenue when a UN vehicle flew past and hit him. Head trauma, died instantly. They're going to take his organs tomorrow morning, he's on a respirator right now."

"So there's still a chance?" I ask. The bartender sets my whiskey down. Without looking I grab the glass and drink.

"Where do you live?" the woman asks, shaking her small clutch purse, disinterested.

"I live on Eighty-Fourth Street, but I plan on moving out once the lease is up. You should have seen the place when my ex-wife and I moved in. The tenants before were artists and they painted all this crap on the walls. The place still smells like turpentine."

"How very cozy," the woman replies. Her name is Rebecca, I know her name is Rebecca, she told me and I do not forget these things. I'm a lawyer, I go to parties, I shake hands with men in suits and women wearing nice dresses, drinks in hand. You have to be good at names to get by in my world. But it's her hair, her dress, the fact that her husband has just died (and I've decided, for the sake of argument, for the sake of all that is holy, to just believe her), she's the woman in the red dress. I live in clichés. Life is better here.

I take a swig of my whiskey and leave the rest. Going into my wallet I remove a wad of bills, placing it on the counter, one action begetting another. Usually when I come here I pay with a credit card, but I'd had to take a certain amount of cash out of my ATM this evening, on my way home from work, before the bar, and it is just easier to pay with the rest. I hate having paper money and prefer to get rid of it as quickly as possible. It, shall we say, burns a gaping hole in my pocket. I can see, feel it smoking before I can smell it.

"I'm going to head out," I say, and the woman nods. At this point she's expecting it.

"Are you going to be okay?" I ask at the last minute. "I mean, can I call you a cab, a grief counselor?"

She laughs and shakes her head.

"No, please, go home." She does not go on and faces the bar as I head out, her eyes on the bartender.

It's a short walk home, a few blocks, and I honestly don't feel it. I don't feel the booze and the bitter taste in my mouth. I don't feel the concrete under my feet, and I can't hear a car honking when I walk right in front of it as a big orange hand signals Don't Walk from across the street. Maybe I'll go the way of the woman in the bar's dead husband.

I walk home and it's like time has clicked shut. I go from one space to another like warp drive, like the transporters. All my molecules are mixed up and I wonder when I became the kind of guy who references *Star Trek*. I never used to watch it and then I started staying up late. I couldn't sleep, and it's the only thing on at four in the morning. I swear, it's either Captain Kirk or How to Sell Seventeen Houses in Three Weeks and Keep All the Profit Without Having to Worry About a Mortgage.

My apartment is dark when I enter. I don't click on a light, but the red flash of the answering machine beckons like that dress Rebecca, her name was Rebecca (I said I was good with names), was wearing. I press the play button without thinking.

"Hi, Ryan. Ryan are you home? It's your wife, Claire. I was just calling to see how you were. You had me worried last night. Please call me. I have my cell, you know my cell."

I walk away before the machine beeps the end of the call, first toward the bathroom, where I urinate briefly, and then into the back room. It's been dark back there for a while, and when I turn on the light a giant octopus stares back at me. He is green with long painted tentacles that go all the way up one wall. Its eyes are black and light blue and the creepy thing smiles at me. It just keeps smiling and I wish I had some paint, anything to wipe that smirk away.

I turn off the lights in the back room. It's better this way. There's nothing here. Leftovers, remnants. I live in the living room (aptly named), sometimes the kitchen. I haven't even slept in my bed in three months. It's too hot, too cold in there, depending on my mood, a regular rainstorm ripe for unimaginable chaos. I've been passing out in front of the television every night. Thank God I set up an alarm out there. There's no reason to stay here so I walk out, back through the living room.

I pat myself down for the night, keys, business cards I've collected at work (we had a meeting with the Boston branch, that many more names to remember). My wallet is not in my pants pocket, couldn't be anywhere else. I pat myself again, panicked. A flash of heat rages through my stomach, tingling down my arms and legs and then I'm fine, calm, relaxed. Sure there's a lot of money in my wallet right now, and my driver's license, but my credit cards are replaceable and I can always take a Saturday trip to the DMV. It'll be a hassle, but I have nothing better to do.

First, better go back to the bar. It's two in the morning; they'll still be open, and I need to go, just to see if they have it. No matter what happens, life goes on. Different plot points connect no matter how many times you try to shred the strings, take each aspect and throw it away. So I have to go find my wallet, you see, I have to make sure it's not there before I give it up for lost. Because really, truly, who wants to spend their entire Saturday at the DMV if they don't have to?

The phone rings. Just like that. It is shrill and comical, my black rotary phone, the one in the living room, just in front of the television. I answer it. Only people who are trying to hide something don't answer a ringing phone. I pick it up. "Hello?"

"Ryan, Ryan, are you there?" a voice asks, coming from beyond the something or other, beyond time and space and energy. Am I there? Does it seem as if I'm not there? "Ryan, I've been trying to get a hold of you all night, where were you?"

"I was at a bar. Why?"

"Ryan, last night, what you said, I mean, you're not still doing that, are you? You're not still...are you okay?"

"I'm okay," I reply, standing near the couch, slouched, the phone to my ear, waiting, just waiting for the apartment to cave in on me, to get a bucket of turpentine to wipe that silly smirk of that octopus's face.

"How are you? Still at the Natural History Museum?" I say, making general conversation, small talk. I was going to use an expletive here, but some people just don't understand those types of things. I've never understood those types of people. I think they need to get over themselves.

"I am. They want me to revamp the Whale Room, but not so much so that anyone actually notices - the octopus exhibit." My wife, my former wife, my soon-to-be ex-wife has a thing for octopuses ("octopi?") She's got some marine biology degree. I swear there was a time when I paid more attention.

"It's just that...I know we'll never get over it, this is not something that you just deal with, but I mean, still ... I want you to be able to move on ... have a life ..."

"Nothing happened!" I cry, and I can see her face dying, shriveling up and dying, on the other end. "Nothing ever happened, Claire. Will you shut up?"

"Ryan, I'm worried. I think maybe I should come by."

"I think you should stay at your sister's," I reply, replacing my nice rotary

94

phone into its cradle. There, the phone is on the hook. Claire does not call back, she stays where she is and so I walk out, grabbing my house keys as I make it to the door. At least I remembered to bring them home with me from the bar.

It's dark when I reenter the bar, coming back as if I've never left. Still in my rumpled suit, as if I were simply in the bathroom. I reclaim my seat across from the old man, who is half asleep but still drinking, and the bartender nods to me, handing me a whiskey I don't want a whiskey, I want to be home, but when he gives it to me I don't see the point in refusing. I'm sure I can get a tab if all else fails.

"I left my wallet here," I say and he shrugs, looks away, turns around, starts helping the redhead with the dead husband.

"You're back," she says, nimble fingers, jumpy fingers, on the counter before she reaches for her martini. It can't be the same drink; she has to have gone through at least two since I left. Life did not stop, time did not stand still. Then again, it looks like it did.

"I left my wallet, have you seen it?" I ask. She nods, turns around, grabs something from under the bar, as if there's a secret compartment, and produces it.

"Here you go," she says and I take it, look inside, just in case. The money is there, so is my license and credit cards and the picture of a six-week-old little boy named Caleb ...

"I didn't go though it or anything, I figured you'd be back. If you didn't return for it, I would have checked out the ID," the redhead says and I remember, again, because I am great with names, that she is Rebecca.

"That's very logical of you, Rebecca."

"Thank you," she replies.

"So how are you doing, I mean, you said your husband ..."

"I did, didn't I?" she replies very seriously, though she has this look on her face that suggests she might be acting coy, that she might start giggling at any second. Instead she lowers her eyes and I finish my whiskey Throwing another wad of bills on the bar, I stand up and she follows me as if it had all been planned out this way in rehearsals the night before. She comes in, I leave, I come back, and we go out together.

"You want to get out of here, just for a little while?" I don't normally do this. I'm really not that guy, with the rumbled suit and shaggy hair, hair that's going to get him called into the boss's office in a few days if he's not careful. I'm not going to take her home. Her husband has just died. And I've already decided to buy that story. Whether it's helpful or not, real or no, I see no reason to go around doubting people. It just doesn't make for pleasant conversation.

"I do," she replies and wrapping an arm around mine, she walks out, attached to me. We move fluidly through the bar and out into the street. It's chilly. It's always chilly at night, the moon is constantly full, and it's perpetually midnight. Scene set. We wander up Broadway for a while and take a right down to Central Park West. We don't go into the park. We have reached that time of night where it is dangerous to go certain places in New York City. Its funny how life hits you that way. How you can be in one place and it's sunny and bright and beautiful and five seconds later the apartment is empty, the doors are all closed and you can see lines where the wires are running up the walls. That's what it's like in Manhattan at three a.m. ... not for the faint of heart.

We walk more slowly, still arm in arm, I with my precious wallet back in my pants pocket and she with a somber look upon her face.

"You forgot your hat, where'd you put it?" I ask and she looks at me.

"I left it at the bar."

"Should we go back for it?"

"Why would we do that?" she asks as if I've just suggested something silly.

Her red dress sways in the breeze and I wonder what it would take to hear a saxophone go off right about now. It's always midnight, the moon is constantly full, what's wrong with a little jazz?

"He was forty-five years old," she says and I turn to look at her. "I'm only twenty-nine, but he was forty-five. We didn't have any children."

"Why not?" I ask. "I like kids, always have. I was hoping to have a big family someday."

"We'd only met a short time ago. Then, he went out for a walk in the middle of the day. We had the day off and had just had lunch when he announced that he was feeling a little full, that he wanted to walk off the weight. Not the calories, the weight, as if something were holding him back. Then I get a call at four in the afternoon, when I'm already a little worried; a walk does not take hours. And, when I got to the hospital they said there was brain damage. They waited until midnight, until I called his parents, they're at the hospital with him now, to let me know that there was no use trying. They drove in from West Hartford, his parents."

"Oh my," I say, because really, what is there?

"We hadn't had a fight or anything. Our relationship was just as it was and all of a sudden, he goes out for a walk and never comes home; gets struck down by a silly UN vehicle."

"You know those things have diplomatic immunity, they probably won't be able to do anything to the driver," the lawyer in me says. And it's like its not me. Ryan is not talking, Ryan is stuck in his own head and this guy in a freshly laundered three piece suit, with a nice haircut, is calling the shots.

"I wasn't thinking about that," she says, still stone-faced. I'm expecting her to break down. Claire used to break down all the time before she left. I'm sure she still does. It's only been something like seven months. I haven't been counting the days; I haven't even been keeping track of what time of year it is. It's always midnight.

"I know, I'm sorry, I'm just saying. I mean ... sometimes someone has to think of those things, so that other people, people like you, can think of the big picture." Now the philosopher in me is talking, the kid who wanted to go to law school to debate the point of the universe. That never happened. No one wanted to talk about anything except tort law and clerkships, myself included.

"It's just that terrible things happen, they happen all the time and sometimes it's to a distant stranger and sometimes it's to you. That is what I thought when they told me, the first time, that there was nothing they could do. That he was probably going to die, barring some miracle."

"Don't you believe there could be—,"

"Miracles," she cuts in, shaking her head. This time she really does laugh. This time she pulls a cigarette out of her purse and lights it in one fluid motion, like those women back in Hollywood circa 1930-something.

"No, I don't believe in them. My husband is dead, he's gone and all that is left now is me, here on earth; my life, his parents and their lives. He has a sister in Florida I never met. They were estranged. I'm sure this will affect her as well. But, when horrible things happen, I mean ... sometimes we deal with them and some things ... they are not said. I prefer to talk about my husband. I prefer to meet a man at a bar and tell him his story. It's either this or waiting around a lonely apartment, or sitting in the waiting room with his parents."

"And what's his story?" I ask. "Your husband, his story?"

"It's not so complicated," Rebecca replies. "He went to college, got a degree in business, worked on Wall Street, quit after September 11th and started teaching in Harlem. He met me at a party at one of his former Wall Street buddies' apartments and we married, honeymooned in Greece, came home and resumed our life together until ... you know."

"I see," I reply. No speed bumps, no pit stops. "It must have been a nice life, uncomplicated."

We stop walking down Central Park West and instead move upward, doing a complete turn around, back toward my apartment. It is not said, it is simply done, as if we are reading each others' minds.

"Some things we do not talk about, we hold them in," she goes on and I wonder what she means. There must be something in the back of her mind, something more dreadful than getting a call saying that your husband is in critical condition four hours after he's gone out for a walk.

"Some things are too horrific, like when you think back to an embarrassing moment, when you said something to a girl in bed and she laughed at you. The memory creeps back into your skull and you push it back, right away, before it can do any harm. We look away, we don't watch. We love to read about it, to hear some nice man in a fancy suit tell us about it, but we can't handle it when it's there, when we actually have to look."

I nod, say something encouraging, something having to do with new media and the grand scheme of the rest of the world. She smiles back at me and maybe this might turn into something, maybe I'll open my mouth and say to the redhead something I've never said before.

Then we get mugged. A guy comes up, asks me for my wallet. I don't hand it over. He takes out a knife and pulls an arm around Rebecca's neck. I try to give him the wallet. I scream for him to take it, beg him to rob me, but he takes Rebecca's purse instead and runs off, into Central Park; that simple.

I don't have my cell phone on me. I am not the kind of guy, anymore, who has his cell phone on him at all times and that guy has just taken Rebecca's purse.

"Oh my God," she screams into the chilly New York air. "I can't believe on this night of all nights." She runs up the street in her clunky heels and I chase after her. She doesn't seem like the type to carry cash and cards are replaceable. It's the humiliation of having a knife to your throat, of having a man take what's yours and run with it. It's having to wait in a hospital for something to happen only to have Worst Case Scenario stare you in the face. Her hair is a mess. It's coming out in Medusa strands from the side of her head, and her dress is torn near the left shoulder from the struggle.

"I'm sorry, we should go to the police. I don't have my cell phone," I go on, helpless. Because, what does it mean for my manhood that a damsel is in distress and I do nothing for her? I don't even hand over my wallet, I just stand there looking dumb while a crazy person takes a knife to her throat.

"No, that's okay, I'll go down to the station myself," she calls. "I never should have come out here tonight. I never should have left the hospital. And giving you your wallet; what do you care, who are you to deserve your wallet back?"

"I'm sorry," I say it like it's nothing, because it is nothing. It's just a single, solitary word falling from my mouth and into the confines of outer space; no more, no less.

"I'll go to the police on my own, thank you," she says and I hand her a wad of bills. She looks at the money and shakes her head, takes it anyway. She sticks her hand out and a cab appears. They come out of the woodwork at night, those New York City cabbies.

I try to stand at the door, to let her in, to help her with her dress, but she disappears inside the car and it drives off. There is no goodbye, no thanks for the cash; it was nice to meet you. I stand in the street for a while. It's still cold. The moon is out, it is always midnight and a sax is playing up the street. Some guy with a beard and an open case at his feet. I go into my wallet and take out another wad of cash as I walk by, throw it in his case and move on. He doesn't say a word, he's too busy playing.

When I reach my apartment, it's dark. Nothing is there. The wires run up the walls like mice chasing; getting ahead of themselves, as if to finish this rat race means something, means anything. My bedroom is cold, I've left a window open, and I don't feel like warming it up. I don't feel like closing the window and seeing that the heater is working. Instead, I meander over to the back room. I don't turn the lights on, that octopus will only stare me in the face. It's stuffy back here and the closet door is open. I consider sleeping in there, on the carpet Claire had put in when we were redecorating, but I can't wait that long and fall to my knees, then on all fours, until I have slowly and systematically sprawled myself out on the hardwood floor. From there the ceiling spins.

The next morning I hit my head on the crib while trying to stretch. I stand up and light comes through the window, illuminating the mobile over the crib, trains and trucks for a little boy. My hand on my head, my spinning head, I walk straight toward the window and hit my shin on the changing table, painted white with a drawer full of bibs and burp rags and a section for diapers and wipes, little baby onesies and pajama pieces. There's a large stuffed Snoopy doll, and that octopus, the one Claire painted on the wall facing the crib, is still looking at me. He won't stop. I told Claire when she did the thing that it would start to scare him when he got older, but she said he'd be used to it by then. By then, as if by then was a time, a concrete place on the calendar.

The sun is still in my eyes, it's burning holes in the back of my head. I am still in my suit, wallet burrowing into my leg, when I enter the living room. My dinner from the night before, some kind of glorified TV dinner circa 1953 complete with powdered mashed potatoes and Salisbury something or other, is still on the coffee table, half eaten, and I've kept the television on. Some courtroom drama has been playing for the last half hour. It's after nine, I have to be at work, but it looks like I'm going to be late, it looks like I'm not going. My boss is going to call me in for this, but I let that slip from my mind.

"You're up," I hear a female voice come from the couch and I stop, petrified. Did I bring Rebecca home with me? Did she come back to the apartment? Did I forget that? What is wrong with me; how could I forget that? I turn to the couch and it's Claire, sitting up, her shoulder-length blond hair a little ratty. She's wearing a white sweater and jeans. She looks like Thanksgiving. She smells like Thanksgiving and if I went so far as to touch her, I'm sure she'd feel like it too. There is no jazz in her bones; it's all big blue eyes, creamy skin, smooth and wholesome like hot apple pie.

"I was worried about you last night, after what you said the night before, after the way you acted on the phone."

"So you decided to sleep here?" I ask, walking further into the living room. I catch the white powder, just sitting out. There's not much of it, I took most of it, but there's the mirror, the straw. I just left it sitting there. By the look on her face I can tell that Claire sees it too. She's been seeing it all night.

"When I got here you were already asleep in the nursery. I thought it would be best to leave you alone, after I saw that you were breathing. I mean, Ryan, really, you need to stop."

I'm fine. The light is a little much right now, my head hurts, but I don't do it that often and I'm just a little dizzy. I look at her funny, like she's just said something crazy, something stupid, but Claire knows me and she doesn't back down.

"What?" I ask and I know as I say it that I sound ridiculous. "All right, whatever."

"You can't be all right, *I'm* not all right. But you need to see a professional. You need to talk to someone, talk to me. You have to stop blaming yourself."

"Nothing happened!" I scream at her and Claire shakes her head. "Tell me what happened?"

"I don't have to, Ryan. I just don't think you should do that," Claire goes on, pointing to the mirror lying on a speaker near my easy chair.

"I went to the bar last night, I met a woman, we got mugged."

"Are you all right, is she all right?" Claire asks, not even flinching when I say I met a woman. This infuriates me.

"She was fine, I was fine."

"You know, I don't care if you go to bars. I mean, you need to have something, I just wish you'd see a doctor. Understand that it's not your fault."

"Not my fault, what's not my fault?" I ask her, confused. "Nothing happened."

"Really, Ryan, if everything is so fine, if nothing is so wrong, then why am I filing for divorce? Why is your mother calling me every day, worried sick. Why are you spending all your money on that junk?"

"I don't know," I reply. What do you say to that? It makes no sense. None of it does. Rebecca makes no sense; Claire makes no sense, the bar and the little old man who is always there, and the octopus on the wall of the back room.

"Ryan, you have to deal with it. I know you think it's your fault. I know that you can see it in your mind; you can see it happening over and over. I can see it happening and I wasn't even there for it. But it's over, it's been seven months, and soon you'll have to deal with it."

"With what, " I ask her, question marks in my eyes. I stare at her, and she looks back. And I know this isn't over; not this conversation, not my nights out at that bar, not us. Rebecca's husband is dead but Claire isn't, I'm not.

"Ryan, I just wish you'd talk to me, I wish you'd let me know ..."

"But nothing happened," I say to her and she nods, sinking further into the couch and closing her eyes. I think she might leave but she doesn't. She's going to stay here, and I am not going to work today. These things don't end. Not like this. Nothing ever does.

Heat Stress

By Claire Ibarra

It was an Indian summer almost as hot as that record-breaking year when coyotes came out of the wilderness in droves looking for reprieve. The animals went crazy from the heat, and in some cases gnawed their way through screen doors and broke windows to get indoors. Others ran in front of moving cars to end their misery.

Now along the outskirts of Moab, the Canyon Lands in the distance shimmered like a mirage in the scorching heat. The dark reds, yellows and oranges of the surrounding desert merged into a single flame, and Kiran felt like the hot winds were incinerating her spirit. It was a cleansing baptism of fire, turning her insides into dry ash.

Kiran drove along a wide dirt road until she reached the state park entrance. She pulled up to the stationhouse and a stout-bellied ranger walked out.

"How long?" he asked.

"We'll be camping for two nights."

"Your pass will be good for a week," the ranger said as he approached the car.

While Kiran asked him questions about fresh water, bathrooms, and trails to the Arches, Sam and Zadie began to argue.

Zadie yelled at her brother, "Why did you take your shoes off? Your feet stink like a dead animal."

"Shut up. It's because these sandals are plastic. It's not my fault Mom's so cheap," Sam responded.

Sam was sprawled out on the backseat, but when the ranger tapped, he scooted upright and rolled down the window.

"Looks like you're the man of this small expedition. You gonna look out for these gals?" the ranger asked as he leaned inside the window.

Sam rubbed his bare knees. The air conditioning was sucked out in an instant, and his legs were already slick from sweat.

"Yes, sir."

"Good. Now, I should warn you all, this heat can be dangerous. You have to make sure you have plenty of drinking water—there are faucets located throughout the grounds. I've highlighted them on this map. If you go hiking, well heck, I'd just rather you didn't."

Zadie put her feet on the dashboard and her long, slender legs scrunched in the tight space.

"We came to see the famous Arches. It took us plenty of time to get here," Zadie said.

"You can drive right up to them. No need to hike the trail—I don't recommend it in this weather. Even the wildlife tends to get loony when it's this hot."

"Don't worry, we'll be careful," Kiran interrupted

Kiran was starting to get irritated; she had had enough of controlling men to last a lifetime.

"Let's go, kids," she said.

Kiran slowly pulled out, forcing the ranger to take a few steps back or be dragged away with the car.

"What a jerk," Zadie said as she twirled her long hair into a bun, looping and tucking the ends tight.

They drove through the grounds, and Zadie began reading from the park guide.

"It says here, we can see Devils Garden and Fiery Furnace; and here's another, Dark Angel. My God, this place is hell." Zadie laughed nervously.

"I came here with your dad once," Kiran told her kids as they made their way along the snaking dirt road. Memories of Doug began to spark and flicker like lit candles in the dark. Kiran saw his image illuminated in her mind's eye.

"But Dad told me he's never been west of the Mississippi," Sam corrected her.

"Not John, I mean your real dad." Kiran was afraid that Sam would forget his father. Sam had been only five years old when Doug crashed his small plane in the middle of an orange grove. She kept photos around the house so the kids would remember his face.

"Daddy was here. When was that?" Zadie asked. Zadie was a few years older than Sam, so Kiran hoped her daughter could still recall Doug's boisterous nature, his soft burliness and deep, reassuring voice.

"We came here before you were born," Kiran said.

Now all three were quiet, and the tires crackled over the dry, sun-baked earth. It sounded like the ground was ripping open underneath them, and Kiran imagined falling through a crack of the earth, into a fiery abyss, and she shuddered.

"Here's a good spot. What do you guys think?"

She pulled into a site surrounded by large reddish boulders and a few small trees with dry leaves. It looked tidy and fake, like a campsite at Disney. Kiran began to question why she was there, as she did when arriving at every new destination.

They had just spent a week in Colorado, now Utah, and after that she had thought maybe they would head south to Arizona. So many places, sometimes it felt like they were on the run. In some elusive way they were. The summer vacation had already come to an end, and they hadn't even reached California yet.

"Yeah, it looks good, Ma," Sam said in an easygoing manner.

"Wait, how far are the bathrooms? I won't trek to go pee." Zadie whined.

"They're around that bend. The bathrooms are the blue square on the map," Kiran said as she watched a Jeep pull into the campsite next to them.

Three young guys climbed out and began unloading the bags strapped to the roof. Kiran noticed they were good-looking. They had longish hair and scruffy chins.

Zadie stared out the window, then suddenly opened the door and jumped out. This was her opportunity. She walked around the car, so she would be in full view. She stretched forward and backward, touching her toes and leaning back--while her long, tan legs glistened with sweat. Her bun had come undone, so her thick mane of dark hair hung down her back.

It didn't take long for the guys to nod and smile at each other like they had just spotted a rare species in the wild. Maybe they had; Zadie was that beautiful and she knew it. There was a time when Kiran got the same reaction from men. Now Kiran admired her daughter.

Sam got out of the car and moaned,

"My God, this really is hell. I can't even breathe, it's so hot." His t-shirt was soaked in the armpits, and it clung to his scrawny frame. Kiran worried that the heat would make Sam's acne worse.

Kiran felt the heat singe her own skin. Sweat dripped down her back, a slow trickle that caressed her spine and almost titillated. It had been that long, so long ago that a drop of water mimicked a human fingertip, a human stroke. She glanced at one of the young men as he strolled across the dirt road, checking out the area.

The camper noticed Kiran watching him.

"Hey there, neighbors. Looks like we're the only ones braving this heat wave," he said.

"We must be crazy," Kiran replied as she began to help Sam unload.

"Where you guys from?" the young man asked as he took a few steps closer. Kiran rapidly assessed that he was well built, with reddish hair and blue eyes.

Zadie jumped into the conversation.

"We're from Orlando, Florida," she said.

"Orlando? You mean Walt Disney's home-turf? Do people actually live there?"

"Of course people live there. It's a real city, you know," Zadie replied. She had heard this reaction often while driving across the country, usually from waitresses in small town diners and clerks in run-down souvenir shops. Many of the families they chatted with at motel pools had been to Magic Kingdom but didn't notice the suburban sprawl beyond the gates.

"What are you doing all the way out here in the Wild West?" he asked, walking right up to their car and leaning on it.

"Hey, Jim, get over here and help with the tent," One of his buddies called, jogging over.

"Sorry to interrupt, ladies, but this is a classic Jim move, checking out the hot chicks while I do all the work."

The friend noticed Sam for the first time. "Oh hey, sorry dude. I didn't see you."

Sam muttered under his breath, "That's okay." His acne was inflamed bright red and his stringy hair was plastered to his forehead.

"You can't blame me; I'd be an idiot to ignore these beautiful ladies," Jim said while looking directly at Kiran.

Kiran was single now, but she had no confidence in flirting. Maybe if she were ten years younger, she would have enjoyed the banter. John, her second husband, took off with a woman ten years younger than her. Kiran caught him and the woman, a teller, holding hands and kissing in the parking lot of the bank where she worked. She wasn't even that surprised.

Kiran felt a rush of adrenaline as she locked eyes with Jim. She felt nervous, yet excited at being watched by him. Zadie flipped her hair indifferently; she was used to the attention. Then Kiran noticed Sam struggle, trying to be cool while suppressing the discomfort of strangers in a desolate area hitting on his mother and sister.

"We'll catch you later. Maybe we could have a beer," Jim said as he walked away. Kiran wondered if it was a real invitation.

The three worked to pitch the tent and set up the sleeping bags and stove. Kiran rummaged through the ice chest. She took a piece of ice and let it melt on her forehead. She felt slightly nauseous, but soon they were sitting at the picnic table, eating pasta and tuna doused with salad dressing.

It was too hot to build a campfire, so after they ate Sam and Zadie played backgammon while Kiran pretended to read a book.

She worked to collect her thoughts, review her plan. Here they were in the middle of nowhere, a beautiful yet broiling middle of nowhere; a nowhere with Arches formed of sandstone, wondrous pieces of God's handiwork plopped down straight from heaven; a nowhere with an expanse of canyons so impressive Kiran had cried the first time she saw them. Doug had stood at her side, wrapped his arms around her and cried too.

The memory flickered.

She had been able to convince the kids that a cross-country drive for the summer would be a decent family vacation, camping in state parks, visiting such Americana marvels as Graceland and Dodge City.

What else could she have done with their real father dead and their stepfather having run out on them for another woman? It was the only thing Kiran could think to do, run away and leave it all behind. She had taken a leave of absence from the bank and locked up the house, the same house where she and Doug had planned to raise a family. She now remembered the nights when she had reached across the bed to caress Doug, only to wake-up and find John there instead.

Kiran hadn't calculated the time it would take to drive home. She didn't want to go back to a place tainted with so many memories. She wanted a fresh start. Whenever the kids brought up the fact that school had already started weeks ago, Kiran drifted further into dreams of making it to California, a place where anything was possible.

Now it was dusk, and the light was pink and golden. Everything appeared to glow, but the heat was still thick and syrupy, as if Kiran had to swim through the air every time she moved. She looked up to see Jim standing in front of them. He had approached stealthily. Kiran was startled.

Lit by the glow of the sunset, his reddish hair now looked vibrant orange. Dark freckles covered his face and arms, and when he smiled, his teeth were unnaturally white. Kiran didn't find him as attractive as she had just an hour before.

"Hey there. You guys about ready for that beer?" Jim lifted a bottle of Heineken, dripping with condensation.

"Come on, I won't bite."

Zadie jumped to her feet and began to bounce around Jim. "And your friends? Where are they?"

"We drove a straight forty-six hours to get here, they're wiped. They crashed out a few minutes ago." Jim flashed a neon-white smile.

Zadie slouched her shoulders and moped back to the picnic table, disappointed that the cute one wouldn't be stopping by. Sam awaited her next move.

"Well then, how about you, Mom?" Jim handed the beer to Kiran. She took it reluctantly, but then lifted the bottle to her lips. The beer was warm and bitter. By the time she finished it off, Jim had settled in and was telling stories about surfing in Hawaii and Baja.

His stories were stirring memories, and Kiran sighed as she thought about the days she spent hitchhiking through California with her friends. She had been so young and reckless, and unimaginably free. Later she met Doug there and fell madly in love.

Kiran thought she might be able to recapture her spirit, if she could just make it there in time.

"Hey, shouldn't you guys be in school?" Jim asked curiously.

Sam began to fidget. Every day he reminded his mom that truancy was breaking the law. He believed they were going to be busted at any moment.

"Yeah, we should. Ask my mom why I'm not enrolled in the eighth grade."

Kiran's throat tightened because she knew Sam was right, not because she could hardly breathe in the stifling heat.

"Well, I had this plan to get us to California. I really wanted Sam and Zadie to see it," she tried to explain, knowing how foolish she must sound to Jim and her kids.

It wasn't really California she wanted them to know and see—she wanted them to know Doug, as well as the person she used to be. Now, the absurdity of her plan weighed on her, and Kiran needed to be alone to collect her thoughts. She suddenly rose and walked away, toward a dark path just beyond their campsite.

"Hey, wait up." Jim had to trot to catch up because of her long, quick strides. "You're not bandits on the run, are you? Did you rob a bank or something?" Jim called out jokingly.

"I worked in a bank. I should have thought of that," Kiran replied. She was reminded of John and the bank teller leaning up against a car with their arms wrapped around each other.

Kiran walked with her eyes on the moon. It wasn't full and spectacular, just lopsided and hazy, yet it lit the path so that she could dodge rocks and sticks. Although it was still hot and muggy, she felt less claustrophobic, like the world had expanded slightly. She could sense Jim behind her.

"You didn't need to come," she called back to Jim. Then she remembered what the ranger had said about the wildlife getting loony from the heat. Maybe it was better he was there.

"I wouldn't want you to get lost," Jim said. "It's better to hike in pairs. Anyway, I'd be an idiot to leave a lovely lady all alone out here."

Kiran couldn't think of a clever comeback. She wondered where his eyes rested: on the path, the sky, or on her. She hadn't felt desirable to a man in a long time.

Doug had made her feel beautiful every day, until the day he crashed his plane. John was the kind of man who stared at other women in her presence and was quick to notice when she gained a couple pounds. She knew he was good to the kids though.

Kiran was sweaty and breathing hard. She became more determined to reach the trail's end as the sky cleared and stars glimmered overhead.

Jim had been quiet, but now he said, "I guess you have your mind set on seeing the Delicate Arch tonight."

Kiran kept walking until she finally came onto a clearing. She held her breath when she saw it. Under the lopsided moon, it looked immense yet worn, sublime and flawed at the same time. Over the eons, the arch had eroded and morphed into a blazing, drastic structure, teetering between omnipotence and destruction.

"I didn't think we'd make it," Jim stood with his hands on his hips, panting and then bending backward to let out a bellowing yelp. He mimicked the coyotes howling in the distance. Kiran stood motionless while Jim began to explore, walking over the sandstone plateau in large circles around her.

"I thought if I got to California, my kids might know their father better. They were so young when he died," Kiran said suddenly. "But now I've run out of time."

Jim stopped roaming and approached her.

"I met Doug at a Grateful Dead concert. Jerry was still alive then," Kiran continued to explain in a low voice.

"You saw Jerry Garcia? I would die to have seen him play. I have some of my dad's old bootlegs. They're so awesome. Space was psychedelic!" Jim was laughing and whooping.

"Your dad's bootlegs?" Kiran looked at him mockingly. "You're just a kid, aren't you?" She calculated that she was nearly twice his age.

"I guess to you and my parents, I am," Jim said. He had lost his playful tone.

Kiran suddenly felt angry. She was annoyed with this cocky kid, but really she was angry with John. Kiran gradually came to realize during the cross-country trip that she never even loved John; she had just been lonely and scared.

Doug was the love of her life, and he died. How could he leave her and the kids like that? Kiran felt her insides constrict and ache.

"Why did you follow me?" Kiran asked. She now regretted being so far away from camp with Jim.

"Follow you? Come on, Mom, I thought I was keeping you company. I thought we might have something going."

It got darker as a cloud rolled over the moon. Kiran could see Jim's silhouette, as if he were only a dark spirit with no substance.

Kiran's heart beat fiercely in her chest. She was frightened by his shadow.

"I want to be alone. Maybe you should leave."

"Leave, to where? You're crazy, lady."

Kiran knew she was crazy. What kind of mother keeps her kids out of school to chase some dream of California? Zadie should be going to Homecoming, taking her SATs and applying to colleges. But Kiran couldn't bring herself to turn the car around and go home. She would have to face friends and coworkers and explain John's decision to leave with the young bank teller.

Sam had needed a father so desperately, and he looked up to John. Now she would have to watch her kids be fatherless once again. She stood near the Arch and her body shook.

"Listen, I'm sorry. I didn't mean to upset you." Jim tried to approach her with concern.

"Stay away." Kiran glared at him.

"Okay, just stay calm. I can't let you walk back by yourself." Jim rubbed his elbows nervously. "Let's just head back. I'm sure your kids are worried about you."

"My kids, what do you know about my kids?" Kiran saw Jim's face more clearly as the moon reappeared, brighter and larger than before. She couldn't stand the thought of this young person judging her. He didn't even know her name.

"I told you I want to be alone."

"Oh man, lady. I thought you were cool." Jim paced and clenched his fists. "You start back, and I'll stay here and wait. Is that okay with you?"

Without answering, Kiran walked to the trail and once there she moved briskly despite the weight of the heat clinging to her back, which made her hunch slightly. Her legs felt swollen and thick, but she nearly trotted to get back to the campsite. After a few minutes, she sensed Jim behind her. His steps made a scratching sound against the dry, rocky trail. As the moon hid and it darkened around her once again, she quickened her pace even more. She remembered the coyotes in the distance and felt real fear.

Suddenly, she lost her balance. She tried to catch herself, but the crack of her ankle resounded in her ears. She didn't let out a scream, just a quiet whimper. Then she was seated on the ground, her chest heaving with tearless cries. Jim halted his steps and whispered curses, which sounded to Kiran like some kind of incantation.

She moaned. "Just leave me alone." She looked down and the ankle was swelling.

Jim stood over her and said, "Listen, I don't know how this happened, but you've got me all wrong. I'm not a bad guy, lady. And listen, I can help. You just have to trust me."

Kiran imagined coyotes circling in on them, going mad from the heat.

She knew she couldn't make it back by herself; she had no choice. She lifted her arms and Jim gently pulled her up, wrapping an arm around her shoulder. She clung to him as they made their way along the trail, her leg lifted behind her. The ankle throbbed and a sharp, hot pain ran up her leg.

As they walked together, Jim began, "My mom had this friend. I was in high school, and, man, I fantasized about that woman. Ann was her name. I can't tell you how many times alone in my bed ... you can use your imagination. She was older, but very beautiful and kind-of mysterious. Anyway, you remind me of her."

Jim was speaking so close that Kiran could feel his warm breath brush against her cheek. He held onto her, nearly carrying her along the trail.

Kiran had thought she wanted to be desirable to a man who wouldn't die on her, to a man who wouldn't cheat. Instead, she began to imagine her life without a man in it. She felt tired, tired to the bone, and the pain in her ankle made her want to be home.

They neared the campsite, and as Kiran listened to Jim's fantasies about a woman named Ann, she thought how pathetic it all had been. She began to calculate the trip back. Her ankle hurt, but she could suddenly breathe easier, deep into her belly, which felt soothing. She realized it would take less than a week if they made a straight shot for it. Kiran decided she was ready to let go of memories and make a new home for Zadie and Sam.

Martina Gets the Last Word

C.B.. Calsing

Here, Aldo."I raised my head from the cradle of my hands and

looked at my girlfriend's... dead girlfriend's sister, Maia. She held out a journal.

"She wanted you to have this."

I took it from her hand. Nothing special. Brown leather binding, with a brown ribbon to mark the pages. I flipped through it. Martina had filled in about two-thirds before she...passed. Passed away today. I sighed. I hadn't wanted to be in that room right when she'd gone over. It felt like something just for family, and I didn't really *feel* like family. Martina had gotten weird toward the end: hanging out with the fortunetellers in the French Quarter, mixing herbs she bought at the Botanica on St. Claude Avenue into weird concoctions, following the phases of the moon, reading about Houdini. Before I knew she was sick, I'd meant to call the relationship off, but with the illness... I didn't want her to die feeling unloved, so I stuck it out. Sort of heroic, I guess.

The rest of her family came out of the hospital room into the sterile, gray hall where I waited. Martina's father had his arm around her mother's shoulder. While her Mother cried into a rough hospital tissue.

"She said you should read it," Maia said. "She said...it's special. Only for you." Tears welled in her eyes. She must not have gotten a journal of her own from Martina. Martina had had a hard time balancing relationships. I'd liked it at first, that she was so devoted to me to the point of neglecting her family, but then it had started to wear me out.

I didn't know what to say to Maia right then; I guess it's sort of selfish, but I felt a little better now that Martina had finally moved on. I could get on with my life too. But Maia would never have another sister. I stood to hug her. Maia had never liked me and could probably tell I wasn't madly in love with her sister, but giving her a hug seemed like the right thing to do at the time.

She patted me halfheartedly on the back and pushed away. "I need to see about arrangements."

That's Maia, always the practical one.

After I left the hospital I stopped in at the neighborhood bar to tell the regulars -- my friends, really -- the news; some of them had known Maia, and some had even liked her. She used to cook whole pans of ziti and feed everybody. Sometimes we threw parties at the bar. It was like a community living room, and Martina had always made the most of it. I'd miss that about her. We toasted a few rounds to her memory. As I drank, I felt the weight of the journal tucked inside my jacket like a warm lump of something, almost alive. That feeling compelled me to leave the bar.

I walked through the humid New Orleans night, thinking about Martina. We'd had fun. She'd even been a good friend, even though I didn't love her. I finally stumbled in to my one-room corner apartment. It took up the back quarter of an old house. I took my jacket off and set the journal on the one table in my tiny living space. I didn't want to read it at all, really. I definitely had too much to drink to tackle it tonight. Instead, I went to bed, falling onto the mattress I had shoved into the far corner.

When I woke up, well after sunrise, I found the journal sitting on the floor beside my mattress. I could have sworn I left it on the table, but maybe at some point in the night, I'd grabbed it. I picked the journal up. Perhaps if I read it before the funeral on Monday, I could say something witty and loving about her and get closure.

I tucked my extra pillow under my head and opened the book.

I just met you, the journal began, *and I think you must be THE ONE!*

I checked the date. Sure enough, the day I'd met Martina.

After reading a good chunk of it, I couldn't help but realize how right I'd been about her mental state... Jesus. What Martina wrote in that journal... I'm surprised she died of cervical cancer and not brain cancer. I started to doubt even the good stuff about her. I looked at the clock. Nearly noon. I decided to go to the corner store and get a roast beef Po-boy for lunch. I threw the journal on the bedspread, dressed, and left. When I came back, I sat down at the table to eat. The journal lay there now. I knew I hadn't moved it. Something was going on. I eyed it as I ate, but it just sat there looking like a plain old diary: nothing special about it at all.

When I'd finished my sandwich, I picked the journal back up and started reading it again. By five o'clock, I'd made it halfway through her entries, to the time her doctor diagnosed her cancer. She talked about how great I'd been, how supportive. She seemed saner for a few pages as she came to terms with her prognosis, but then...

I shut the journal. I still had a whole day until the funeral. I could finish it on Sunday. I needed a drink.

I walked to the neighborhood bar and took a seat on a stool.

"Hey," the bartender Owen said as he wiped down the spot in front of me.

"PBR, please," I said.

Owen swiftly delivered the brew, and I took a long drink.

"Tough day?" he asked.

"Martina left me a journal to read." I shook my head. "She'd gone nuts, man. I mean off the deep end. I thought she was a little crazy, but there's material in there I thought only happened in B horror movies, and the whole thing's addressed to me. She's doing...*did* all of it for me, she says." I took another drink. "I didn't notice what was going on. The late nights she was out doing God knows what I thought she'd been with her sister." I paused, afraid to say anything else out loud, but Owen was my friend. "Calling it off earlier would have been better than...this."

I think Owen could tell I didn't want to go into any further detail, but that I'd sufficiently scared him. He kept the beers coming, and after a few hours and a couple bags of potato chips from behind the bar, I felt I could go home and pass out without thinking about the journal.

Next morning, though, it lay right there by the bed again. Some kind of sick joke, I thought, but I decided to keep reading. I don't really know what compelled me to do it, but I wanted to get to the end. I thought closure would come if I just got to the end. Maybe she'd repent or something.

By mid-afternoon in journal-time, Martina had arrived at the hospital. I was within days of her death in the text. I kept reading. The day before my now...Thursday...Then in a weak, faint hand, *I love you, Aldo. I will ALWAYS love you. M.* I turned the page.

More?

Dated yesterday, Saturday, near midnight, when I'd been at the bar.

What a flipping D-bag you turned out to be, eh, Aldo? You think I'm nuts? And you're going around telling your friends that. Thanks a lot, you A-hole. I thought you loved me.

I slammed the journal closed without finishing the entry and threw it across the room.

The phone rang.

I picked it up. "Hello?" I said; my voice sounded shaky even to myself.

"Aldo?"

That voice. So familiar. Calling me from the grave too? "Martina?"

"No, this is Maia."

"Oh...sorry."

"I'm calling about the funeral arrangements. You need to write this down."

I got a pen and an old receipt and wrote down when and where I needed to be the next day.

Before I hung up, I asked Maia, "Did Martina say anything else about that diary?"

Maia was silent for a moment. "No. Exactly what I told you." She sighed on the other end. "I'll see you tomorrow, okay?"

"Yeah." I hung up the phone and turned to look back at where I'd thrown the journal. I didn't see it. I went back to my bed, and the book was sitting there, ready for reading.

But I'd gotten to the end, right? I must have. I picked the book up and decided to finish the last entry. Maybe it was some kind of joke or something.

The entry dated from yesterday finished, *I'm sorry. I got a little angry. I know how hard this must be for you. Maybe thinking I'm crazy is your way of distancing yourself from my death. That's fine. I do love you. We'll get through this together.*

I turned the page. Another entry, from today! *You thought Maia sounds like me? Priceless. I always thought she sounded like a cow. A BIG, FAT lowing cow. But I love her. LOL. Wait until you see the dress they put me in for the funeral. It's GORGEOUS!*

I slammed the book closed again. Some kind of sick joke. But how? There was no one here but me. I looked around the room. There had to be someplace to put the journal, someplace to keep it safe.

Aha. I had a bookshelf constructed of one by eight and cinderblocks. I put the journal on the table and started dismantling the shelf, throwing the books, magazines, and knickknacks onto the floor. I grabbed the journal, dropped it in the middle of the floor, and then stacked cinderblock after cinderblock on top of it. I got the stack four high. That seemed adequate. I didn't move my eyes from the journal, pressed under the weight of all those blocks. There's no way it could get out from under that.

I kept staring at it, never took my eyes off it. I ate dinner staring at it. I brushed my teeth in the kitchen sink staring at it. I had to take my eyes off it for a moment when I pulled my pajamas over my head, but it was still there afterward.

I climbed into bed, still staring at the journal.

I left the lights on.

At some point, I fell asleep.

The next morning, I woke up to the phone ringing.

Groggily, feeling as if I had a hangover, even though I hadn't drunk anything the night before, I pulled myself out of bed to answer it. "Hello?"

"Aldo? It's Maia. I just wanted to make sure you were on your way."

"Just getting in the shower now." I looked at the clock. Owen was coming to pick me up in fifteen minutes. "Don't worry."

"Don't blow this, or I swear I'll rip your heart out and bury you with my sister, though she deserves better than that."

Ah, there was the Maia I knew, the one that hated my guts for monopolizing her sister's time. I showered, dressed, and searched the fridge for something to take the edge off my gnawing hunger. I knew there'd be lots of food at the various services, wakes, and mourning rituals scheduled for today, but I didn't want to start it all on an empty stomach. I grabbed a rather soft apple, bit into it as I closed the fridge, and turned.

On top of the stack of cinderblocks sat -- looking very smug, if a book can look smug -- the journal.

Somebody knocked on my door.

I grabbed the journal to take with me. I opened the front door, and Owen stood there. He took me to the vigil.

The services -- vigil, mass, burial, and wake -- took all day. Owen said he'd drive and that the family probably expected me to drink a few toasts with them in Martina's memory. I did, and the journal sat in my jacket pocket the entire night. I had a sneaking suspicion that Maia had something to do with the journal's movement. Maybe she was trying to get me to confess to something by playing with my mind. Finally, after a few whiskeys, I pulled her to the side.

"What do you want?" she asked. I think she could tell I was not happy.

"This." I held up the journal.

"Martina's journal." A tear rolled down her cheek. "What about it?"

"Is this some kind of joke you're playing on me?"

"What?"

I showed her the journal entry dated from yesterday, the one from when I'd been on the phone with her.

"That's Martina's handwriting," she said. She read it. "A *cow*?" She started sobbing. "What kind of sicko are you, Aldo?" she cried. "I mean, Jesus, that's not funny. How can you play a joke like that at a...a...wake? She's just died, for Christ's sake."

She pushed past me and ran to her mother, crying hysterically.

"You don't understand," I said after her. "I didn't do this."

"I think it's time to go, man," Owen said, putting his hand on my shoulder. I nodded and dropped the journal right there on the floor, pretty much done with the whole thing. Let them deal with it.

That Tuesday I had to go to work. On autopilot, I got ready, ate, and left. I rode my bicycle to the real estate office in the French Quarter where I helped out: making copies, filing, typing up forms. Everyone was really sympathetic. My boss even let me leave early.

When I went outside to unlock my bicycle from the lamppost, I saw something in the basket wrapped in pretty paper, like for a wedding. I looked up and down the street, but I saw no one who could have left it. *Must have happened earlier in the day.* I picked up the small package, and immediately, the weight of the object felt familiar. I ripped the paper off. *Martina's journal.*

That bitch, I thought. Maia knew where I worked. She probably did this to mess with me. I locked the bike back up, walked to Canal Street, and took a bus to the house where she lived with her parents.

I pounded on the door. Eventually, Maia answered it, dressed in PJ's.

"What do you want?" she asked.

"This is not funny." I shook the journal in her face.

"That again?" She paused. "How did you get it back? I found it last night and put it in my vanity drawer..."

"Right," I said. "And then you wrapped it in wedding paper and left if for me to find."

"No. *You* must have broken in and taken it from me to mess with *me*."

"Alarm system, big dog?" I reminded her. Her parents kept their house like a fortress during a war.

"Well, then..."

"I know what you're doing," I said quietly. "You're trying to make me feel guilty."

"Feel guilty about what, Aldo?"

"You know." I knew she knew.

"No, I don't. What is it you feel guilty about?"

"You know I didn't...love her. That I stayed with her because I didn't want her to feel bad."

"Really?"

"Take the journal, okay?"

I handed it to her and left. Hopefully, that would be the end of it.

When I finally got home that night, after taking a return bus and fetching my bike, the journal was sitting there on my table, waiting for me. It would have a new entry, I knew. I turned to the last page.

Didn't love me? Really? Like, ever? I wasted my last months on this earth with a D-bag that not only thought I was crazy, but also didn't love me. YOU'LL BE SORRY.

I'd had enough. I went over to the small gas range and lit a burner. I grabbed some barbecue tongs and used them to pick up the journal. I lit the journal with the flame. As I held it there, it flopped open to a blank page.

Pages began to singe and curl, and as I watched, bold, dark words appeared on the paper as if hastily but emphatically scribbled. As if someone's life depended on that note. *Why are you doing this? I'm sorry. It's just I'm so lonely, and I need you. I really need you. Please, Aldo, don't*

123

do this. Please.

A sound of gentle weeping filled the air, and I could almost feel the pain of the pages as they slowly burned.

I couldn't do it.

I threw the journal in the sink and doused it with water. Then I spread it open on the dish rack to dry. I sat down at the kitchen table and, finally, cried too.

Six months later:

I got home from my date. The journal sat on the kitchen table, waiting for me, right where I knew it would be. Right where I'd left it. Fire had singed and burned its corners, and the pages had warped from water, but I could still read every word.

Tonight's entry read:

She's cute, but I don't know that she's right for you. Plus she laughs like a HYENA! LOL. And couldn't she shut up about herself just once? Let's go get a beer.

I put the journal in my jacket pocket and headed out to the bar. Martina had been and still was a great friend, but I wondered what would happen when we ran out of pages. I know she worried about it too, but we didn't waste pages discussing it.

Monkey Love

Jess Dunn

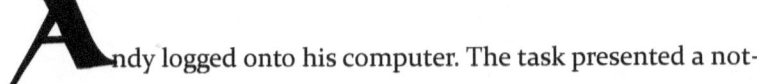**A**ndy logged onto his computer. The task presented a not-

inconsiderable amount of anxiety, because it brought him one step closer to checking his email. His clammy fingers left tiny drops of condensation glistening on the top of each key. It was Monday, so his inbox would be filled with the minutes of meetings and unfinished assignments from the previous week, all marked with little red exclamation points. Judging by the number of exclamation points in his inbox this morning, Andy was certain that he would be in the office until late that night. His hands trembled as he scrolled down the list of subject headings, not daring to open even one.

The office was filled with voices, all melding into a single, unintelligible mumble, amplified by the sounds of thousands of fingers running over hundreds of keyboards. Overhead, muzak spewed forth in an unstaunchable flow. Suddenly, a shrill chirp cut through the cacophony. Marie, the chipper, cherub-faced woman who occupied the cubicle across the aisle from him huffed down the hallway, humming the overhead tune. The chair heaved a sigh as she lowered her ample frame down into it. She spent the next few moments adjusting the height on her chair. The lever squeaked with each jerk of her hand. Her The humming did not waver, except for the heavy sounds of Marie inhaling to fuel her serenade.

Andy felt the familiar sensation of pressure behind his eyes, followed by a dull, unrelenting ache. He grabbed the bottle of generic aspirin next to his computer. He struggled for a few moments with the childproof top, but finally managed to shake out two white pills. He proceeded to chew them. After a few moments, the humming stopped and Andy cringed at the awkward conversation that would surely follow. Her chair groaned as she turned to face him.

"How's the new cube?" she said.

He hated whenever anyone called it that, "cube". It made him queasy. Andy remembered a movie he'd seen in the middle of the night, some night when he couldn't sleep. It was one of those shoe-string budget, sci-fi, gore-fests where a group of test subjects were trapped in a cube and died messily, hideously, at each others' hands. At the time, the blood and viscera had disgusted him. But as he stared across the aisle at Marie's wide smile, he appreciated the film's sentiment.

"Isn't it much brighter in here now?" she said.

"Huh?"

"The walls."

Andy spun in his chair and looked at the walls of his cubicle. Over the weekend, the grey felt had been replaced with reddish- brown felt, the color of an angry scab. His calendar, all the little comics and sticky notes he had collected over the years were gone. There had been a postcard pinned just above his computer. It was a picture of a monkey sitting at a desk, holding a telephone to its ear, with the caption *Monkey Business* across the bottom. Now there was nothing but scabby red.

"Isn't it so much nicer than before? I just love red."

Andy pulled open his drawers, but there were only crumpled documents and dead pens inside. He scoured the top of his desk, lifting stacks of papers and unopened packets of yellow sticky notes. He even pulled his computer away from the wall in the hopes that his postcard had fallen behind it, but drew back nothing except a hand covered in dust.

Marie's face contorted into an exaggerated pout.

"Oh no," she said, "Did you lose all the stuff on your walls?"

Andy leaned back in his chair and put his hands over his face. The pain behind his eyes intensified and he rubbed them, making furious circles with his fingers. After a few moments, his neighbor realized she was not going to get a response, and resumed her humming. The overhead speaker droned a watery rendition of Simon and Garfunkel's greatest hits on a loop.

By lunch time, Andy had consumed three more bitter little pills, but his headache raged on. His emails remained mostly unread. Now and then, a window popped up informing him that he had new mail, which he would quickly close, as though the veracity of the statement would increase the longer it remained on the screen. Marie's high-pitched tunes had been replaced with the sounds of chewing. He looked over at her; "special sauce" dribbled down her chin as she bit into the a greasy double-decker burger. The stench of oil and meat invaded his nostrils, and sour acid rose up the back of his throat and into his mouth. He swallowed it down. Marie nodded to him, and attempted to smile while chewing. Andy spun his chair abruptly and stared into the cold glow of his computer. The red exclamation points throbbed.

Andy spun around again, facing the aisle. He pushed himself up out of his chair and quelled the urge to throw his body down the hallway in desperate flight. He managed to force himself to move slowly, mechanically, between the rows of cubes. He walked to the window at the end of the aisle, so far away that it looked like a picture from where he sat.

The wet sounds of Marie's smacking lips faded into the distance, only to be replaced by the hum of florescent lights. He looked out the window, down at the masses below him. A group of small children crossed the street, careening toward the zoo just a few blocks away. Andy couldn't remember the last time he had gone to the zoo; it must have been when he was a child. All he could remember was the primate house with all the monkeys and orangutans in their little habitats, behind glass so that people could see inside, like peering into your neighbor's window.

He had the vague feeling that he might have enjoyed the zoo; that he might enjoy it again, but he didn't have any children, or a girlfriend, or any friends to go with him, and he couldn't go on his own. He couldn't bear standing by himself, surrounded by children's birthday parties and couples with their arms around each other's waists. There was something so pathetic about a grown man, alone, at the zoo, watching the monkeys masturbate.

Andy placed his hand on the cold window, longing to throw it open and let the chilling wind outside wash over his face. But, none of the windows in the building opened; forcing all those inside to breathe recycled air, unbearably hot or cold depending on the season. Instead, he pressed the side of his face against the glass and closed his eyes. He imagined that he was looking at himself from the building across the street, staring at the side of his distorted face, fog from his nostrils steaming up the glass. He shivered.

"Are you all right?"

Andy jerked to attention and bumped the window with his forehead. He turned and met watery blue eyes, eyes that did not look a bit concerned as to whether or not he was all right. They belonged to his manager's personal assistant, a man who had never remembered his name, after five years of working in the same office. The eyes had a quality of impatient boredom, designed to make all who fell under their gaze instantly apologetic.

"No ... I mean, yes," he stammered in response.

The eyes were unmoved.

"I just, I was hot and I wanted ..." Andy said, "Can I ... do you need something?"

"Yeah ... um ..." His eyes wavered for a moment, then narrowed, as though offended that Andy's name had intentionally eluded him. "... Mike. Ken wants the quotes for the Peterson account before five."

"I'm ..."

"Look, I've got a lot to do. What do you want me to tell him?"

"Well ...," Andy said.

"Should I tell him you don't have it? Or what?"

"I ... um ... sure."

"I should tell him you don't have it." The assistant's eyes cut through him.

"I ... uh ... no."

"Great, I'll let him know that you'll have it by five."

Andy, who was positive that his name was not Mike, was almost just as certain that he had never heard of the Peterson account before this moment. But like a tortured prisoner, he would have said anything to bring an end to this encounter. He mentally calculated the number of sick days he had left and found himself wondering if anyone would even notice if he went on break and never came back. His paycheck was direct deposit. It could be a matter of weeks before the checks stopped coming, even months.

When Andy returned to his desk, the breathless humming had returned in full force. Only now, Marie would occasionally sing the words that were absent in the muzak rendition. *Someone told me it's all happening at the zoo.* The sharps and flats bored into him like a dentist's drill. Andy gaped at the space above his computer through the stuporous pain. An expanse of red felt stretched in front of him. Andy's insides sank. In its absence, he now realized how much that trivial picture had made him laugh. The monkey's eyes had looked back at him with a mischievous sparkle. He imagined that the picture had been taken right before the little brown hands had chucked the phone across the room and had proceeded to climb up the set and swing from the ceiling.

Andy began to reexamine his desk, in the hopes that maybe he had just overlooked the postcard amidst all the refuse of his work. He rummaged through the papers on his desk. Finding nothing, Andy swept the papers off his desk with a single movement of his arm. They descended in a whirling torrent of white and yellow. He yanked the drawers off their metal tracks and overturned them onto the floor. Marie looked over from her work, her eyes bulged a bit as she watched him squatting on the floor.

"Did you lose something?"

He furiously grasped at papers and threw them over his shoulder.

When she got no reply, she spoke a bit louder, "Do you need help?"

Andy stood up and surveyed the carnage. The floor of his cube was completely covered. Endless reams of Times New Roman stared back at him.

"Did you ..." Marie began.

"No!" He yelled.

He stepped sideways out of his cubicle and walked down the aisle once again. Away from the mess, and the muzak and the humming, away from the sounds of clacking key boards. Andy stepped into the single-occupancy handicapped bathroom and pressed his body against the heavy door, sealing silence in with him. He clicked the lock firmly and flipped on the lights. The overhead florescent sputtered and blinked at seizure-inducing intervals, and he flipped them off again. He sat down on the seat of the toilet and basked in the quiet darkness. Even the sterile scent of ammonia and hand soap soothed him.

He leaned back against the cool porcelain and the pounding in his head faded to a dull roar. Andy let his mind drift through the darkness. He thought about the couple he'd seen on the light rail that morning on his way to work. They were just a pair of hipsters, like the hundreds of others who attended the local art school. They rode the line with him almost every morning, and he always looked forward to seeing them, despite the fact they had never spoken.

This morning he had sat directly behind them, staring at the backs of the two heads with their near-identical asymmetrical haircuts. Their ears were encased in oversized, retro-style headphones. They bobbed their heads, keeping time with the music he couldn't hear. Their skinny jeans and zipped motorcycle jackets made it impossible for him to determine the gender of either one. This fact had not dissuaded him from glancing covetously over their shoulders at their clasped hands. He longed to be holding hands with anyone at all. He longed to be one of two people, alone in their separate worlds, holding hands together.

Andy unzipped his pants and closed his eyes. He pictured the couple from the light rail. They were standing across from him, slouched against the tile, naked, except for their headphones. Side by side, they held hands, heads bobbing in unison. Up and down, they mesmerized him with their cool nihilism. Their bodies were sexless and smooth, like plastic dolls. He felt his heart race as his hand moved. Up and down. After a few minutes, he ejaculated into his cupped hand.

After he finished washing up Andy sat back down and stared at the place where the two androgynes had been. He thought again, about monkeys. Not just the monkey from his picture, screeching and swinging from the rafters, but all the monkeys he'd ever seen on commercials or nature shows, behind glass. Hairy, humanoid faces pressed up against their windows, stroking themselves while crowds gaped and left sticky fingerprints on the other side. He didn't remember where he had heard that they masturbated. It was something about them masturbating in front of schoolchildren, much to the horror of on-looking members of the PTA. As though the monkeys' behavior was maliciously aimed at, forcing parents to discuss sex with their children. He found himself wondering what else a caged animal with four hands and no mating opportunities was supposed to do. After a while, Andy took a deep breath and opened the bathroom door, light and noise streamed in, striking him full force. He made his way back to his desk and picked the papers off the floor around him, depositing them into his quickly overflowing trash can.

That evening, as he predicted, while most of his colleagues were buttoning their coats and twining scarves around their necks, he sat hunched over his computer furiously typing. The blue-eyed assistant had not resurfaced and Andy felt safe in the assurance that his assailant had no idea where his desk was. Occasionally, Andy stopped and held his forehead in his hands in an attempt to quiet the throbbing as blood pounded through his skull. Even after his colleagues had finished filing out of their cubicles, the noise in his head continued and he glanced up at his computer screen. The black letters seemed to blur and run together against the painfully white background of the screen. Andy stood up at his desk, forcing his chair against the back wall of the cube. He walked down the aisle and stopped when he reached the window.

As he looked out, his forehead rested on the black glass. He had to struggle to look past his own reflection. When he looked down, he could see the lights of cars moving below him and the streetlights bathing small circles of the sidewalk in a sallow glow. Squinting through his reflection at the moving lights below nauseated him. He stood back from the window to find his equilibrium.

From this distance, he was able to see his entire body in the glass. He didn't own a full-length mirror, and this was the first time he had seen his complete reflection in a while. His slight frame swam inside the belted khakis and gaping button-down shirt. A sense of agnosia came over him, as though he was unable to recognize this figure in front of him while still plagued with a sense of odd familiarity. He reached out to the window, placing his fingertips against the glass. He crouched down and stared into the familiar eyes that were cast into shadow by the overhead lights. A tight darkness grew inside him as he watched the figure in the window.

He stood suddenly, and stumbled back as the blood rushed through his head. He backed away from the window, slowly at first, then turned and ran toward the elevator. He pressed the button repeatedly. The little light at the top of the elevator blinked, indicating that it was five stories above him. The elevator descended toward him for eons. He abandoned it and threw his body against the door to the stairway.

Andy felt weightless as he picked up speed down the stairs. He gripped the banister and propelled himself around the corner of the stairwell and down the next flight. As he reached the ground level of the building, there was a box with a glass front on the wall. Inside was a red fire axe. The letters painted on the outside simply read *IN CASE OF EMERGENCY BREAK GLASS*. Andy stepped back and elbowed the glass, putting the full weight of his slender frame behind it. With the glass broken, he wrapped the axe in his coat and tucked it under his arm.

Andy thrust the door open and flew into the main lobby. He ran past the empty reception desk to the revolving doors, which deposited him out into the night. For a moment, he stood and breathed in the chilly air, happy to be free of reflections and fluorescent lights. But,, as the initial wash of relief soon began to dissipate, every muscle fiber in his body seemed to twitch to the same agitated rhythm. Images of hairy primates flashed through his mind. They were jumping and shrieking, howling and gnashing their teeth, going "ape-shit". That was the only phrase he could conjure to describe it. With a sudden decisiveness, unlike anything Andy had ever experienced before that moment, he began to run. His muscles burned from their unprecedented use. His nose and lungs stung with every breath he took.

As he approached the front gates of the zoo, Andy realized that they were locked. He looked at the turnstiles and ticket booths thoughtfully. He remembered that one of the bike paths at the nearby park winded wound along the back of the zoo. When he had first moved to the city, he used to take his bike to the park and ride. The bike had been in storage for several years now, but he remembered that the fences along the bike paths had been chain -link.

Following a few wrong turns, Andy finally found the path that ran behind the zoo. As he had remembered, the fence consisted of wide links that could easily accommodate fingers and shoes. The axe made a soft thud as it hit the grass on the other side of the fence. Andy followed closely behind. Once inside the perimeter, he picked up his weapon and began to wander around in the shadows, not sure of where to go. He did not see any security patrols, but tried to quiet his thunderous breathing anyway. His exhalations seemed to roar from his chest, but in reality it came to barely a whisper.

Finally, Andy found a sign with an arrow pointing toward the monkey "neighborhood," as they called the cluster of primate houses up ahead. Suddenly finding his second wind, he jogged in the direction the arrow indicated. He approached the first house and tried to pull open the double glass doors, but they were held together with a heavy chain. Andy unsheathed his axe, and, stepping back a moment to get his footing, struck the chain. On the fourth strike, the chain unraveled and clanged onto the cement.

Andy entered the dim hall of the primate house, which had dark glass windows running down both sides. He was able to make out at least ten small, black monkeys lying on wooden beams designed to mimic tree branches. The plaque next to the window labeled them as spider monkeys. He squinted myopically through his reflection and tried to make out the details of the sleeping monkey closest to him. Its tiny, humanoid hand was wrapped instinctively around the fake branch. He tapped gently on the glass and the monkey sat up. Two black eyes shone back at him through the darkness. Andy was touched by the warm brilliance of those eyes. They seemed to soothe him,; quiet the tremulous anxiety that racked his body.

Placing his hand on the glass, he mouthed, "I'm going to get you out of here."

His heart fluttered a bit at the sight of his gaunt face in the glass. He stood back and looked at his reflection. He scanned the sickly pallor of his flesh, his twisted, poorly nourished frame. That same darkness he felt in the office earlier that night gnawed at him. He tried to swallow the terrible sensation down, but it flowed out of him, through his arms, into the axe. *IN CASE OF EMERGENCY, BREAK GLASS.* Andy swung with everything inside him. The blade of the axe impacted against his reflection. Andy watched his face crack, distorting more and more with every strike.

Two security guards came running down the hallway.

"Sir," the first guard said firmly, "put down your weapon and back away."

The second guard stopped. "I'm going to radio the police."

Andy did not hear them. He saw his face disappear, swallowed by the black behind the window. As Andy knocked away the remaining glass, the pungent odor of urine and feces wafted through the void. Andy breathed in deeply.; It smelled good to him:, visceral, primal. He stepped into the darkness. The monkeys drew themselves back on their perches, chattering and grunting.

"Come on," Andy whispered, waving his hand emphatically.

The monkeys continued to chatter and moved toward the other side of the cage. He walked toward them. Tarry feces squelching under his shoes. The monkeys began to chatter louder and jumped irritably up and down on their branches. He reached up to the one closest to him; it puffed up its chest and pressed its back against the wall. But, Andy would not be dissuaded. He stretched his arm and his fingers brushed a furry limb. The primate released a heart-chilling shriek and sunk its teeth into the offending hand. Andy mimicked the shriek of his attacker. Red spurted from the wound as the little teeth released, then latched onto his pale wrist. The other monkeys, empowered by their comrade, followed in kind. Andy fell backwards as they descended upon him. They sank their teeth into him, through his pants, into the prominent mound of cartilage on the front of his neck. Chunks of his flesh came away in their clenched teeth. He tried to crawl away; pulling them off as he went, but they were unrelenting. As soon as they found their footing, they pounced on him again.

The guard that had been talking to Andy ran into the cage. He waved at the monkeys emphatically, but they would not be dissuaded. The guard stepped back when a hairy, humanoid face looked up at him, baring red-tinged teeth. Andy continued to scream. Blood poured from his wounds and oozed across the ground. The guard could see shocking white peeking through the unstaunchable fountains. A few of Andy's fingers were hanging on by threads of sinew.

"Tell them to bring the paramedics," the guard called to his partner, who was bent over, vomiting.

Then, suddenly, Andy stopped shrieking and struggling. A calm weightlessness washed over him. He felt small and far away as his vision was consumed by an ever- contracting tunnel. He couldn't feel the tiny teeth ripping out chunks of his warm flesh. The throbbing in his head that had been his constant companion throughout the day was gone. The sounds of screeching and retching faded into the background and even the sirens that were drawing closer fell silent. He watched pieces of himself disappear into their red-frothed mouths and he knew that now he was a part of them. He was the monkeys and they were he. And, as the tunnel closed in, enveloping him in hushed black, Andy couldn't help but smile.

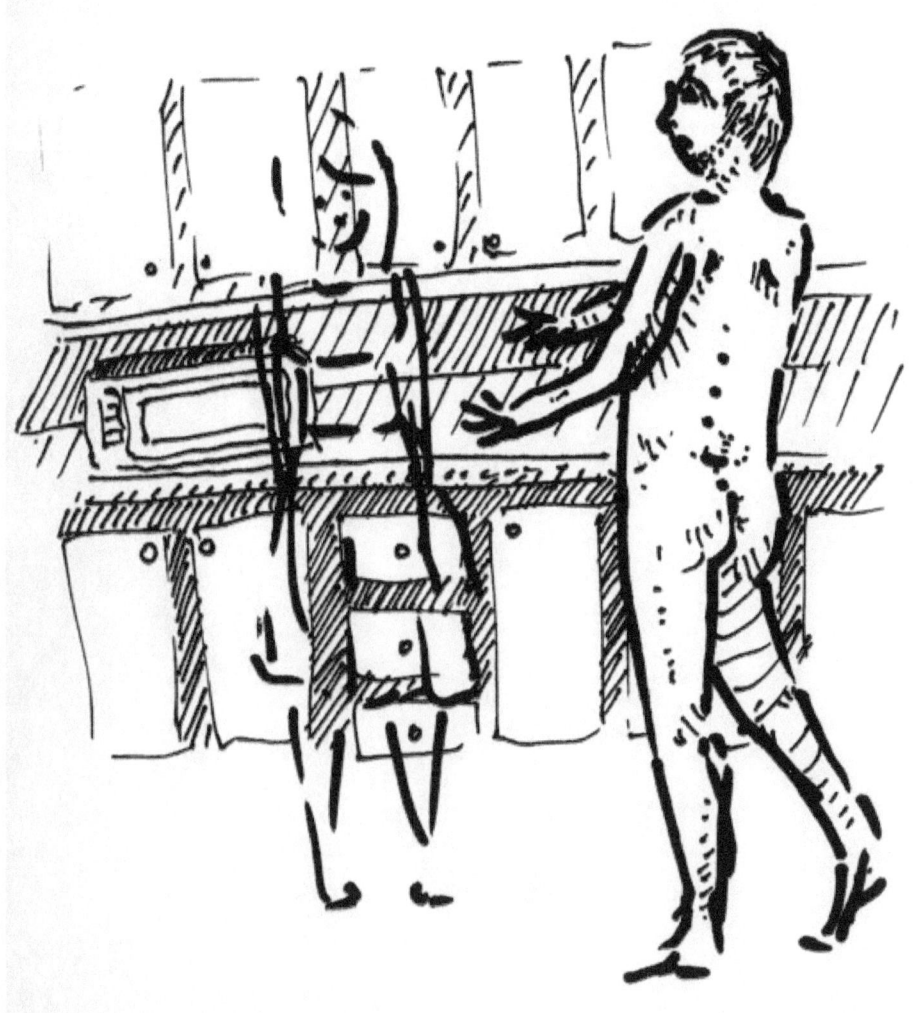

After It All Ends

Davin Kimble

Brian stood before the mirror in his bathroom. He was freshly

showered and he stood dripping on the shag rug Dana had bought one sunny Saturday afternoon. Dana would have scolded him for standing wet from the shower without even a towel to stem the flow, ruining the carpet. He would have argued with her about it, maybe even called her "stupid girl," in jest of course. Something like, "you say the stupidest things sometimes, how will my few drops on this carpet ruin it? It's a bathroom carpet; it's supposed to stand up to a bit of shower water."

But she wasn't going to scold him, she was dead. She died of cancer in the bed they shared, the same bed he was going to die in, soon, finally.

He could still remember the day they had bought that bed. It was awkward lying there in a bed while some guy in a tie stood over you reciting a bunch of specs and tech stuff you didn't care about. All he could do to stem the tide was envision what it would be like to live in this bed. With the sales guy hovering and pattering, Brian thought about reading, eating, watching television in this bed with Dana by his side.

"We're gonna need a frame," He said.

"And maybe some of those little bed chairs," She had turned onto her side and so he turned onto his side spooning her. "Or a headboard," she finished.

"We can get you into a pretty good package deal if you wanted some furniture and pillows." The helpful khaki clad sales crotch slid into view.

"Will we need to buy new sheets?" Dana asked him.

"So this is the one you want?" He asked in return.

It turned out that that mattress was the one they wanted and over the course of the sales transaction they learned that they would need new sheets and that the furniture they had in the mattress store wasn't half bad nor were the pillows. They left that afternoon with a smile on their faces and a hefty bill in their pockets.

The one bill he'd left unpaid...the bill for the bed.

After Dana passed Brian had roamed around the house constantly reminded of her. He knew that these things that had made up their home should bring a smile to his face but they'd brought only constant pain. He confined himself to the bedroom, to the bed. Eventually he'd sold all of the décor Dana and he had purchased after moving into this house. He had thought to just box it up, but once he'd decided to follow her he concluded that those things would do better enriching someone else's life. When they shopped together they bought what they liked and it worked well for them. The house had been cozy, homey.

When Brian decided he was going to do it, he decided it like he decided everything else. He first made the plans. He knew what he'd use (pills, her pain medication) he knew where it would be done; and he knew if he did it that the pain would stop. It would be a fitting end for him. Numbing the pain of his loss with the medication that helped Dana remain pain free at the end.

He'd put in his notice at work and no one seemed surprised. Brian was "in a funk" and it was going to take more than going to work every day to shake him out of it. He was the type of guy that left nothing unfinished, but after Dana's death his job held no joy for him. Still, he'd come to work every day and put in his sixty days, doing his job as well as he ever had. When he was asked to stay an extra thirty days in order to train the new guy, Brian never hesitated. During that time period he used his time productively, selling and donating what he couldn't bear to throw away. Everything was in place, now there only remained the deed.

Brian wiped the condensation from the bathroom mirror and looked into his own eyes. He choked a bit on his sorrow as he looked at himself in the mirror. He felt older than he looked though there was a noticeable sag in his cheeks and sadness in his eyes. Brown, a deeper brown than you'd first realize. Or, that's how Brian liked to think of them. No one had ever looked into his eyes like Dana had; at least not that he knew or anyone said. She used to tell him he had beautiful eyes. She said they were deep and thick like molasses.

"A girl could get herself trapped in those eyes," She'd say, "forever trapped in amber." It used to embarrass him. It made him feel weak, like a girl, to be attractive. And maybe his eyes had once been beautiful, but he'd ruined that. Now they were just tired and washed out; the brown was watery like cheap whiskey. They'd discussed naming their first daughter Amber in honor of her father's eyes. But they were never able to have a child. Brian could remember that first trip to the doctor. Dana had been sick in the mornings, and with anticipation in her heart, took a home pregnancy test to see if she was going to be a mother. When after a few minutes the result showed positive Dana was elated. So was he, to tell the truth, but he kept it under wraps just a bit. They waited a week and went together to the doctor's office. It was a Friday.

When the doctor came into the exam room following the initial test, they'd been sitting together on the exam table chatting into each other's ears; him into her left, her into his right. It was something they'd always done; it was the thing, he thought, that had pulled them together in the first place. He'd seen her sitting at the bar. She was beautiful and sitting on a barstool enjoying a beer. To him she looked as if she belonged there, sweaty and panting, turning her beer up as she fanned her neck. He leaned over and whispered into her left ear.

"So, I know you're not here alone," he'd said feeling fully confident in his boozy haze, "but I was hoping that by the time tonight is over you'd be willing to share some of your togetherness with me."

She had leaned into him resting one hand on his chest.

"That was the stupidest thing I've ever heard." She said, but she'd stayed there, close to him and he talked to her. He said all kinds of stupid stuff that night, but by degrees she drew herself closer and closer to him always, always whispering into his ear.

They were together from that night, Brian and Dana, Dana and Brian, depending on whose friends they were hanging with. Two became one and he'd always thought, and they often laughed about, being joined at the ear.

"Excuse me," Doctor Brightman said, slightly embarrassed at finding the couple in such an intimate moment. "I uhh, have to tell you that the test results are negative. You are not pregnant Mrs. Suber but there is an anomaly in the results that is going to require some lab work. I'm sorry you didn't get the good news you were looking for. For now, don't worry."Don't worry she'd said. They worried. Anyone would worry. Anomaly, negative it was the opposite of what they wanted. It was uncertainty.

Brian took a deep breath. They had been uncertain then. He was sure of his path now. He left the bathroom he didn't take the bottle of pills with him to the kitchen. Not yet, those would join him in the bedroom later, for now he had to eat.

He worked pulling out bread, ham and condiments. The windows were bare but Brian took no notice as he prepared his last meal. As he slathered on Miracle Whip and carefully positioned his ham on the bread, followed by cheese and pickles, he wondered if eating first would affect the pills. Would it take him longer to die because he had food on his stomach? He knew that the last thing he wanted to do before he died was puke. He hated it. He remembered Dana holding his hair back as he puked one night after a Christmas party. There was no way he wanted to die choking on his own vomit.

"You're spilling crumbs all over the floor." Her voice was so clear in his head he whipped around at the sound of it.

"Dana?" She stood in the kitchen, a beam of sunlight playing over her pale shoulders and reflecting off the yellow flowers on her dress. She'd been buried in that dress and those sandals. She refused to spend all eternity in a stuffy old dress. She insisted on being buried in her favorite summer dress. She was real, but not real. He could see, faintly, the refrigerator behind her, but she was almost solid, almost real. She shimmered, no, wobbled like the world did when he was on Peyote.

"Dana, how-"

"Why don't you sit properly at the table to eat Brian? Where is your plate? I can't believe you."

"Brian," she stopped and looked around. When she did the world shimmered and she wobbled and almost blinked out. Brian held his breath and waited his stomach clenched at the thought of her leaving again so soon. When she spoke he took a breath and almost collapsed.

"I see now. Maybe this is why I am here."

'What? Dana this makes no sense, how can this be possible?"

"I don't know either Brian. I know this is possible, but I don't understand why. What are you doing here Brian?"

"Finishing it," he said.

"I see..." She seemed to grey as she thought about this. It was as if a cloud outside had covered the sun, but that wasn't it. Dana physically went almost black and white. "Oh, Brian, darling, it's not what you think."

"What isn't?" He moved towards her, when she didn't retreat he walked right up to her and spoke into her left ear. "What do I think?"

"You think that if you do this, this horrible thing, to yourself that you are going to be with me again. But it doesn't work like that in the end. This is more than I ever expected." Her voice was cold in his ear but familiar.

142

"Aren't you happy to see me?"

"I am ... more sorrowful than you can imagine. You can't do this to yourself."

"Why not, this is my life isn't it? It's mine to do with what I please."

"It is," she said, "this is your life. It's also mine and everyone else's. Please understand Brian that all death is an accident. Mine was sad, a tragedy, but if you kill yourself-"

"What, Hell and eternal punishment?"

"No, that's silly, nothing like that Brian. It's different over there. It's the same sometimes, but not, it's odd. I'm still getting used to it."

"And you don't think we'd see one another?"

She laughed at this. Not a full laugh, a small chuckle as if the thought of trying to relay this idea was too much. Brian knew her, he caught it but he didn't like it any more for the knowledge of it. He stepped back a pace, she looked past him into the distance. What did she see with her dead eyes? Was there another reality just over his shoulder, something that, had he been able to tear his eyes from her perfect form, he would still never see?

"Well?" He said. She looked at him then, her eyes were still gray but her form became vibrant.

"Brian, as much as I love you I believe that I should be able to find you in the midst of all those souls. Your life force radiates over there Brian. It's like a static that draws you together. Sometimes there are dozens of us all intertwined. It's ecstasy."

"So...what does that mean?" He was confused. He had no way to relate to what she was saying to him. "You have some cosmic lovers or something?"

"You drift there Brian, in places you recognize and in some you don't. But always there are others, once living, but now dead, that are the same as you. You are drawn together. I would like to believe that somewhere in the ether, I would find your *feel*, but I can't say. I am alone here and your *feel* is all I know. It's like being alive again."

"And that's worse."

"Yes..."

Two months after Dana got the news from the doctor, she and Brian had had a conversation about mortality. They were sitting on the balcony of a

143

small bookstore in Greene Texas. She was wearing a flowing hemp dress and she had her hair tied up with a ribbon from the honeymoon bouquet the hotel left in their room. She had been sad that morning so he'd ordered a platter of fresh fruit and some cold green tea. To make her happy he ordered flowers as well.

"Did you order green tea because we are in Greene Texas?" she had asked.

"Hummm...maybe, you know what a romantic I am."

"Is it going to hurt you?" She'd asked biting into a strawberry. Her lips were a bit puffy, maybe from crying, but the juice on her lips made him stir.

"Is what going to hurt baby?" He couldn't peal his eyes from her mouth. She was so sweet, his perfect woman.

"When I die," she asked. His eyes snapped to her face, she looked so unhappy. "When I die, is it going to hurt you?"

"Yes," he'd said taking her hand. "More than anything it's going to break my heart. We are not supposed to be talking about that now. This is us time."

"But in our lives, *I* am the one dying and if I want to talk about it I will."

"Okay, then what do you want to talk about?" He'd said relinquishing her hand.

"Your attitude says a lot. I want to know if you are going to miss me and you are attacking me for caring."

"Baby, I'm not attacking you. We had just agreed to-"

"Not talk about the end of *MY* life, for a whole week. Well excuse me if it occupies some of my mind most of the time."

"I was just trying to help you forget." He'd stormed out and walked on the beach for an hour. When he returned to the hotel she was gone.

He never knew where she went. When she got home they fell into each other and they'd never talked about it again, until she brought it up now.

"Brian, do you remember our trip; the one where I disappeared?"

"I do." He still stood a bit apart from her, no longer connected at the ear. He feared never again to be so.

"That trip, that time in my life I wanted to be something else, someone

144

else. I wanted to share that with you, but you wanted to cocoon me. You thought it best that we forget and live as if we had our whole lives in front of us. But Brian, only you had that reality. Only you had that luxury. I wanted to share that with you."

"What? What is it you wanted to share with me?"

"I did things that day Brian, things I may never have done otherwise. I was still strong enough to do them and I had no more reason to be afraid, so I did them. I wanted to share it with you but you were so closed. I knew I couldn't. Dying for me was like that day, it was ... is, a freedom unlike any I felt before that day."

"And there was no way we could have shared this mysterious day of yours together?" Brian was angry. He didn't want to be angry with her.

"We could have Brian if you'd been willing."

"What did you do Dana?"

"It doesn't matter." She wavered, her form seeming to ripple as if she lay just under the surface of water. "Death is different for us all. I died in one place in my life. My heart was in a certain *place*, your's is in a different place, it's darker. All there is in death is love."

"I'm lonely without you."

"Then LIVE your life Brian, find another me. Don't drag me here."

"But I love you."

"I know," she moved towards him, he could tell it was an effort for her. She wobbled again but his time the world didn't shimmer. She leaned into his ear, "are you going to go through with this Brian?"

"I am kind-of committed--"

"--Like you were to me. Your loyalty, your ability to commit is why I married you, you know? It was selfish of me. I loved you but I knew you loved me so much more. I died, and for you ... there was nothing more. But for me my life continued, the greater part of me became clear over there, and I found there never really was an "us"."

"And there never will be." Brian pouted at the thought. His heart was breaking and there was nothing he could do to stop it.

"You are so sad." She wobbled again; he thought he could feel her hand on his face. "I don't know how I ever loved you."

"Don't you still?" He sobbed into her ghostly shoulder.

"I do, and that is the sadness of it all. I died loving you and so I always shall, even though I know the truth."

"And the truth is?"

"You don't matter Brian. You never did."

Brian couldn't speak. He looked at her, his breath leaking from his open mouth in a low hiss. With his breath his legs were losing their strength. He felt he was going to fall. He wanted to fall and keep falling forever, the world blurred and he thought it was strange. Then he realized he was crying. Only tears.

He turned fully away from her then. He went back to his sandwich and shoveled it down only chewing enough to keep from choking on his own sobs. His whole life had been dedicated to finding and keeping that one perfect love, and here she stood in his kitchen, their kitchen, dead and telling him that it had never mattered, that it never should have been. SHE was happy knowing that she should have been someone else, or something else. He whirled around to confront her but his voice caught in his throat; bits of bread fell from his mouth. She was standing in the same place, in the sun from the window. Her face was turned into the light and she was smiling. Her shadow fell over the counter. Brian wondered how this was possible, but only for a moment. It didn't matter how this happened, only that it had. His feet moved him into her arms of their own accord. She pulled him close and for a long time he just cried.

She was warm, her skin sun kissed as he held her. She smelled like he remembered her, lilacs and mangoes, but it was now mingled with a hint of earth, or corruption.

"Brian, I love you. I loved you in life and so I love you in death."

"I'm confused."

"I know honey," She held him. "The only way you could know would be to die and I'm telling you that would be a mistake."

"Why? If all there is in death is love then what difference does it make?

"I don't know. I died in love. If you kill yourself over me ... you will die in sorrow."

She stood back from him again. He let her go; he looked at her closely like he used to do. He could see that one of her eyelashes was off, poking out

146

from the others at an odd angle. He could see the smile on the corners of her mouth. The smile she would wear when she was truly having a good day. She walked away from him and she didn't wobble the world didn't shimmer. She danced in the sunlight from the window, so happy, dead but so alive.

"I do love you Dana. You were my first and only true love."

"Oh, Brian; you were always so sad. It's why I loved you, you made me see my tender heart and I enjoyed it."

"What are you talking about?" Brian paused. Somewhere in his head something she said made him feel sick. He wanted to run to the bathroom and puke. He looked up at her standing in her bit of light. She looked so happy.

"I can feel the sun on my skin." Dana whispered.

"You don't have any skin, you're dead. What did you say a minute ago?"

"That you were ... are a sad little bit of a man, Brian. I always knew it. I loved you in spite of your weakness. It was love still, but you never inspired passion in me."

"You don't have to sound so disappointed."

"But it was disappointing. It was, and it wasn't completely depressing. Yes I wanted everything you were. But, I also wanted you to boil over and sweep me away. I wanted to wake up next to a magnetic animal of a man."

"And I'm not that."

"No,-"

"Stupid girl, it wasn't a question."

"Stupid girl...I am so glad you said that. You used to call me stupid girl and at no time in our relationship did I ever feel more distant from you." She stretched as she spoke and began fading again, her form becoming less substantial as he watched.

"Wait!" Brian screamed willing her to stay.

"There is nothing left to wait for, Brian. It's all up to you now."

And then she was gone. She was gone but her image remained like a shadow on a piece of film, faint, thin, like a true ghost. Residual, his mind told him. This was the last bit of her image he would ever see, and nothing else of her would ever be his again. She looked directly at him, and though

147

her last words had been full of spite, her eyes were full of love.

Brian could still remember the morning her test results came in. They had been getting ready to leave for work. The house phone had rung and they each looked at the other. Only bill collectors called on that line.

"Answer it," She said. He reached out and answered the phone without further thought; "Hello?"

After listening for a moment, he carried the handset over to Dana and handed it to her.

"It's the hospital..."

Dana muted the television, and said hello; then she went silent. He could tell something was wrong. She held one hand over her mouth as she listened and her eyes were on the floor. After a moment she thanked the voice on the other end and ended the call.

"So...?" He inquired sitting on the arm of the couch at her elbow.

"I'm dying." She said. He walked into her arms and pulled her in. She wrapped her arms around him and leaned into his chest. He could feel the sorrow in her body. She was holding him tightly. Every inch of her frame was strained, but she wasn't crying only breathing hard.

"I need time," she'd said and with that she'd pulled away from him and walked into the bedroom. Later when he tried the door it was locked. Instead of harassing her, he let her be alone. He called into work, made sure her bosses knew she wouldn't be making it in and stayed in that house waiting to serve her.

For two days he'd watched over her. On the first night he slept on the floor outside the door. The second night he didn't sleep at all. On the third morning she came out and she'd said ... what--? He thought he knew but in his mind the memory was fuzzy. In his mind she had clung to him and begged him to help her through this. But she hadn't said that had she? He didn't think so.

He looked around the kitchen the memory fading as he tried to recall the truth. She had emerged from the room her eyes puffy and red from crying. She hadn't slept and she refused to eat, or allow him to comfort or soothe her. Instead she'd insisted they sit. They sat together on the couch. The way she'd looked at him and placed her palms on his knees he'd thought she was about to tell him she wanted a divorce. He'd smiled and held her hands in his.

"What is it baby? I'm here for you whatever you need."

"I am dying Brian, and I am not going to let the thought of it kill me. You can continue to be a part of my life, but you are not obligated to come along with me. I wish you would, but I understand if you can't."

He didn't even understand what she meant. He only wanted to be with her. He wanted to be a part of her life no matter what that meant.

"I will do anything you need Dana. I love you with all my heart and whatever this thing is, we can beat it."

"I knew you'd say that." She replied.

I knew you'd say that. That was what she'd said. He had failed before the bad news even reached their ears. Years before the cancer and Dana passing from his life, he'd failed her. She was right, he was a weak man. The only thing that crossed his mind the whole time Dana died at his side was helping her die comfortably. He never thought that she might want to dance her way into death. In spite of it all she'd loved him and remained loyal to their bond. Whatever she'd done that day in Greene he would never have been able to follow her. He didn't, he ran instead, he'd pouted and she'd left him. He believed that if she'd have lived, if their lives had turned out differently, she would still have left him eventually. He felt like such a fool. Standing in the sunlight where she'd stood at her most solid, he felt the sun on his skin. Standing in their kitchen he had the greatest epiphany of his life. He was what Dana wanted in a man, but not what she'd needed. If it wasn't death something else would have taken her from him. She never found in life what she truly was, but in death she'd found peace.

Brian walked back to his bathroom. Everything was in place and there was really no turning back now. His eyes flickered over every inch of his naked form in the mirror. Now and then they would, as if instinctually saying I'm still here, look at me, look at me, they would lock on themselves. It was at these moments Brian would want to cry. There was no soul, no light, and no depth in those eyes any more. They could no more preserve a woman than they could shoot beams.

He turned from himself, snatching the bottle from the counter as he went. He stood for a moment looking at that bed. It would be the last one he ever laid in but it was hers ... theirs. He walked over and sat on the edge. His usual bottle of water was by the bedside and he twisted the cap off of that and the pill bottle. With that done he sat up on the bed his back pressed to the cool headboard.

When Dana was towards the end Brian spent a lot of time lying by her side in the bed they bought together. He'd sleep next to her even when she was almost comatose with pain pills. She'd decided to die at home rather than in a hospital surrounded by strangers and he, like in everything else, had supported her. He was there when her family visited her. He fielded all the angry phone calls, returned all of the emails and warded off the quacks and lawyers. He, Brian Suber, was her husband and he knew what she wanted. Sitting up in that bed now he wondered if he knew anything at all. His wife that he loved so much loved him, but her ghostly apparition told him he was a waste of a man. He'd started to believe that was true.

As he took the first of the pills he thought about what she'd said in the kitchen about love. She'd said that there was only love over there. There was a chance, she'd said, with our connection we might find one another. He was afraid, but he swallowed a few more pills, knowing there were twenty in the bottle, counting down, fourteen left. He was afraid because he did see the life he could have, but this vague vision was over shadowed by his own reality. Only an hour ago he had been convinced that he'd suffered loss. Now he was certain of it.

Brian popped pills into his mouth one handful at a time swallowing them with deep gulps of water. He lay down; the memory foam pillow they'd bought that day in the mattress store cradled his head. It was so comfortable. His body sank into the softness of the pillow top. For a moment he was afraid he was going to puke, but his body didn't seem to completely connect with his mind, his thoughts. He opened his eyes and the ceiling swam away before him and there was cloudless blue sky above him.

How beautiful, he thought. Gradually the blue spread across his vision until it was all he could see. A breeze blew across his face, it smelled like artificial Fall and he knew, somewhere in his mind, that he'd left the air conditioner on. The thought of it running brought his mind back into focus. The blue wobbled like the kitchen had when Dana first arrived but it didn't vanish. The room didn't come back into focus.

Brian tried to move but his body wouldn't listen to him. He screamed, but no sound came from his lips the scream only echoed in his head. I'm dying, he thought, and then he was truly afraid. With the fear came a gradual blackness. The blue started to dissipate before it and Brian panicked.

"I don't want to die!" His mind screamed over and over.

I DON'T WANT TO DIE! I DON'T WANT TO DIE! IDON'TWANTTODIE! IDON'TWANTTODIE!

But it was too late, the blackness had almost defeated the blue. His heart seemed to thunder in his chest, once, twice and then there was nothing more ... only death.

A Taste of Death

By Bob Clark

153

T hough the temperature was in the upper fifties when Arthur M.

Rykowski stumbled into the giant Santos Supertienda, he was on fire inside and exuded sweat as if it were the middle of August. Within fifteen minutes however, the fifty-seven-year old's body would be heading toward room temperature.

"Merry Christmas and welcome to the grand opening month here at Harlingen's Santos Supertienda. Is there anything I can help you with?" asked the greeter at the door as she handed him a map of the store's departments.

"Yeah, you can," he said. He peeled off his winter overcoat to reveal a plaid flannel lumberjack shirt buttoned up to the collar. "I heard you got free food here."

"Oh yes indeed," beamed the greeter. "All throughout the store there are foods being made and served just for you to sample. Go right in and enjoy the Santos Supertienda experience. It's the greatest store on the border."

Before he shuffled forward another five feet, a familiar voice called out, "Hey Michigan. I see you made it."

Rykowski turned in the direction of a stack of pineapples and saw Rusty, a transient from Ohio. Rusty ignored the sign taped to a plastic half globe to his left. The admonition urged the customers to "Please use tissue." Instead, with his grimy hands, he scooped out chunks of the bright yellow fruit from the sample display. "I told you. It's all free for the taking. They say it's been like this all through December."

Rykowski licked his dry and chapped lips. He needed something to eat. Last night's scraps from a fast food restaurant dumpster weren't filling and his belly growled. So did he, "Why you always on my ass? I'm not your wife."

"Hey dude, no need to get all riled up. I thought since we partnered up in Kansas and we was buddies, you might be cool. After that groundhog bit you outside of Texarkana the other day you been hard to live with."

The man from Michigan responded by resuming his straight ahead course. He thought, *I've been doing this for years. I don't need his help.*

The male voice of a food preparer halted his inner discussion. "You are going to love the taste. All I did was to take the natural Angus beef rib eye steak on sale here at the Supertienda Butcher Shop, add the all-purpose Greek seasoning and some coarse ground pepper. Then I grilled the meat for five minutes. Let your eyes drink it in. Mmmm. Smell it. I know you want some."

Rykowski did want some, and he angled over to the sample kiosk, which sported a small kitchen with a grill atop the built-in stove.

"Well, looky here. My first customer of the day," said the man with the microphone in his mouth. In a cheery voice, he asked, "Would you care for a sample?"

"Yeah, yeah. I need to eat something. Gimme what you got."

The preparer used tongs to take one of the steaks off the grill and moved it to a cutting board. He sliced the savory steak into small dice-sized morsels, placed three on a paper plate, and offered up the sample. "Medium rare. Take a bite."

The hungry man vacuumed the food off the plate and asked, "Is that all?"

The server watched the man suck the food into his mouth and never saw him chew. He remarked to the customers who passed, "Look at that. It melts in your mouth and it's so good the man wants more."

"Yeah. More. Gimme another one."

In haste, a second paper plate was handed over. The server turned off his mike and said in a low voice, "Sir, there are others who would like a taste."

Rykowski glared at the man, but moved back, and a fat woman took the next plate. He stepped away from the rib eye meal as drops of salty sweat from his forehead seeped into his eyes. Though his vision was blurred, his ears worked fine. He heard another microphone-enhanced voice and made his way to a second kitchen island in the sea of groceries.

"You like pork, sir?"

His head turned in the direction of the voice and he rubbed his eyes. A tall man in a blue Santos Supertienda apron smiled at him. "You got that right," he said. "If a pig walked out here now, I could eat it, snout to tail."

"Then you are going to fall in love with our lemon pistachio pork over fresh picked lettuce. I can tell by the look on your face you want a taste."

With the worn cuff of his lumberjack shirt, he wiped away the perspiration and looked down at a paper plate covered with leafy green

156

lettuce. "Don't look like no pork there and you don't have to give me none of that lemon or pistachio crap neither."

"No sir, it's still all in the bowl here. Let me put some on the lettuce and your taste buds will thank me for the rest of the day." An ice cream scoop carved out a walnut-sized sample of the pork dish and plopped it down in the middle of the fresh lettuce.

Before the man could hand the sample to him, Rykowski snatched it up and downed it. "Yeah, good. I uh, I got a wife. Can I have another plate for her?"

"Certainly, sir, and she can come back to our Butcher Shop later and get all the ingredients too," said the preparer as he used the scoop again. "For this tasty dish, I used cornflakes, shelled pistachios, fresh lemon zest..."

"Okay, okay. I'll tell her." To his right, a tall customer stared at him as he ate the second sample and turned to move on. A few aisles away, he bumped into Gerardo Martinez who was in the midst of chatting up a lovely young thing who had paused to compare calorie counts in the margarine cooler.

When Rykowski jostled Martinez, it was Martinez who said, "Excuse me," although he had nothing to excuse himself for.

Unsure on his feet, Rykowski leaned on the open-air cooler and asked, "You know where any more free food places are in this airplane hangar?"

Martinez shook his head, but Linda, his pretty quarry, said, "There's one at the end of this cooler. The lady is cooking some Southwestern Fajitas. It looks good."

Rykowski fought the urge to take off his shirt. The tip of Texas felt like a boiling cauldron to him. He knew they would toss him out of the store and the feast would be over if he began to disrobe, so he staggered on to where sixty-year-old Elinor Lezcano uncovered a skillet and started to ladle her freshly cooked food into mini sample containers. Wisps of scented steam danced over each sample and he wanted all of them, every last bite.

Her amplified voice said, "What I did was to take a fifteen-ounce can of whole kernel corn and a can of black beans. I mixed them together, and then I diced whole tomatoes freshly picked at the store's own nearby farm. I added cooked rice, a cup of Southwest marinade, and the fajita meat. I put it all in this skillet and after five minutes, just sniff at the result." With a twinkle in her eye, she added, "You can tell by the smell, it's going to be

157

yummy in the tummy."

"Gimme some," ordered Rykowski as he swayed to the left, then to the right.

He reached out to the display in order to regain his balance and knocked two cans of black beans to the floor.

Elinor just knew the man was drunk from his slurred speech, but she had her orders from the top. She forced a smile and said, "Yes sir. I think one taste and you'll want more."

"Okay. Gimme two then. I want more now."

She made an inward chuckle at his demand. She didn't want to antagonize the drunk by telling him it was only one sample for everyone, so she spooned the fragrant food into two mini containers and pushed them across the display toward the man.

He wolfed down the first and coughed. A small, red piece of food shot out of his mouth and landed in the uncovered food on the counter. She sighed and covered it. He tilted the second container so the portion of Southwestern Fajitas funneled into his open mouth.

"All right. Now there is a man who knows good food and he can't get enough of it," she said into the microphone which was held close to her lips by a band of steel over her head. She looked around and spotted a woman with a child in the plastic seat of a shopping cart. "Ma'am, this feeds a family of four to six in just five minutes and you can..."

She was interrupted by Rykowski, who coughed twice and crumpled to the floor. The unchewed meal portion in his mouth dribbled out on one side of his face. The woman with the shopping cart screamed and her little boy began to cry. Out of the corner of Elinor's eyes, she saw a man and a woman moving toward the drunk on the floor. "Security!" she spoke into the microphone. Her voice was louder the second time. "Security. Sample display, aisle number six."

By this time, the man on the floor was making hoarse coughing noises and had turned whiter than a glass of milk. She knew he was seriously ill, and all she could think of was her new job going down the drain. *It isn't fair,* she thought. *I didn't like the look of him, but Mr. Santos said we had to give out samples to all no matter whether they looked rich or poor. All customers were to be treated equally he said. I was just doing my job and now I will be fired. How am I going to pay for the light bill? This fool on the floor is responsible for ruining my life.*

The coughing stopped and Rykowski became motionless as Gerardo Martinez knelt down next to him. Linda, the young woman he had struck up a conversation with stood there with her pretty eyes wide open. He turned his head and looked up at her. By her expression, he saw she wanted him to do something. He gazed down at Rykowski, bent over to put his face close to the fallen man's ear, and muttered, "I got no idea what to do, but I have seen stuff on TV. Be good to me, man. A date with an angel is hanging on you." He sat upright and put his hands on the man's chest. With all his might, he pushed down and then relaxed. Again he pushed on the chest.

Someone in the gathering crowd called out, "Mouth to mouth," and he slammed his eyes shut. The thought of putting his lips to those of this man, this revolting homeless bum, sickened him. Once again, he turned his eyes upward to Linda.

She nodded and whispered, "Go ahead."

Without her there coaxing him, he would've bolted for the door, but instead he reached up with a hand and pinched the man's nose, then took a gulp of air. As he blew the contents of his lungs into the man, he thought the feel of male lips against his wasn't much different from those of the women he had kissed, although the guy needed a shave. There was no change in the man's condition, until he tried a second time. Rykowski coughed up undigested bits of tomato, fajita meat, and tortilla pieces into Gerardo's open mouth. He rolled off the man and vomited onto the floor.

He was oblivious to the small crowd that ringed the two men. They began to applaud and shouts of "Hero" sprang up. Linda took a roll of paper towels out of the nearby cart with the crying boy and knelt down next to Gerardo so she could clean off the vomit on his face.

A man in a white shirt and tie hurried toward them trailed by two security people, one in a blue rent-a-cop uniform, the other a tall woman who appeared to be an ordinary shopper. The man with the tie started giving orders. "All right. It's over now. Please break up this crowd. We are in charge." He turned to Elinor and said, "You there. Close this kitchen down, but don't leave the store. We will have questions for you." He looked down and said, "You two down there on your knees, get up and step back from the mess on the floor. I think we need to ask you questions also, so stay right here. The EMS people have been called and will take over."

The man's ID tag stated in bold print, "Tomas Ysunza," and in smaller letters, the words "public relations." It was Ysunza's job to create

159

promotions like the sample kitchens and carry them out. He also handled advertising, and was the man the media talked to when they wanted a story about any of the store's operations. The 22-year-old was a recent graduate of the University of Texas-Pan American in nearby Edinburg and had been given the task of bringing bold new ideas to the Santos chain. He never faced a challenge like this in the classroom, but he knew he was up to it. His grades at school gave him all the confidence he needed.

A familiar ring tone jangled in the cell phone on his belt and he answered it. "Boss, I am on the scene now, and I will have a full report as soon as the EMS unit shows up."

On the other end of the line was Salvador Santos. "I'm counting on you, boy. So is your Aunt Regina. She was the one who convinced me you were the right man for the job." Santos clicked off and began to check the figures for produce inventory at the warehouse.

Three emergency medical team members rushed through the automatic doors and were met by the greeter, who directed them to the sample kitchen, where Rykowski lay sprawled on the floor in the midst of vomit and the debris of a soiled towel and a spilled cardboard sample container. Within moments, they hooked the man up to their instruments and detected no pulse, breathing, or heartbeat. Several resuscitation attempts were made, but when the leader of the team shook his head, the woman with the crying child screamed, "He's dead!" The shoppers who had formed a circle around his body earlier were now aisles away, but when they heard the shouted words, they drifted back, and brought others with them to see what a dead man in the middle of the new Santos Supertienda looked like. Among them was Rusty, the man's traveling buddy. He took one look at the dead man, decided that discretion was the better part of valor and made a straight line for the exit.

Ysunza told the security personnel to call the police and to cordon off the area. He also attempted to break up the growing crowd again, but they wouldn't move. He picked up his cell phone and called upstairs. "Boss, the man is dead. He was eating a sample of the Southwestern Fajita Skillet meal and he keeled over. The kitchen is closed and..."

Santos sighed and then said, "OK Tommy, tell me the ingredients right now. You handle everything down there. I will take care of the rest. Just tell me what was in the food."

"I have the recipe here, Uncle Salvador. It was made with fajita meat."

"Oh, Maria Madre de Dios. It could be E. Coli. What else was in it?"

"There were fresh tomatoes..."

"This is not good. Might be botulism. I don't need this. You find out if he had any more samples. I'm calling the store manager."

Bobby Padilla's smiling face was on the welcome posters at both entrances to the store, but he wasn't smiling when he entered the office of Mr. Santos. "What's the trouble, boss? Your call sounded urgent."

"Urgent? Do you know there is a dead man in the store?"

"Well no, I was having a bite at the snack bar with a new employee and I wasn't informed of any..."

"Don't give me that 'bite' story again. You were pinching some cashier's buttocks in the break room. I know where all my employees are. I don't care what you were doing. I want to know what you're going to do about the situation."

"Uh... first we need to call the police."

"I already covered that, you idiot. Let's get to the two possible problems that should concern you, meat and tomatoes. There may be more possibilities later when I have all the facts. My cousin, Paquito runs the tomato farm south of the border. I have told that moron time and again not to let the workers piss and crap in the fields and if he got me in a jam today, I am going to cram an entire case of tomatoes up him for this. Immediately, take all the tomatoes out of the produce department."

"But boss, there is a big sale on them during this grand opening. We have at least a hundred pallets in the warehouse."

Salvador Santos pounded his fist hard onto the desk and stood up, "113 pallets, to be exact. I want you to listen to me now. Not one more customer is going to drop dead in my store. Close down the meat counter also and get it done now. Leave the pre-packaged stuff out, but put all fresh meat into coolers immediately."

"Right, boss. Keep this in mind though. It's going to be a big loss at a time when sales are supposed to go up."

"Use the cabbage head on your shoulders, Padilla! Don't you realize that if people die in my stores, we will be out of business? The other big grocers will crush us before January starts. Now get out of my office and get to work."

The next morning, Cameron County medical examiner Percival T. Jennings stepped to the microphone at a hastily assembled press conference in the lobby of the county courthouse. "I have a prepared statement I would like to read to you. It will fill you in on all we know about the death of Arthur Maurice Rykowski yesterday. We have found it necessary to answer the questions that have come up in the last twenty-four hours and try to dispel the countless rumors circulating about the causes."

A reporter from one of the local TV stations called out, "Was it E. coli? Is the meat safe to eat?" A storm of other questions thundered over Jennings and he held up his hands to wave off the reporters.

When they settled down, he said, "I cannot answer any questions in this manner, though E. Coli doesn't usually act that fast, but nothing is off the table. I simply cannot rule out anything at this point in the investigation. I will read the statement and that is all I will say. No questions, please." The crowd grumbled for fifteen seconds. He cleared his throat and his monotone resumed. "We are striving to find the exact cause of the sudden death of Mr. Rykowski, but contrary to popular belief and what you may see on television this county does not have the facilities to do the necessary testing."

For the second time, the medical examiner was deluged with questions and once again, he waited for calm. "We have sent samples of the contents of the stomach of the deceased to the Medical Examiner's Office in San Antonio and to the Center for Disease Control in Atlanta. We have also sent along other samples of body fluids. We will not have a definitive answer back for days, but at this time, I can tell you that the shopping public should avoid tomatoes, beef, pork, and lettuce."

Another round of questions was shouted at Jennings, and he moved two paces to the rear to put distance between himself and the microphones thrust in his face. The Harlingen Police Chief moved forward and began to speak. "The Medical Examiner will distribute the statements to you in just a moment. I have been in contact with the management of the Santos Supertiendas chain and they have taken the items mentioned off store shelves and will continue to stay in operation. Mr. Rykowski's next of kin has also been contacted in this unfortunate tragedy."

In Ypsilanti, Michigan, Doris Rykowski, the common law wife of the deceased, sat in a lawyer's office and inquired about a wrongful death suit on behalf of herself and her son, who was incarcerated in the Michigan

Reformatory in Ionia. "We was together for eleven happy years," she said through her yellowed and crooked teeth. "All of a sudden, he ups and leaves me a year ago. How much do you think eleven years is worth?"

In San Benito, south of Harlingen, Gerardo Martinez made an

emergency visit to his doctor about the food particles he ingested when Rykowski threw up into his mouth. He was agitated about the lovely Linda too, because after the rumors of E. coli and botulism started circulating, she stopped answering his phone calls.

Elinor Lezcano decided not to wait for the store to drop the axe. She called in and resigned. By the next afternoon, she had signed on as a security guard at a large church run by a televangelist. It didn't pay as well as the Supertienda job, but she didn't have to cook or even meet any people on the night shift.

Paquito Rendon, who owned the land around a farming village south of the border, put in a rush order to the Supertienda for fifty dozen packages of male and female adult diapers. He knew his workers would never use the portable toilets cousin Salvador demanded he get for them. They would lose too much picking time in the fields and that would cut into their incomes.

At the Salvation Army in downtown Harlingen, Rusty stuck a spoon in the

stew and told the man next to him, "I knew the guy who dropped dead in the middle of that store yesterday. You ain't never gonna catch me in there again. They done give out poison to him."

Since the day after the news of the man from Michigan's death hit TV and newspapers, Salvador Santos stewed in his office daily and watched the shoppers diminish to a trickle. *Ruined. This will ruin me. The same thing is happening in my stores from Roma to Brownsville. I gotta do something.* A knock on the door took him away from the window that overlooked the empty cashier lanes. "Come in and bring good news," he said to the door.

Store manager Bobby Padilla strode up to the cluttered desk and said, "Good news. I just unloaded the meat and tomatoes to a store in Matamoros. We took a beating, but if we left them in storage much longer, the meat and all the rest would have rotted."

"Ay, Dios Mio. So our problem has moved to Mexico? It could kill people down there. Are we covered? Do they know where it came from?"

Padilla shook his head. "Do I look that stupid? I had it loaded into plain white vans and parked them in a shopping center in Brownsville. Workers from the Mexican side unloaded it and put the cargo in a moving company truck. They paid me cash and drove it across the border. It's no longer our problem."

"How much? How much did you get?" When the store manager told him, Santos leapt to his feet. "I paid four times what you got for that. They screwed us."

"But Boss, you were going to lose all your money if the tests came back positive."

Santos slumped back in his chair, closed his eyes and rubbed his forehead. "OK, but if anybody dies over there and they trace it back here, I didn't tell you to do that. I don't even know you did it." When he saw Padilla nod his head, he smiled and said, "You did good. Now put the money down on the desk and take the rest of the day off."

As he closed the door behind him, a Cheshire Cat grin lit up Padilla's face.

The extra thousand dollars he skimmed off the top was going to buy a lot of sparkly trinkets for his two mistresses, and maybe a new blender for Mrs. Padilla.

In the course of the next four days, Rykowski's wife came down to Harlingen and held a news conference of her own, where she extolled the virtues of her dearly departed husband. Her lawyer, who sensed the Santos chain's deep pockets, weighed in with a scenario describing Mr. Rykowski's possible earning power over the next decade or so.

At the store, Santos read the Mexican newspaper from Matamoros and buzzed Bobby Padilla. The moment he saw the store manager's smiling face, he rolled up the newspaper and threw it at him.

Padilla ducked and asked, "What's wrong, boss?"

"Did you sell that shipment of meat and produce to the Servi-Compra chain across the border?"

"Yeah, why?"

"If you unroll that newspaper and take a look at their ads, you'll see why. They took our beef and pork at a huge discount and now they're undercutting our prices by 30%. No Mexicans are coming across the border and shopping at our stores in Brownsville, Hidalgo, or Roma. I might as well shut those stores down."

164

"But the good news is that nobody died from eating any of it in Mexico."

Eyeball knives flew across the room. "You go tell that news to the dead guy. I'm going bankrupt and you're telling me about the health conditions in Mexico. You know, I am seriously considering sending you to the vacant position of produce manager at the Roma store."

The look on Padilla's face said more than his words. "No boss, please don't do that. This thing will be over soon."

Santos searched his desk for something else to throw, but settled for, "Get out of my sight," and pointed to the door. As Padilla turned to go, he added, "I take back that day off I gave you. You're working both days this weekend."

Gerardo Martinez had surfed the Internet and finally paid an internet search site for Linda's address. He felt it was money well spent as he knocked on the door of her apartment in Combes to the north of the Harlingen city limits. He beamed when the girl of his dreams answered the knock wearing tight shorts and a T-shirt that appeared to be painted on her body.

"What are you doing here?" she inquired.

"I came to see you and show you that I'm okay. I didn't die."

"Yeah. I can see that. Congratulations. I guess you're lucky." She paused a second and pushed open the door so he could see into the living room. "I got company now. You'll have to excuse me."

It was a familiar face, but he couldn't quite place the man sitting on the couch. "Who is that?"

"It's Tommy, the public relations guy at the Supertienda. He's questioning me about the poor guy who died."

"Questioning? The cops asked me about that days ago. You always dress like that to answer questions? I thought you and me had something."

She shrugged. "Um, I don't think so. Look, I'll see you sometime. Bye."

When the door closed in his face, he felt sick to his stomach all of a sudden. He puked on the door. When he was done, he turned and left.

Rusty got tired of South Texas in a hurry. Unemployment was bad and even the people who worked didn't have enough for a panhandler to make an honest living. He packed a gym bag containing all his possessions and caught a ride heading to Houston before the afternoon sun had a chance to kiss his bald spot. He never got to hear the latest news about Rykowski.

Medical Examiner Percival T. Jennings received an e-mail from San Antonio around noon and he called the news media into his office so they could have the story for the air this afternoon and for the paper in the morning. When the details were made public, big changes were to affect Bobby Padilla, Doris Rykowski, and her lawyer. There was no trace of E. coli or botulism in the specimens that were examined. An assistant in the coroner's office in San Antonio washed the body of the victim in the case and discovered a tiny mark on the man's neck. He reported it to the medical examiner for Bexar County and further time consuming tests were ordered there.

"The official cause of death was established this morning," said Jennings. "Mr. Arthur M. Rykowski died of anaphylactic shock brought on by an allergic reaction after being bitten on the neck by an unknown type of rodent."

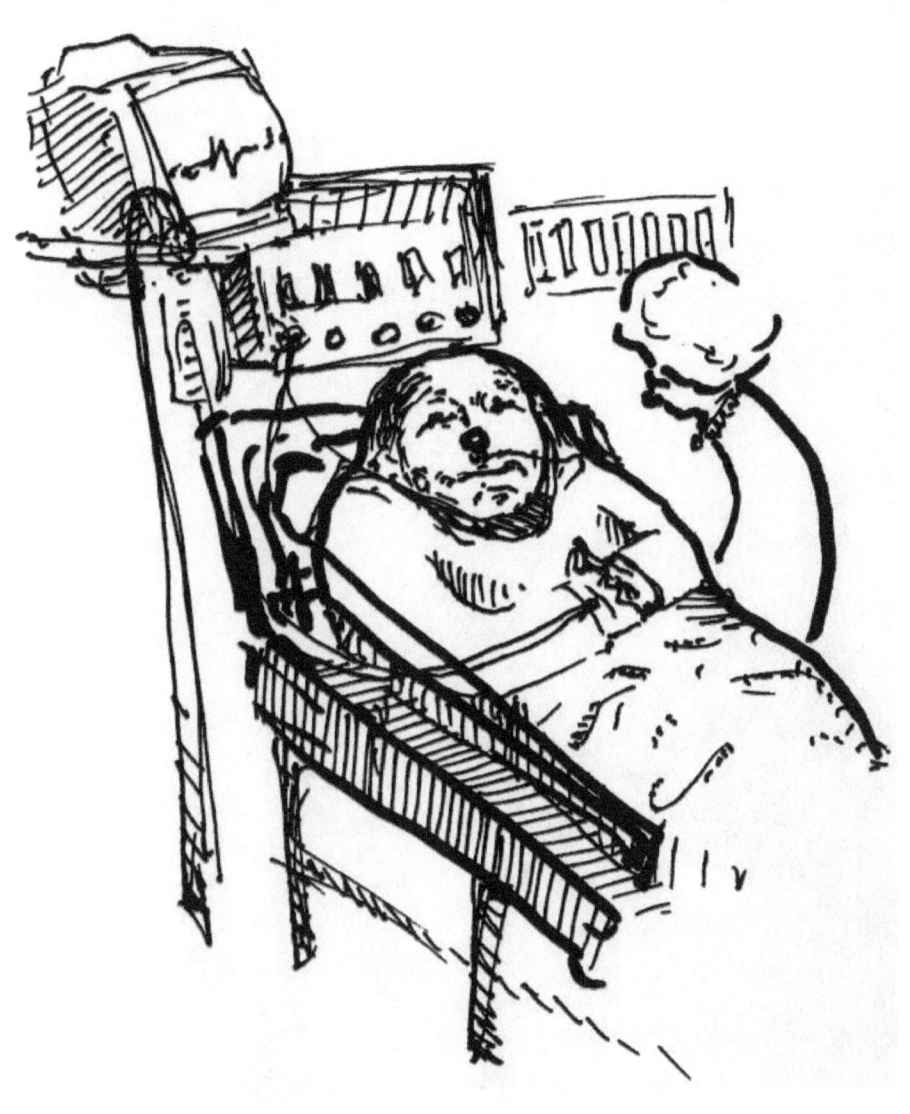

OZZIE THE CLOWN

William Walton

I don't know when I became Ozzie the Clown. Sometimes it seems like it happened over time, other times like it happened in a flash. Once, when I was very young, my mom took me to the circus. That was before she ran away with the real estate man. There were lions, tigers, elephants, and acrobats, but I wasn't very interested in them. Something else caught my eye.

"Who is the funny looking man with the red nose?" I asked.

"He's a clown, Donnie. He makes people laugh."

"How does he make people laugh?"

"Oh, he falls down in funny ways, makes silly faces, and plays tricks. You'll see!" She got kind of excited. He did fall down and make funny faces, but he really didn't make me laugh all that much.

"Well, what do you think, Donnie?" she asked, smiling.

"I've never seen a person with a red nose like that before."

"It's just a painted-on face, with a rubber nose. It's not real."

I liked the idea of a painted-on face. The next day she drew a clown's face on me with red lipstick. She laughed as she painted it on. I didn't mind too much.

Later that year my dad killed my mom and the real estate man. He got put away, and I never saw him again. I went to live with an aunt as a foster child. She got paid to keep me. Her children didn't like me very much, but I had plenty to eat, so I didn't care. I didn't like them either. I spent most of my time in a vacant lot down the street. It was my special place. Anyway, they didn't care where I was.

Things were okay. You know, not good, but I wasn't going to die or anything. Then school started. I didn't want to go, but my aunt made me. I wasn't athletic, smart, or good-looking, so I was not popular. The other kids delighted in ridiculing me, making fun of me all day long. In class it was bad enough, but recess was the worst. I purposely got in trouble with my teachers so I would not be allowed to go for recess, but I couldn't do that all the time. Lots of times at recess kids roughed me up just for their amusement. When they pushed me or spat on me, I just endured it, saying nothing. Then I discovered if I pretended to be happy and made people laugh, they were less likely to bully me. So I did lots of magic tricks, card tricks, and goofy stunts. I guess you could say I learned to "play the clown." It seemed to work pretty well. Nobody wanted to be my friend, but at least they left me alone. That's all I ever wanted.

One day, when I went to the local hobby shop looking for magic tricks, a clown was performing there. His name was Cal, but his clown name was Burpo. I liked it that you couldn't tell what he looked like. I asked him what you had to do to become a clown. He showed me a few tricks. He said there sure was a lot to know, but that if I would come to his place after school he would teach me. I didn't like some of the things he did to me to me there, but I kept going every chance I got because he was teaching me what I needed to know about how to be a clown. He even gave me some of his extra stuff. He showed me how to paint on a clown face, make balloon animals, and to fall down in goofy ways without hurting myself. He taught me to play lots of tricks and many other elements of the clown's trade. I didn't like it when he took his clown suit off because that's when he did the things to me that made me feel funny. But when he had his clown suit on he was okay. He was more than okay. He was special. He had it on when he gave me my wig, my rubber nose, and my very own makeup kit. I believe that was the happiest I have ever been.

"Donnie," he said, "I think you are ready to help do some kids' parties with me. How would you like that?" My heart was pumping so hard I thought it would burst. But it didn't. That would come later.

"Can I have my own clown name?" I asked.

"Do you think you are ready?"

"Do you think I am ready, Burpo?"

"Yes, I do, Donnie. Who would you like to be?

"I'd like to be Ozzie the Clown."

"Ozzie the Clown it is. That settles it." He never called me Donnie again.

I worked with Cal, or Burpo as I knew him, after school, doing mostly kids' birthday parties. After a while I dropped out of school so I could spend more time clowning with him. With the passage of time, Burpo let me take a greater role in his shows. He still did most of his stunts alone, but we started doing a few together. Finally, he even let me do a couple on my own.

"Way to go, Ozzie!"

"Thanks, Burpo!"

"I think you've got what it takes, Kid."

"Thanks, Burpo."

One day, just before one of our birthday appearances, Burpo got sick. He called his clients and told them not to worry about the party. He said he would send over a colleague who would do a great job for them. He called me a colleague! I wasn't sure what that was, but I knew it was good. I was still uneasy, though.

"Burpo, I'm not sure I can do it by myself."

"Sure, you can. Do it for me." I would have done anything for Burpo.

"But, Burpo, I don't even like kids. I just like being a clown."

"What's liking kids got to do with anything? Do you think I like the little buggers? It's our craft that matters."

"You really don't like them either?"

"No. I can't stand them. Never could." I know he liked me though.

"Okay, Burpo, I'll do it, but you'll have to tell me what to do."

"Just do what we always do. You know the drill as well as I do."

That's how I came to do my first Ozzie the Clown Show. I did it for Burpo. I started out pretending to be Burpo in my head to help with my nervousness, but as the show progressed, I was just Ozzie the Clown. It went okay I guess. The kids laughed and hollered, and the adults seemed satisfied, satisfied enough to pay me anyway. I guess that made me a professional. I can't say that I particularly enjoyed myself, but I couldn't imagine any other way I could make a living, let alone get through life. It was the only way for me.

Burpo had given me a gift no one could take away. Without him I could never have become a clown. I could count on Burpo to support and teach me, to never leave me like my mom and dad did. With him I was safe, or at least as safe as it was possible to be.

It turns out that Burpo was very sick with some kind of lung disease. He had always looked kind of funny smoking in his clown outfit. I never really thought much about it. Even as he lay in his hospital bed, he had his clown nose on. He didn't have his makeup, but he had that big, red nose,

171

even if it did have oxygen tubes running under it. When I went to see him the first time, he took my hand, squeezed it hard, and made me promise to bring him his orange wig. Of course I did, and he wore it along with his red nose. The hospital staff tried to get him to take them off, but he wouldn't. Once, after he had gotten weaker, they managed to get them off while he was asleep. I brought him an identical set, and they never got them off him again. He died with them on. I know, because I was sleeping there when he died, to protect him from the nurses taking them off. You could say he died with his boots on.

I took it pretty hard when Burpo died. He had stopped doing the uncomfortable things he used to do to me years before. Besides, it was Cal, not Burpo, who did them to me. A few days after Burpo was buried, I got a call from his lawyer who told me that he had left me his house, his car, and all his clown equipment. I moved in that day. I only had two suitcases of clothes and a few boxes of my clown stuff, most of which Burpo had given me, so it was easy. Burpo's house, now my house, was overflowing with the tools of the clown's trade. It was like the Mecca of Clowndom. I could wear my now much-embellished, full-fledged clown outfit around the house as much as I wanted, which was pretty much all the time. I was in heaven, or at least as close as I will probably ever get. But, I'd rather that Burpo were still alive. We were a team. But he was not, and that was that. It was time to move on. Goodbye, Burpo.

I applied for Burpo's old job with Party Town. That's where he got most of his birthday engagements. I applied in my clown outfit. I filled out the job application as Ozzie the Clown, although they had to get my given name too, for tax purposes. I got the job.

One day, when I was doing a private birthday party for Party Town, I was approached by a woman I remembered from school. Hazel had been a homely wallflower back then, and time hadn't done her any favors. But she had always been kind to me. There hadn't been many kids like that. She, of course, didn't recognize me in my clown suit. The party I was doing was for her nephew, to whom she felt particularly attached because she couldn't have any children of her own. That made her instantly more attractive to me. I can actually carry on a pretty good conversation when I am Ozzie the Clown, so we hit it off pretty well. Finally, I told her who I was. Well, not who I was, but who I had been. I had to identify myself for obvious reasons. I couldn't ask to see her again as Ozzie the Clown. Even I understood that.

"Donnie, I can't believe it's you. I shouldn't be surprised, though. You were

172

always funnier than a barrel of monkeys."

"You can call me Ozzie."

"Actually, I'd rather call you Donnie, although I will call you Ozzie when you are dressed up in your clown outfit if you like. Will that be okay?"

"I would appreciate that."

She asked me if I would like to go out to dinner with her. I said sure, and we set a date, time, and place. When she left, I wasn't really sure I could go through with it. I wondered if I could get away with showing up in my clown outfit. Maybe she would think it was really funny. Not likely. Believe it or not, I managed to show up in street clothes and without my face painted. It wasn't easy. I felt like an impostor, like I was in disguise. I didn't think it went very well. I never have very much to say when wearing street clothes, but things must have gone better than I thought. She invited me to her home for dinner. After that, I began to visit her fairly regularly. Sometimes I went in my clown suit, and she seemed to enjoy it. Once, when she had her nephew visiting, she even asked me to come over as Ozzie. I liked hearing her laugh. Once, when I was in my street clothes, she did some things like Burpo---no, Cal---used to do. It made me uncomfortable, but I tolerated it because she tolerated me. But, when I wore my real clothes, when I was Ozzie the Clown, all we did was laugh and talk and kid each other. It was fun.

Things went surprisingly well, and in the spring Hazel and I were married. She wanted me to move into her place, but there was no way I was moving out of Burpo's. It was a Clown Shrine. I didn't like moving all my clown stuff out of our bedroom, but I did. She had no idea how hard it was for me. She wasn't trying to be mean. She was just trying to make the place more livable. I understood that. She wanted all my clown gear out of the living room, too, but I was able to keep some clown memorabilia as decorating items. Most of my clown stuff went into the guest bedroom, which we called my Clown Room. It was floor to ceiling with clown stuff. I spent a lot of time there. It was my favorite place in the world, and the truth is that I hated it when Hazel came in. Of course, I never told her so. But I would be wearing my clown clothes, so it was usually okay. Nobody else but Hazel was ever allowed in.

I wore my clown clothes a lot in the rest of the house, too. After all, I was usually getting ready to go to work at Party Town, or returning from one of my birthday gigs. At first, Hazel was pretty tolerant of what she called my eccentricity. She was glad that I had what she thought was such a passion for my work. After a while, however, she insisted that I take off my clown face and clothes for dinner. Lots of times I called to say that I couldn't make dinner, that I was working late, but, from time to time, I had to put on my phony street clothes and Donnie face to make her happy. I did it as often as I could, for as long as I could, but it wasn't good enough. Later I created a clown mask that I could wear around the house instead. It wouldn't do for work, but it was okay for around the house. She didn't seem to mind that as much, and I could take it off for just long enough to have dinner.

The straw that broke the camel's back was bedtime. I took off my clown suit, but I often left my face on, telling her that I wouldn't have time to do a full makeup in the morning. This had the additional benefit of preventing her from doing those things to me that I didn't like. My painted face seemed to offer some sort of protection from that. But she kept pressuring me, and I switched to the mask, which could be taken off. It didn't offer the protection of the makeup, but it helped some. She tolerated this for a while, but then she told me that if I was going to wear my Ozzie mask to bed I would have to sleep in the guest bedroom. I guess she thought I would quit wearing my Ozzie face so I could remain in our bed. Instead I started sleeping in the guest bedroom, my Clown Room. Hazel left me.

"Donnie, I can't take this anymore."

"Please don't call me Donnie. I'm Ozzie."

"That's what I mean. You're not even here anymore. I've lost you. Lord, Donnie, *you've* lost you."

Being the kind, gentle person she was, she told me she still loved me and, if I was willing to work on my problems, we might still have a chance together. I thought that was wishful thinking, but somewhere deep inside of me I was pleased that she felt that way. I guess I cared about her some. Not like I cared about Burpo, but some. Yet in some ways I felt relief that she was leaving. I hadn't lost myself. I knew exactly who I was. I was Ozzie, Ozzie the Clown, that's who.

I threw myself totally into my work. I even tried to be enthusiastic when Party Town had a special promotion and I had to meet and greet the kids. Thankfully, that didn't happen very often because it was all I could manage just to get through it. At least I didn't yell at them or anything.

"Ozzie! Ozzie! Me! Me!" they'd shout as they came storming into the building the instant the doors opened.

Yeah, yeah, sure you little snots, I'd think. But I just said, "Hi, boys and girls," and hid behind my painted-on smile. At least I didn't have to take the little buggers home with me. I reminded myself of that very consoling fact every time I reported for duty as the Party Town greeter.

"Don, I've got a couple of home party jobs for you today. Should keep you busy all afternoon," my boss, Leland, said. I'd tried to get him to call me Ozzie, but he wouldn't. I finally gave up.

"Great," I answered, taking the sheet of information about the number of kids, the party themes, if any, and the times and addresses. More friggin' balloon animals, but at least it was a living.

It wasn't long before I ran into some problems in my job with Party Town, too.

"Don, we've been getting some complaints from parents that your costume is sloppy and that your makeup runs down your cheeks and stuff," said Leland.

"They say you are a pretty sorry specimen of a clown. Some of them are asking that we send someone else. I'm not sure your heart is in this anymore."

"Leland, I haven't told you, but Hazel left me a while back, and I've had a hard time coping."

I thought that might buy me some wiggle room.

"Just bear with me for a little while, if you can. I just need a little time. I'll do better. I promise." Actually, I had been kind of relieved Hazel left, but that clearly wasn't going to play.

"Well, I wish it were that simple," Leland said, "but it is worse than that. Some of the parents feel that the children are uncomfortable with you. One even used the word frightened. Surely you can see we can't have a clown representing Party Town who actually scares the children."

"I don't think I scare the children."

"I think you do, Donnie, and it can't be tolerated."

"Please, Leland, give me another chance."

I was in a panic. Without being Ozzie the Clown, I was nothing. It was about far more than just being able to earn enough to put food on the

175

table. It was about my very being. It was about my being able to carry on at all.

"Please, tell me what I need to do. I will do anything. Please, just give me another chance."

"Of course we'll give you another chance, Donnie. Do you think we would just cut you loose without trying everything possible to keep you as part of our Party Town family? I'm not without a heart."

"Thank you, Leland. I really mean that. What do you want me to do? Just tell me, and I'll do the very best that I can. Thank you. Oh God, thank you."

"Well, Donnie, there is even better news. We have been in contact with Hazel who, like us, wants to keep you as her family. We have made arrangements for what is called an intervention with a psychologist, Dr. Abrams. He will be awaiting your call to set up an appointment in which we can all participate in getting you back on track. I am confident that, if we all do our part, everything will work out fine. Donnie, I believe that the best is yet to come for you."

"I don't know what to say."

"You don't have to say anything. Let's just move forward."

Needless to say, I cringed at the thought of this intervention thing. But what choice did I have? I'm Ozzie the Clown, and if I'm not, I'm nothing. So what else could I do but cooperate, or at least pretend to?

So I phoned Dr. Abram's office to make the appointment. His secretary said he wanted to talk to me.

"Is this Donnie?" he asked.

"No. It's Ozzie. Ozzie the Clown."

"Okay, Ozzie, how do you feel about participating in the intervention? Has it been explained to you?"

"Kind of. But I'm not very comfortable with it."

"Would you like to meet with me privately first, so we can make sure you understand what to expect and we can establish some ground rules that might make you more comfortable with the process?"

"Yes. Would it be okay if I wear my clown clothes?

"Would that make you more comfortable?"

"Oh, yes, very much."

"Then sure, that would be fine. How about 9:30 a.m. next Monday? That would give us a full hour and a half. Will that work for you?"

"Yeah, I guess."

"And, Ozzie, don't worry about the cost. Your employer, Party Town, is paying for everything."

"Okay."

"Terrific, Ozzie. I am looking forward to meeting you."

"Thanks," I said. I wasn't looking forward to the appointment, but it certainly put me more at ease that he called me by my real name, Ozzie, and that I could wear my clown clothes, my real clothes.

I was on time for my appointment with Dr. Abrams. I had on my clown clothes and face. Dr. Abrams didn't seem to notice.

"Come in, Ozzie. Have a seat."

I sat down, but didn't say anything.

"Would you like me to explain what an intervention is?"

"Yes, please."

"It's where all the people who care about you meet with you and tell you how they see your behavior as self-destructive. They will also tell you how it has a negative impact on them. They will assure you of their caring, but insist that you make some changes. If they were to continue to go along with your destructive behavior, they would be what we call enablers. That is, their behavior would actually support the continuation of your self-destructive behavior. Be prepared to hear some hard things. I don't usually meet with a client before the actual intervention, but this is a very unusual situation."

"Can I come in my real face and clothes?" I ask.

"What do you mean---'real'---Ozzie?"

"These are my real face and clothes. I can be myself when I am wearing them."

"Sure you can. Then if you are willing, we will remove them one step at a time, so you have a chance to adjust gradually. Which is more important to you, your clown suit or clown face?"

177

"Well, both of course. But if I had to keep just one or the other, I would keep my clown face."

"Okay, let's do it this way. The first time we meet you can wear both your clown face and costume."

"These are my clothes. Please don't call them a costume."

"I beg your pardon, Ozzie, your clown clothes. We may have to do that a few times before we go any further. Then we will try it with just your clown face---excuse me, I mean your real face---but without your clown clothes. I know that will be hard, but I think if we take it slow enough you can do it. Finally, and only when you are ready, we will meet having you wear street clothes and no makeup. And, Ozzie, during all these stages those who care about you will be offering you reassurance. You will be happy to know that they have already agreed to call you Ozzie, not Donnie. Everybody ought to be called what he chooses."

I told him I would give it a try. It was more than I could take in all at once. I couldn't imagine that I could ever get to a point at which I could meet with a group of people in my street clothes and without makeup. That's just not Ozzie. It's just not who I am. But I needed my job at Party Town. I mean, really needed it. I also have to admit that I was touched---well, as close to touched as I can be---by the fact that Hazel and Leland were concerned enough to do all of this. Could it be that I was actually developing feelings for people? No, let's not get carried away. Let's just do what we have to do, and let it go at that.

Let me tell you that it was not easy, even in my real clown clothes and makeup, but I showed up. Everyone, even Hazel, called me Ozzie. Hazel told me that she didn't care if I was Ozzie, so long as I didn't shut her out. She didn't think it was too much to ask just to see what she called my real face once in a while. Although we didn't agree on which was my real face, I understood what she meant. I thought I could compromise a little bit, if she could. Leland told me that I was very much valued as an employee and more than that, as a member of the Party Town family. I hadn't thought of Party Town as a family, but when I think about it, it was more of a family than anything I had ever had except for Burpo and, to a lesser extent, Hazel. I thanked them and promised to try to change. After several weeks, I even agreed to come to the next session without my Ozzie clothes, as long as I could keep my real clown face. They praised me for my courage, and when they said goodbye, they all called me Ozzie. That was progress, don't you think?

For the next several weeks, I met with the group wearing my phony Donnie clothes, but with full makeup. At least they called me Ozzie. We discussed the problems that my obsession (that's what they called it) with being Ozzie the Clown posed for both them and me. Behind the protection of my Ozzie face I was able to be at least minimally responsive, although I have to admit I pretty much told them what I thought they wanted to hear.

Finally, after about a month, Dr. Abrams asked me if I would be willing to come to the next appointment without makeup. They all said they thought I was ready. I told them I needed more time, a lot more time.

"How do the rest of you feel about that?" Dr. Abrams asked.

"If Ozzie needs more time, I'm willing to give it to him," Hazel replied. Hearing her call me Ozzie was music to my ears.

"I'm willing to give him more time too," said Leland, "but I've got to find someone to fill in for him. I'll hold his job for him as long as I can, but I can't make any guarantees. I've got a business to run." That really scared me.

"Okay, okay, I'll do it," I said.

Hazel kissed me on the cheek and told me how proud she was. Leland shook my hand and told me he thought the Party Town job would be mine for a long, long time. Dr. Abrams told me that he knew that it wasn't easy, but at some point I just had to take a leap of faith. Leap of faith, my ass. I just wanted to keep my job at Party Town. I just wanted to be Ozzie the Clown.

I spent the whole week leading up to our next session holed up in Burpo's, I mean my, house. I never once took off my Ozzie suit or face, although I did have to touch up my makeup once in a while. A couple of times I thought about preparing for Dr. Abram's intervention group by practicing going outside and walking around in my street clothes and fake Donnie face, maybe buying a newspaper or a pack of gum or something. But that's all I did, think about it. I kept putting it off, until I finally decided to wait to do it on the day of the meeting. Why do it before? I was just jumping through the hoops required to keep my job. That's all. It didn't really change who I was. I was Ozzie the Clown, and nothing could change that. Nothing.

The day of the session, I was really scared. At first, I couldn't get out of bed. Then I couldn't stay still. I paced back and forth across Burpo's

Shrine, my legs pumping like pistons, my heart beating heavily in my chest. Finally, I took off my Ozzie clothes and put on a pair of slacks and a dress shirt.

The moment I dreaded most had arrived. I went into the bathroom to remove my makeup. I must have stood in front of the mirror for half an hour before I finally picked up a washcloth and started scrubbing my face. My Ozzie makeup would not come off. I scrubbed harder, but it remained unchanged. I looked through Burpo's things and found a bottle of cosmetic remover. I put some on a cloth and rubbed and scrubbed, but the makeup refused to come off. Then I leaned very close to the mirror and looked at my reflection. It was then I realized that there was no makeup, that this was really my face. Like I said, I don't know exactly when I became Ozzie the Clown. Maybe it happened over time, maybe in just a flash. But that's who I am, Ozzie the Clown. Nothing can change that. As Burpo would have said, "and that settles it."

The Not — So - Merry — Go — Round

Dennis Thompson

S*tan Snow couldn't breathe--there was some kind of film over his face.*

He clawed at it and felt it rip away like peeling flesh. Air rushed in and he gulped it greedily. Then someone pushed him in the chest. He fell backwards, kept falling, landed in something soft, wet. He smelled . . . fresh concrete? Some of the slop hit him in the face. He looked up and saw a looming figure. More mix hit him in the chest, in the shoulder, covered him. He started to scream.

"Daddy! Daddy! Daddy!"
Tiny fingers grasped at his arm and startled Stan from a deep sleep. Moonlight illuminated his bedroom and he could see a small form standing at the head of the bed—one of his twin daughters.
"What is it, babe?" he asked, looking around.
"I have to go to the bathroom," the child said urgently.
It was Kaitlyn, as usual. Stan shook the fog from his head.
"What time is it?" He reached over on the nightstand and peered at the florescent dials on his wristwatch—4 a.m. "Katie, for God's sake, when are you going to learn to go on your own?"
"I'm scared, Daddy," she replied.
"Scared of what? It's light as day outside."
"Monsters."
Monsters? The only monsters Stan knew were the monster headaches he got each time he had to escort one of his seven-year-olds to the outhouse at such a godforsaken hour.
"Fine," he said, "Let's go." He threw the sheets off as his wife Monica snored (or was it giggled) and snuggled deeper into her cocoon. He mashed his feet into his boots and clomped after his pint-sized daughter. Newly confident, she opened the back door of the cabin and strode out into the gloom ahead.
The full moon illuminated the well-worn path to the outdoor toilet. Frost glimmered on the flattened grass and Kaitlyn's bare feet left prints. Stan blew an icy breath as he urinated on a dead rose bush. The sky was clear. Stars competed with the moon. It was October 31, Halloween morning. Stan zipped his pants and shivered, "Hurry up."
"Gotta wipe," Kaitlyn replied, her voice muffled. She finished her business and sprinted past her father to the cabin. Once there, the diminutive blonde clambered up the wooden ladder to the warmth of the loft she

shared with her sister Ashleigh.

Stan felt the top of the wood stove. It was just barely warm. He opened the door and shoved in a pine round. The stove began to tick in time with the wall clock. Stan decided not to bother returning to bed; he and Monica had agreed to be up by five anyway for the trip to Spokane .

He walked into the small kitchen, lit a match, and started a burner on the propane stove. The aluminum coffeepot was nearly empty so he stepped out on the front porch to get some water from the rain barrel. He nearly tripped over a pumpkin one of the girls had carved the night before. Cursing under his breath, he righted the grinning Jack-o-lantern, then got eggs and bacon from the small propane refrigerator that sat on the concrete patio. He went back inside, placed the pot on the burner. Once the coffee perked and the bacon sizzled, Monica poked her nose through the low doorway that separated the small master bedroom from the main room of the cabin.

"Smells good," she yawned.

"Morning," Stan said. "Cinnamon and whipped cream on your latte?"

"Sounds great," she replied.

"Oops. Forgot. No cinnamon, no whipped cream. How about coffee— black?"

She walked over and hugged him from behind. "It's okay, goofball," she said. "You can take me to Starbucks later."

Stan handed her a cup and poured one for him. After the bacon was done, he fried a couple of eggs. Stan placed Monica's plate in front of her. They sat at the dining room table and watched the mountains lighten on the horizon.

"Gonna be a beautiful day," Monica said.

"Yep," Stan replied, "Cold and beautiful."

Monica rubbed her eyes and peered at the outdoor thermometer mounted on the sill. It read thirty-four degrees.

Stan shook his head in disbelief, "Summer evaporated."

"That'll happen when all you do is cut firewood, pick rock, and slave on the house."

She was right about that, Stan thought. It was hard work living in Goldpan County . The cabin went through eight cords of wood a winter, the surrounding alfalfa field he and his wife farmed had been aptly renamed the " Garden of Stone ," and the new home they were building a mile from the cabin occupied every spare moment. The house had to be finished soon—his girls were getting tired of no electricity or running water.

"Guess we'll have to try and have some fun in Spokane ," Monica said as she yawned. She smiled wanly, and took a sip of her coffee.

"Speaking of fun," Stan replied, "you wanna wake the girls?"

His wife looked at him in mock horror. "Girls," she intoned, "time to rise and shine."

Groans of dismay issued from the loft.

"Long trip ahead of us," Monica continued, "You don't get up, means less time at Riverfront Park and Northtown Mall . . . ."

"Nooo," the twins said, but this time feet hit the planks. Moments later, the disheveled blondes descended sleepily from their cozy room. Each girl had a blanket wrapped around her shoulders. They moved quickly in front of the crackling wood stove.

"Ready to go?" Stan asked.

They looked at him with sleep-blurred eyes, smiled vaguely and nodded.

"Costumes and stuff are in the bag at your feet," Monica said to her husband.

Stan finished his coffee, then set his mug down on the table and picked up the bag. "Better grab some breakfast, ladies. We're outta here in ten minutes."

Stan went outside and finished loading the van. Monica and the girls soon piled out of the cabin and climbed into their seats. Two cattle guards and fifteen minutes later they were at the bottom of Thor Mountain where dusty April Creek Road met the asphalt of Highway 20.

The first leg of their trip took them over Falling Rock Pass. Autumn colors were nearly gone and the snow line hovered precariously at five thousand feet.

"The trees look like Christmas cookies, Daddy," Kaitlyn said.

"They sure do, honey," Stan replied.

"I have to pee," Ashleigh said.

Stan sighed and pulled the van over at the rest area near the summit. "How come you girls can go to the bathroom by yourselves up here on the big scary mountain?" Stan asked when the twins clambered back aboard.

"Because it's totally light, duh," Ashleigh replied. She stomped snow off her tennis shoes and buckled up.

Kaitlyn climbed in behind her sister and shut the van door. "Yeah, and it's pretty," she chirped.

Stan smiled. Kaitlyn reminded him of a dachshund he used to have as a kid. Its favorite pastime had been to chase flies—duh-duh-duh, chase the fly. The dog had been a bubble-head, but Stan had loved it dearly.

Next stop, thirty miles away, was the small town of Salmon Falls. Stan gassed the van up at the Chevron mini-mart and bought a few snacks for the road. He passed the treats around and then pulled back into traffic. The rough country ended and civilization began.

The family gawked at the unfamiliar bustle. The number of people and cars gradually increased for the next hundred miles. The towns got bigger —Couchville, Tulip, Bear Park —with the promise of Spokane 's urban sprawl lurking on the horizon. Excitement built in the van.

"Can we eat at McDonald's?" the twins asked in unison. "Can we? Can we?"

"We'll see," Stan replied, shooting a mortified glance at Monica. "We have a lot of shopping to do first. It'll mean less time at Riverfront Park ."

"I don't care," Kaitlyn said, sticking out her lower lip. "I want a chicken nuggets kid's meal."

"You know what they put in those?" Stan asked.

Monica put a hand on his arm.

"What?" Ashleigh asked, always on the lookout for weighty information.

"Nevermind," Stan sighed. Monica batted her eyes.

Stan met the first traffic light on the northern edge of Spokane 's commercially-clogged Division Street . He had to focus now. Not a single stop light in the entire county back home and taking turns took some getting used to.

Suddenly Ashleigh yelped as if she'd been bee-stung. Stan jammed on the brakes. The driver behind him honked angrily.

"What the hell?" Stan exclaimed.

"Carnival!" Ashleigh yelled. She pointed to the flashing lights of a seedy production in the K-Mart parking lot.

Stan growled and sped up.

"That's odd," Monica said, "a little late in the season."

"Yeah. And nothing to make noise over," Stan said. He looked in the rear-view mirror, "Next girl who screams is gonna get something to scream about."

"You take us, Daddy?" Ashleigh pleaded.

"No more asking for anything, got it? This traffic is making me crazy."

Stan soon spotted the large red and white Costco sign. He pulled into the massive lot and found a parking space. The family bailed out and stretched their stiff muscles. While Stan locked up, Monica and the twins found some shopping carts.

Two hours and a thousand dollars later the family returned to the van. Stan and Monica loaded a three-month's supply of bulk food into the rear compartment. The twins excitedly unboxed the portable DVD player their parents had splurged on for the return trip.

"She's sittin' a little low," Monica remarked as she wedged one last case of canned vegetables between a fifty-pound bag of cat food and the van's ceiling.

Stan dropped to one knee and peered under the wheel well, "Clear by two inches. We'll be fine."

The chant started low, then gained volume, "McDonald's. McDonald's. MCDONALD'S!" The girls pounded the backs of their seats.

"Okay," Stan said. "Calm yourselves or no movie on the way home." A few minutes later, they pushed through the doors of McDonald's. It wasn't quite lunchtime, but the restaurant was already crowded with families. Some of the children sported Halloween costumes.

"Can we put our costumes on too, Daddy?" Kaitlyn asked.

"Sure, honey," he said. "After we eat."
"Now."

Stan sighed and looked up at the wall menu. "Number six," he said to Monica. "Be right back."

He stepped out of the over-heated foyer and into the late morning air. A massive 747 rumbled overhead on the last leg of its descent into Spokane International Airport a few miles away. Stan tilted his head to watch it. A man and his young son noticed and followed his gaze. They frowned as if to say, "What's the big deal?"

Chagrined, Stan moved to the van, retrieved the costume bag, and returned to the restaurant. He spotted Monica struggling with a large tray of food and moved to help her. She retrieved straws and napkins while he fumbled with the paper thimbles of ketchup. They sat at a table and watched the twins run around the indoor playground with a screaming mob of over-stimulated ghouls.

"Riverfront Park next?" Monica inquired.

"Mmm-hmmn," Stan replied around a mouthful of burger. He took a sip of soda and mentally reviewed the itinerary: find a parking place at the Flour Mill Mini-Mall, walk across the swinging bridge to the Imax Theater and watch the newest movie, play a round of miniature golf, feed the ducks, ride the carousel. Afterward, take the twins trick-or-treating at Northtown Mall and then get the heck out of Dodge.

Kaitlyn pounded on the playroom glass, mouthed something. Stan shrugged. Kaitlyn opened the playroom door and walked over to the table, Ashleigh behind her.

"Come to the bathroom with me," she said. "So I can put on my costume."

"Huh?" Stan replied. "We're right here. You'll be fine."

"I don't care, I'm scared."

"Of what?"

The blonde waif thought for a moment, then mumbled shyly, "Kidnappers."

Stan shook his head. He'd been taking the girls to the outhouse for too many years. He grabbed his food, rolled his eyes at Monica. She tilted her head and smiled as if to say, "Better you than me!"

Stan watched Ashleigh pick up the costume bag. She was the brains of the outfit, made Kaitlyn ask the dumb questions that brought the heat. She was just as much a chicken-heart— just wasn't her style to broadcast it.

Stan slid into one of the molded plastic booths next to the ladies room and waited. Ten minutes later, out walked the bride and groom of the dead. He and Monica had tried to steer the twins in a less gruesome direction, but they had seen *Beetlejuice* for the first time the week before and would consider no alternative. Stan feigned shock and then guided the twins back to their kid's meals.

After another ten minutes of food and talk, the family left. It was exactly noon. A dozen traffic lights later, Stan pulled the minivan into the parking lot of the Flour Mill.

"Put on your jackets, girls," he said.

"Not over our costumes," the girls' whined.

"You'll thank me later," Stan said. "It's gonna get a lot cooler this afternoon."

188

The family crossed the swinging bridge that spanned the Spokane River and then followed the path that paralleled Riverfront Park's outdoor amphitheater. They crossed a second bridge that led to the rear of the Imax complex and the local YMCA.

"Look, Daddy, an ambulance," Ashleigh said.

"I see it," Stan replied.

A small crowd had gathered. Two ambulance attendants wheeled a gurney down a handicap ramp at the back of the theater. A blanket shrouded the small body on the gurney. Stan and Monica hustled the girls by.

Suddenly, the medical technician guiding the rear of the gurney stumbled and lost his grip. His partner over-corrected and a back wheel slipped over the edge of the ramp. The heavy cart careened sideways against the guardrail, hit an upright, and tipped. The corpse slid from under the single strap that held it, bounced twice, then rolled the remainder of the way down the ramp. It stopped at Ashleigh's feet.

It was a little Down's syndrome boy. His eyes were open, his mouth twisted abnormally. His face had suffered an odd paroxysm in death and somehow frozen itself in a macabre mask of fear.
From the doorway of the theater came a low moan. An elderly woman, presumably the child's mother, was just waking up to her second shock of the day. The ambulance attendants scrambled to remedy their mistake. Ashleigh gasped and Stan swept her into his arms. He glanced once more at the dead boy's features, puzzled over what sort of malady could cause such a distortion.

A few minutes later, Stan and Monica sat on a park bench and held their girls. Kaitlyn sobbed quietly. Stan pulled out his handkerchief and handed it to Monica. She took it and dabbed at Kaitlyn's sodden cheeks. Ashleigh had not shed a tear.

"What was wrong with that boy, Daddy?" she asked.

"What do you mean, honey?"

"With his face."

"He had Down's, Ash."

"I know that, Daddy," she said. "Just like baby brother, when he died," she clamped her hands over her mouth, "Oh."

Stan's forehead wrinkled into a frown for an instant, then relaxed. He glanced at Monica. She squeezed her eyes shut. Stan smoothed his daughter's hair. "It's okay, honey. You didn't mean to talk about brother. Go ahead."

"What I mean is," she continued hesitantly, "why did he *look* like that? His face was really scary."

"I'm not sure, babe," Stan replied. He glanced at Monica again. She shook her head. "Let's try and forget about it, shall we?"

Just then, a group of young boys swaggered past. One of them wore the black and white mask from the movie *Scream*. He jumped at the girls and made a hissing sound. The twins yelped and this time Ashleigh burst into tears.

"Get the hell out of here," Stan snarled, waving a hand at the boy.

"Fuck you, old man," the boy said, his voice muffled by the frozen-grinned mask. He gave Stan the finger.

In one quick movement, Stan slid Ashleigh from his lap and was up off the bench. The boys scattered like a flock of crows, laughing and waving middle fingers in the air.

"Forget it," Monica said. She stood up, Kaitlyn still in her arms.

"Little jerks," Stan replied.

"Don't make things worse."

Ashleigh tugged on Stan's sleeve, "Daddy—can we go ride the carousel?" She sniffled and dried her tears with the back of her hand.

"The carousel?" Stan looked across the river at the lights of the park's signature ride. Cheerful calliope music tinkled through the crisp air. "You bet," he replied. "That's exactly what the doctor ordered."

The next three hours passed smoothly. After watching the girls take a half-dozen rides on the gaily-painted horses, Stan walked across the street from the park to a small novelty store; Ashleigh needed a fresh tube of fake blood and Kaitlyn had misplaced her vampire teeth. Monica took the twins to a cotton candy vendor. When Stan returned, he also had tickets to the sky tram and two sacks of breadcrumbs to feed the ducks.

After a picturesque ride over the park, Stan and Monica sat on the grass and watched the girls scatter morsels to the various waterfowl in an eddy of the river. A trio of young men played Frisbee on the park's expansive central lawn, and a group of Japanese tourists chattered by, their camera's clicking furiously.

Kaitlyn and Ashleigh soon tired of the ducks and enthusiastically agreed to try their hand at a round of mini-golf. Afterward, they conned Stan out of ten dollars worth of quarters and played video games for an hour in the arcade.

Before long, the twins were hungry again. Their favorite sit-down restaurant was an Italian place in the bowels of the Flour Mill. Rather than return the way they had come, Stan hailed a taxi. The trip took less than five minutes. When the driver pulled in front of the Flour Mill, Stan thanked him, gave him a small tip, and followed his family inside.

An hour later, they exited, their stomachs round from pasta and Italian sodas. They piled into the van.

"A bit early for Northtown, isn't it?" Monica asked as she pulled on her seat belt.

Stan glanced at his watch: "Not quite five yet. The trick-or-treating doesn't start till six. Why don't we drive down Division a ways and see what catches our fancy?"

"What about the carnival, Daddy?" Kaitlyn inquired. "Remember the carnival?" Her cheeks were smeared with a combination of face paint, cotton candy, and spaghetti sauce.

"How could I forget?" he replied sarcastically. "But it's getting a little cold, isn't it?"

"We got our jackets," the twins reminded him.

"What do you think, Mother?" Stan asked.

"I think it's a little strange--a carnival this late in the year," Monica replied, "but it's fine with me."

Fifteen minutes later, Stan turned into the K-Mart parking lot. The sun had dipped below the horizon and the multi-colored carnival lights blinked against the dark backdrop of distant hills. There weren't many people, but the rides churned away.

"I wanna go on the Hammerhead," Kaitlyn said.

"I wanna go on the Octopus," Ashleigh argued.

"Better choose," Stan said. "We only have time for two or three. I'll get some tickets." He walked over to the booth where a wizened old woman with severe scoliosis peered from behind grimy Plexiglas. At first Stan thought she was wearing a mask. But then she grinned, revealing toothless gums.

She peered at him with glittering eyes as she took his money. She handed him a string of tickets and pulled four pieces of bubble gum out of a plastic skull. "Happy Halloween," she croaked.

Stan thanked her quickly and returned to his family. He gave each of the twins a few tickets and a piece of gum. They scampered ahead. "Creepy old bag," he muttered to Monica as they started down the midway. He unwrapped his gum and popped it in his mouth.

"Look around," she said.

Stan appraised his surroundings. Nothing seemed out of the ordinary. Barkers touted their games, young men worked hard to impress their girlfriends, families waited in line at the food trailers and ride queues. But then Stan saw it--the carnival employees. Most were deformed, uncommonly ugly.

And the deformities somehow seemed appropriate for each post. A grotesquely obese woman with a neck hugely swollen from goiter manned the Octopus. A bearded dwarf who was as wide as he was tall coaxed passersby into the House of Mirrors. The man operating the Hammerhead was over seven feet tall and had a bald, egg-shaped cranium.

"I think we should go," Monica said, spitting her gum into a nearby waste-barrel. "I have a bad feeling about this place." She glanced over at the Goldfish Toss where the twins were handing tickets to a hairless albino with abnormally large lips.

"What," Stan replied, "Freaks aren't people, too?"

"You know what I mean," she said., "and what's with the goofy names on the rides?"

Stan looked at the crude signs wired to each platform—full sheets of sun-warped plywood with red block letters a foot high: "TALL ED'S BOLD-O-RIDE" for the Hammerhead, "MOTHER SOYRUB'S RIDE" for the Octopus, "AUNT SASS-R-LOT'S RIDE" for the Tilt-o-Whirl.

"Dunno," Stan replied. He held up his hands and made ghost parentheses, "Guess they take a lot of 'PRIDE IN THE RIDE.'"

Monica tittered nervously and grabbed her husband's hand.

Suddenly Ashleigh squealed in delight. She bounced up and down as the albino handed her a water-filled Zip-lock baggie. She came running over.

"I did it, Daddy! I won a goldfish!" She held up her prize.

"Great," Stan replied. "Hope this guy makes it longer than Gill did."

Kaitlyn walked over. She didn't seem too happy her twin had won a goldfish and she hadn't. "I wanna go on a ride," she pouted.

"The Hammerhead, then?" Stan said.

Kaitlyn looked over at the giant running the controls. She shook her head. "Something easier first."

"How about the Tilt-A-Whirl?" Monica suggested. She nodded at the massive spinning disc. The operator, a severely-hunched octogenarian cackled toothlessly as she manipulated the joystick and elicited screams from a half-dozen riders.

"Waittaminnit," Stan said, "Isn't that the hag from the . . . ." His voice trailed off as he looked behind them. The dimly-lit ticket booth was vacant.

"I want the carousel," Kaitlyn said, and pointed.

"Another carousel, Katie? You sure?" her mother asked.

Everyone turned to see the ride Kaitlyn referred to. It was offset from the harsh glow of the midway.

"Cool," Ashleigh said. "It looks like a UFO!"

Stan smiled, but she was right. The swirling lights seemed otherworldly. And they illuminated the man running the ride--if he could be called a man. Even from fifty feet away it was easy to tell something was off about him. He gripped the handle of a large wooden cane and stood beside the same style of crudely-lettered sign that accompanied the rest of the rides. This one declared "THING'S ICKUTY-POO RIDE."

Stan and Monica looked at each other and shrugged.

"I assume he must be 'Thing,'" Monica whispered.

"Yeah, and what's 'ickuty-poo', carny for 'grotesque'?" Stan replied.

As they approached, Stan tried to figure out who or *what* the man reminded him of.

"Ooh," Kaitlyn said. "He's dressed like the Grinch."

That was it, Stan thought—the Grinch Who Stole Christmas. Only this wasn't the right holiday and the man wasn't Jim Carrey under latex. The attendant's sallow green face had wrinkles as deep as the bellows of an accordion and his legs were abnormally long compared to his sunken torso. He wore a soiled black t-shirt that read "Old Scratch Daniels." It featured a bottle of liquor whose red-sequined contents gleamed hypnotically in the revolving lights.

There was a small line. A little boy in front of Kaitlyn jumped up and down screaming, "Merry-go-round! Merry-go-round! Merry-go-round!"

"Quiet!" his mother said, popping her gum noisily between drags of a cigarette.

Thing smiled thinly.

Kaitlyn tugged at Stan's elbow: "What's the difference between a merry-go-round and a carousel, Daddy?"

Stan tore his gaze away from the misshapen carny and looked down at daughter.

"I don't know, Katie. Why?"

"Because I think this is the *not*-so-merry-go-round," she whispered. Stan looked at the scarred wooden animals as they whirled by. She was right. These weren't the jolly horses of Riverfront Park. Instead, they were nightmarish creatures of lore, gargoyles and bats and werewolves and trolls, truly realistic. So real, Stan felt sure he saw a massive red dragon cock his head and glance his way.

Thing pulled on a lever and the merry-go-round slowed to a stop. The children getting off seemed dazed. The freakish attendant hustled them along and began ushering in new riders.

"Nice evening for a whirl, isn't it?" Thing's tongue, slightly forked at the end, jerked involuntarily from between thin olive lips. Kaitlyn and Ashleigh stared at him open-mouthed.

"That's a great costume, Mister," Kaitlyn said.

Thing's lidless eyes widened momentarily. "And yours, Little Missy." His snake-like lisp only added to his reptilian appearance.

The twins each handed the carny a ticket. He opened the gate. Ashleigh handed her fish to her mother. Monica placed the Zip-lock gingerly in her purse.

194

"No ride for you tonight then, Missus?" Thing said to Monica, openly leering at her breasts.

"No thanks," Monica replied, pulling her jacket tighter.

"Ah, but this one's on the house," he said, his eyes bulbous and mesmeric.

Monica looked over to where the girls clambered indecisively from one hideous creature to the next.

"C'mon, Momma," Ashleigh yelled.

Stan glanced at his watch, then pushed Monica gently in the small of her back, "Let's do this, babe. We're about out of time, anyway."

The creepy attendant nodded and smiled. "That you are, sir. That you are." He shuffled backward and let the pair by.

Stan helped Monica up on the platform and they joined the girls. They sat together in a sled that doubled as the belly of the giant red dragon. Kaitlyn perched precariously on the back of a winged gargoyle and Ashleigh sat low on a squatty demon-troll.

"Cinch your belts, girls," Monica said. She grabbed Stan's hand and squeezed tightly.

"It's just a merry-go-round, hon," Stan said.

"Yeah, and suddenly I ain't feelin' so goddamn merry, okay?" She let go of Stan's hand and grabbed hold of the bar in front of her.

Stan shot her a puzzled look, but didn't say anything. The calliope music started slowly then matched the speed of the ride as it creaked into motion. The girls screamed and clutched their poles in mock terror as their charges rose and fell on well-oiled gears. Stan peered out into the gloom.

Darkness had fallen and the main pool of carnival lights flashed by intermittently. It was only an optical illusion, but the lights seemed to recede in the distance as the ride gained momentum. The music grew louder. Stan looked up at his girls and over at his wife—their faces skewed as they laughed wildly. Only they weren't laughing. They were screaming. And Stan was screaming too.

Because the dragon he and Monica sat in suddenly unfolded its leathery wings. It reared its head and blew a stream of flame that scorched the ceiling of the merry-go-round. The oil in the gears at the top of the poles ignited. In seconds, a conflagration roiled around the interior of the ride

195

from pole to pole like some kind of stygian maelstrom. The hair of scattered riders burst into flame.

Stan reached for his daughters, but a hand on his shoulder held him back. It was Thing--his head tilted back, his mouth open. Where teeth should have been were two rows of emerald bone connected by a string of saliva that wavered in the unnatural breeze of the careening ride.

For it was a ride no longer. It was a trip into hell. All the creatures morphed from wood to flesh. They ripped the poles from their backs and crawled about the deck. The children on their backs thrashed wildly as they burned.

The beasts unleashed a cacophony of discordant wails. Some began to fly. The gargoyle that Kaitlyn was astride rose into the air. Kaitlyn reached for Stan, her hair aflame. Skin peeled off in layers, revealing her skull. Stan watched helplessly as her eyeballs melted like candle wax down her cheeks.

Suddenly, the gargoyle burst through the roof of the merry-go-round, trailing a shower of sparks. The demon-troll Ashleigh rode ripped his hands and feet from the wooden deck and disappeared into the melee.

Stan shot a horrified glance at Monica. Cinders from the scattered remnants of Kaitlyn's face settled into his wife's hair. Pockets of fire quickly spread in the preternatural wind. Stan frantically tried to smother the flames but Monica's blonde locks disintegrated into ash in his palms. He closed his eyes and screamed his throat raw.

And then Monica had hold of his wrists.

"Stan!" she shouted, "Stan! Stan! Stan!"

Stan opened his eyes. Monica desperately fought to keep his hands from her face. Kaitlyn and Ashleigh watched the scene with horrified expressions.

Stan looked frantically around. Everything was back to normal. The ride slowed and came to a stop. "But . . . but, I saw—I thought . . . ," he stammered.

Monica pressed her fingers to his lips: "It's okay. We saw it too. I think it's all part of the 'ride.'" She motioned to the girls and helped her stunned husband out of his seat and off the edge of the merry-go-round.

"I think we were dosed," Monica said. She reached in her jacket pocket and pulled out the gum wrapper.

Stan grabbed it, glanced at it angrily, then tossed it down and ground it into the dirt. He looked furiously to the gate where Thing had been. "That wicked ..."

"Don't worry about it, Stan." Monica took him by the elbow. "Whatever they intended to do, they've already done it."

"We gotta call the cops," Stan argued.

"And tell them what, exactly?" Monica motioned around.

Stan realized they were standing in the center of the midway. It was deserted. The rides were silent, the booths vacant. The strings of rainbow lights continued to wink, like they harbored some terrible secret. A bulb buzzed, flickered, and went out. The twins looked up at him. They had rubbed most of the Halloween makeup off their tear-stained cheeks.

"I don't feel like trick-or-treating anymore, Daddy," Ashleigh said.

"Neither do I, baby," he replied. "Neither do I." He grabbed her hand. "Let's go home."

The van was almost to the end of North Division before anyone felt like talking. The twins hadn't even bothered to ask if they could watch a DVD on their new player.

"I think those signs were anagrams," Monica said, breaking the silence.

"What?" Stan replied. He had a headache. At the moment, the traffic signals he hated so much were only that much more disturbing.

"Those stupid signs on the rides." Monica said. "I think they were anagrams."

"What's an 'anagram,' Mommy?" Kaitlyn asked, yawning sleepily from her prone position in the middle seat. Ashleigh had already fallen asleep on a pillow in the rear, the day's events too much for her.

"You still awake, baby?" Monica murmured. She looked over her shoulder, "Anagrams are words whose meanings change when the letters are switched around."

Kaitlyn thought for a moment: "You mean like . . . 'dog' and 'god'?" she replied. "I think we learned that in school."

"Exactly, Kaitlyn. Just like that." Monica opened the center console and took out a small spiral notebook and pen. She jotted down some letters. "Like that 'AUNT SASS-R-LOT'S RIDE,'" she said to Stan: "That could've stood for 'ASSAULTS ON RIDERS.'"

Stan scratched his head with his left hand and his eyes lost focus for a moment. "Nope. Don't think so. You forgot a 'T'."

Monica checked her work. "Okay, smarty-pants. You give it a try."

"I will," Stan replied. He pressed his thumb and forefinger on the bridge of his nose and squinted. He drummed his fingers on the steering wheel and whistled tunelessly for a few seconds. "Got it!" he exclaimed.

"What?" Monica replied.

"SERIOUS TAN LARD ASS."

Monica chortled mirthlessly. She scribbled some more letters on the note pad. Then she shook her head: "Huh-uh. Sorry 'Word Doctor'--you not only forgot a 'T,' you *added* an 'A'."

Stan and Monica laughed together. It eased some of the tension. There was a sound of rustling behind them.

"Can I give it a try, Mommy?" Kaitlyn asked.

Monica sighed: "Sure, baby. Here you go." She handed Kaitlyn the spiral, then leaned her head back on the seat and closed her eyes.

It was a long drive back to the cabin. Stan turned the radio to a soft rock station. Gentle snores soon filled the van.

Stan stopped at the Chevron on the way through Salmon Falls and got a cup of coffee, but by the time he turned up April Creek Road, he was so tired he was seeing things. At one point he was sure he spotted a swooping gargoyle. "Big owl," he thought. "Just a big owl."

He pulled into the cabin's driveway and turned off the van's overheated engine. He left the lights on so his family could make their way to the door without tripping over any pumpkins. He shook Monica gently on the shoulder, "We're home, babe."

"Huh? What?" Monica said, sitting up. She looked wildly around, but quickly realized where they were. She began to fumble a few things together.

"Forget the stuff," Stan said. "You head in and I'll get the girls."

Monica nodded sleepily and stumbled toward the cabin. In moments, she was inside and had a propane lantern going.

Stan went around to the side door of the van. He opened it and reached in to unbuckle Kaitlyn's seatbelt. As he moved to lift her, something fell to the floor. The spiral. Stan picked it up. He scanned it in the weak glow of the dome light. Kaitlyn had been playing with the anagrams. She had at least thirty different combinations, all scattered about in her childish scrawl. But in the lower left corner, in big block letters, a random grouping of four caught his eye:

BLOOD'S ALL-RED TIDE

SMOTHERS YOUR BRIDE

SATAN'S SOUL STRIDER

PICKS YOUR NIGHT TO DIE

Stan dropped the notebook like it was hot. *What the heck?* He glanced at Kaitlyn's pale face, then back at the spiral. The sentence fragments fit the names of the rides, perfectly. A chill went down his spine. He shook his head. He quickly picked up his daughter, and carried her into the cabin.

He immediately returned for Ashleigh. The full moon illuminated the surrounding alfalfa. Dark shapes moved at incredible speeds across the lower field. *Deer*, Stan thought. But he gathered his precious cargo with a surge of adrenaline and wasted no time getting back inside.

It was a little past midnight when Stan felt the motion at his shoulder. He was deep into a particularly disturbing nightmare and the pressure on his shoulder didn't help any.

He sat up as if he had been poked by a cattle prod. "What? What is it?" He grabbed for the .22 caliber pistol he had placed on his dresser before going to bed.

It was Kaitlyn again. She held a flashlight. "I have to go to the bathroom, Daddy," she said. Monica groaned in her sleep.

"Okay, okay," Stan said, swinging his legs over the edge of the bed. "No problem." He stood up and realized he had fallen asleep in his boots and jeans. He reached over and jammed the .22 automatic in his back pocket —with the dream he had just been having, he wasn't taking any chances.

Kaitlyn waited by the door. This time she didn't go out first. "What's wrong, Katie Jo?" he asked.

"Noises, Daddy," she replied. "I've been hearing scratching noises on the roof above the loft."

"I'm sure it's just birds, babe," he said. But then he smiled conspiratorially, "I'll tell you what, though, if it's anything else, I'll blast it, okay?" He pulled the pistol out of his pocket, held it chest high with both hands, and looked at his daughter, "Ready?"

Kaitlyn nodded.

They stepped out into the moonlight. Stan glanced around. He gave the thumbs up and gestured for Kaitlyn to follow. He smiled as she grabbed an empty belt-loop on the back of his jeans. They moved toward the outhouse.

Suddenly Stan screamed as he felt the completely unnatural touch of Kaitlyn's bare feet dragging up his back and across his shoulders. He watched the winged gargoyle from the merry-go-round bite his daughter's head off and fling her torso into the moon-drenched alfalfa. Stan's fingers went numb and he dropped the .22 in the grass at his feet.

He fell to his knees. He continued to scream. He tore helplessly at his unbelieving eyes. His screams were matched by those coming from the cabin. The squatty demon-troll was on the roof, clawing through the cedar shakes and spinning them like Frisbees into the night. In seconds, the monster disappeared inside the loft.

Remnants of Stan's protective instinct kicked in and he snatched the pistol off the grass. He flicked the safety on and scrambled to his feet. Just then, the outhouse exploded in a geyser of flame. The force of the explosion hurled Stan against the side of the cabin and partially through a window. He slumped to the ground, rolled onto his back. Dazed and bleeding, he looked into the sky.

Somehow he had managed to hold on to the .22. He pointed the gun at a sight his eyes refused to believe. It was Thing, astride the neck of the giant dragon. The green and red apparitions glowed translucently from some hellish inner fire. The demonic carny was naked. In one hand he held a scythe. In the other, he held the flaming bottle of liquor that had once decorated his shirt. He tipped it to his lips.

Stan's face contorted, his mouth open; he tried to scream but couldn't. There were no screams from the cabin anymore either. Stan emptied the clip from the .22 into the emerald demon's concave chest. He watched as the bullets melted on contact.

Thing laughed maniacally, a thunderous bass that resonated into the night. He pointed the scythe, and the dragon emitted a concentrated stream of flame. It dissolved Stan's pistol and half his arm. Stan stared in disbelief at the smoking stump.

Thing slid from the neck of the dragon. In a flash, he was next to Stan's ear. "Who's 'grotesque' now?" he whispered. His breath smelled like hot blood and charred flesh. He straightened up. "You know who I am, don't you?"

Stan nodded, his teeth chattering uncontrollably. He couldn't talk, but he could think. Old Scratch; Mr. Bojangles; Moloch, The Archfiend.

"I was with you when you used the plastic bag on your baby," Thing said. "And I was with you when you dumped his body into the foundation of your new house." He leaned closer, "I've been part of your name the whole time, Stan . . . just add an 'a'." He raised the scythe.

Stan moved his good hand in front of his face. "No! Don't!" he screamed, finding his voice. "I'm sorry! I'm so sorry!"

"Sorry?" Thing threw his head to the sky, steam roiling from his mouth as laughter echoed across the burning alfalfa fields. "I know you're sorry, Stan. Sorry you're so selfish. Sorry you wanted the perfect family. Sorry your freak baby didn't fit the picture."

"Yes," Stan choked. He lowered his arm and started to sob.

"Ah. Poor Stan," Thing said sarcastically, "The picture of contrition." He took another swig from his steaming bottle of liquor. "What was it you told your girls—'The baby was dead when he came out of Momma' and 'Don't talk about it, 'cuz it makes the angels sad'?" He wiped his mouth with the back of a filth-encrusted hand. "But the girls saw you, Stan. They saw what you did that night."

Thing reached down and pried Stan's mouth open. He poured the molten liquid from the bottle down Stan's throat. Stan gagged and sputtered, tried to scream.

But he saw instead, saw the blood, saw the year-old events unfold like a nightmare.

The baby came prematurely and they were over an hour from the nearest hospital. Stan was in the cabin's master bedroom, bending over Monica as she struggled to complete the birth. In the final moments, she passed out from pain and exhaustion. Stan recoiled in horror and disgust at the writhing baby's abnormal features. He glanced at Monica's motionless form, then took a plastic bag off the floor and wrapped it around the baby's head. When the baby flailed a tiny fist and grabbed Stan's finger, he watched his horrified reaction. He held the bag tight until the baby kicked no longer, then pulled the small tarp from under Monica's hips and wrapped the newborn in it. The twin's watched from the rain-streaked window of the loft as he got on the three-wheeler with his tiny bundle and vanished into the storm. He rode to the new home site, mixed a wheelbarrow load of concrete and sand, and placed the baby between a row of plywood forms. He saw himself throw shovelful after shovelful of fresh concrete into the form and then watched himself fall to his knees and scream into the curtains of rain. He watched it all.

When the hallucination ended, Thing raise the scythe one last time.

The final image Stan Snow's fractured mind allowed was the flash of a razor-sharp blade, stained black by an eternity of souls.

Somewhere . . . in the distance . . . he swore he heard calliope music.

My Own Making

Cynthia Witherspoon

This wasn't lying to lie. Like the time I told my granny that I loved her when I hated every second spent beneath her beady eyes and the threats of repeated swats from her broom handle. Or, the time I told my brother Joey that he was adopted, and spent the afternoon laughing as he ran around the house frantically searching for any evidence of his lineage. He died when he was seven from some kind of children's hospital disease, still trying to find the real parents that were right under his nose. No, this was much more serious. I was in trouble, and I had to find my way out of it.

The white lights of the room made the dingy walls gleam under the layers of dirt and dust that painted them. I squirmed in a chair that refused to mold to my form and wished that they would hurry it up so that I could go home. As if they had heard my thoughts, the man who had led me to the room now entered with a sickly smile on his face. His eyes seemed to search my every move for a hint of deceit. I shuddered beneath his gaze and prayed that he wasn't as good at discovering the truth as I was at distorting it. The slap of his folder against the table ransacked that belief. I stared at his hands before looking to him.

"Miss Samson, my name is Detective Jesse Bowman. You said that you needed to talk to someone." His eyes were trying to search my own once more. I nodded to stop him from seeing something there that I didn't want him to find. And, the knot in my throat was growing larger as I waited.

"Can you tell me what happened the morning of July 3rd? I know the story that your father told us, but I'd like to hear your side of it. Is that what you wanted to talk with us about?" His pudgy fingers flipped through pages that I couldn't see.

"I was at home, sir. I didn't have school since we're out for the summer, so Momma let me sleep in."

"When did you wake up?" Those fingers stopped and skimmed downwards for a moment.

"About eight-thirty, I guess, when I heard the loud bang in the kitchen."

"The kitchen, was it? My notes here say that when you were questioned before, you told Officer Andrews the noise came from the living room."

I frowned, shaking my head as he allowed the silence to balloon throughout the room. "No, sir, it was in the kitchen. I must have been upset when I said the living room. I ..."

My face was a perfect fit against my hands. I willed the tears to form and for my body to shake. All the years of drama camp I had been forced to go to were crucial at this moment. Think of something really sad, like the time you found a dead cat, or when somebody hit you really hard. I felt like somebody had hit me really hard. Just being in the South Kingston Police Station did that. But, I had to keep it together. I had to make them believe me.

"Are you alright?" His words were filled with kindness and the pudgy hand patted my elbow where it was pulled against my waist. I began to breathe as if to control myself. I rubbed my eyes furiously to make them seem red from tears I couldn't muster; to buy time; to find the right tone to make my confession.

"I ... oh, sir ... I can't tell you what I know. He'll kill me!" My voice cracked at just the right moment and had I been on stage, I would have smiled. Not too bad for a fifteen-year-old. Maybe I really could be the actress Momma always wanted me to be.

"There, there. No one will hurt you. I'd just as soon see one of my own two girls hurt than you. Are you afraid of your father?"

I nodded and looked away from him. "I ... I had to lie before.

I couldn't tell the truth with him standing right there.

My voice worked its magic once again. It cracked when I turned towards him."It's so hard to keep it in. Keep the truth in when I know ... "Cue nervous swallowing. Cue flicking at invisible dust from the table.

The man before me smiled again, slick and sweet. I wondered if he was getting the show that he wanted.

"No one is going to hurt you now, Miss. Samson. Your father is locked up in jail and will be for a long time for what he did. You can tell me the truth. I need you to if you want us to find out what happened to your mother."

I let out the breath I'd been holding through cracked lips before nodding. I spilled out the story in low tones that had taken me a week's worth of nights to construct. I told him what he wanted to hear while my eyes examined the fake wood grain of the table. And, the scene fell right into place.

"I heard the two of them arguing over something. That wasn't new, you know. Daddy picked fights with Momma whenever he could. I heard a crash in the kitchen, and snuck downstairs to see if she was ok. He had a habit of doing things, bad things, to her when they fought."

Detective What's-His-Name was too busy recording my words in neat little lines across his yellow notepad to pay attention to the gleam in my eyes and the smoothness of my delivery. For that, I was thankful. The man stopped only when I did, looking up as I turned my eyes away.

"Did he hurt her often?"

I shrugged. "Often enough, but never where she couldn't hide it. You know, she always wanted me to be an actress. She wanted to be one, too. Always laughing and smiling with family members, but ..."

My voice caught again. I swallowed hard at the pretense of my fear. "But I would come home from school to find her crying in the bathroom. He'd been home and had hit her. I tried to tell her to leave him, but she was too scared, said that it wouldn't do any good; that he'd just find us again and do worse."

The scratching of his pen against the page rattled my nerves. I gritted my teeth before continuing with my story. "That morning, he was doing it again. I could hear her crying, and Daddy yelling about something. Then I heard the bang, like a misplaced firecracker. I ran downstairs and ... and ... she was gone."

My fingers found the pattern in the wood and traced figure eights across the smooth surface. "He saw me, and my heart just stopped. Daddy had that gun in his hand and pointed it at me. Told me ... told me ..."

I groaned and started to shake against the chill that the plastic chair provided. That horrible scratching stopped as he let me get my wits back together.

"What did he say, Miss. Samson?" gentle, prodding, patient. My best damned confidante in a rumpled suit and scratchy pen.

"He said he would kill me too if I didn't help him." The words came out in a fearful whisper as I clutched my fingers together. I played with them under the table, watching as they twisted. Then I turned them upwards and outwards in a game I used to play by myself. Here is the church, here is the steeple; open it up, and see all the people! The rhyme wouldn't go away no matter how hard I tried to push it out. I shook my head against it before I turned to Detective Whoever and leaned forward. "Will you swear that he won't know that I told you? Do you pinky swear it?"

His wrinkled hand patted my own. "I can't promise that, Miss Samson. But I can promise that if you testify against your father in court, you'll never have to see him again."

I feigned sadness. I slumped back into my chair in sullen shock as the damned rhyme danced around my thoughts. Focus, girl. Focus! I looked to him. "I have to tell somebody, sir. I can't ... I just can't keep ..."Cue sobbing like mad; few seconds to let the damnable scratching stop, then start up again.

When I calmed myself, he asked me something about continuing, and it turned out I had the strength to do so. "Daddy had me get a knife ... cut ... cut her to pieces. I wasn't strong enough to cut through her ... her bones. He did that part. But I had to clean her up."

I was so proud of the way my voice sounded that I had to keep my face down to hide the satisfaction. "When we got her in the trash bag, he drove me out to Camper's Park and we threw her in the lake."

"My God, child." The detective whose name kept escaping me stared at me for a moment before standing. "Parker's Lake? Near the boat ramp?"

I shook my head and looked away as if ashamed. "No, sir. He threw her down on the side by Mulligan Road, near some big trees that break by the water."

He jotted the words down and reached for the door. The detective's eyes filled with sadness as he spoke words of encouragement, condolences, and the possibility of therapy. I found myself staring into nothing, ignoring the speech that was supposed to help me. I interrupted him with the only question that mattered to me now.

"Can I just go home now?" My eyes shifted to the harsh wrinkles in his shirt. For a moment, I wondered if he owned an iron.

"Of course, Miss. Samson, of course." He opened the door and stood beside it. I was all too careful to not to run for joy, but to act as if my bones were made of lead. I stopped just before I could pass him in the doorway, meeting his eyes as I whispered my words, "I kissed her goodbye before I had to put her head in the bag, sir. It was the last time I would ever get to do so."

And the Oscar goes to ... I left him frozen in place as I headed down a hallway lined with framed faces much too important to be forgotten. I walked into the lobby where my Aunt Phyllis had been waiting. She wrapped her arms around me the moment I approached her side. "Are you ready to go home, dear?" Her busy hands pressed down against my back as she led me through a mass of people waiting to receive services from the dead-eyed girls there to take their complaints. I followed her to the car and rubbed away imaginary tears as I slid into the passenger seat. "Yes, ma'am, I told them, I told them everything."

Phyllis' lips formed a grim line as she locked us both inside against the bright sun that came with a southern afternoon. "You are a good girl, Chelsea. I hope he rots in Hell. Danny Samson was never good enough. I told Amy time and time again to leave him. Now look what happened."

I smiled grimly against my hand as I watched the yellow line that divided the highway pass me by. You never said such a thing. Always 'Amy never could meet a bad man like I do.' or 'Danny's too good for the likes of you, sister.' But now ... oh, now you've always known how bad he was, even when he wasn't bad at all.

I ignored her rants as the car flew past happy houses and pretty lawns to examine the image captured against the window. My reflection showed a pretty girl whose jaw was too sharp to be refined with eyes that blurred against the greens and grays of the landscape outside. But you've got it all wrong, Aunt Phyllis. She wasn't good. She wasn't good at all. Momma tried to turn me into her. She was too hard. And I couldn't take it anymore, not for another single second.

Her voice scratched at my eardrums. I closed my eyes against her voice as my teeth ground together. I hate that noise. I hate it! First the pen, now her. Oh, God, shut her up! Shut her up!

"Aunt Phyllis, when we get home, can I lay down?" My eyes pleaded with her to stop speaking, to give me the silence that I craved. The ruse worked to perfection.

"Oh, of course, dear. After having to talk to the police again and having to tell them that horrible story. Why, I just couldn't imagine ..."

Her voice trailed off and I loved her for it. The thin skin of my bottom lip found itself wedged between my teeth as I bit back the smile that was threatening. The old cow. I had to run my story by somebody first. And she thinks she's so special because she was the first one to hear it. Now she pities me and thinks that I love her best! I guess that's what happens when you live alone for twenty years. You want anybody to make you feel wanted. Even if they do it just to use you.

The car stopped and I treaded along after her. I kissed her on the cheek before I walked upstairs, throwing my bag onto the desk she had placed up in the bedroom that had become mine the day my mother disappeared. I grimaced against the bright pink and yellow flowers that dominated every wall, every picture frame and every pillow in sight. But, I had to be careful, tell her that I loved it, that I was grateful for it. *Don't want to end up in the State Home.* I chuckled as I fell back against the bed. I wouldn't have a bit of freedom in doing that.

I breathed with ease for the first time that morning as my eyes closed. After I had 'confessed' to Phyllis, she made me go down to the Police Station and tell them my story. I didn't know if I could pull it off until Detective Whoever began to pat my elbow. He didn't have a chance. I smiled as I snuggled down into the pillows. Then again, neither did she.

My mother had been a beautiful woman who had found the man of her dreams at the age of twenty. The two settled down, had two kids, and tried to live happily ever after. Even after Joey died, Helen and Danny Samson were the envy of all who knew them. Helen was a combination of strength and beauty that she tried to pass on to me. But she couldn't know that I would use those lessons against her.

The people outside our house envied my mother, but they didn't know the real Helen, the Helen that dominated every conversation, the one whose husband cowered under her every command, the woman who forced me to excel in all the things she failed at beneath the threats of sullen silences or sharp shakings. I hated her! My mind screamed as my smile faded into the drawn line of tightened teeth. I still hate her! I'd do it again and again and again if I could!

Three weeks ago, she had finished breakfast and was telling me what I would be doing that summer. "Chelsea, I have signed you up for the Advanced Playwright's Classes down at the University for next month. It's quite the honor, you know. Only the best girls in your class will be eligible. Until then, I want you to study everything you can about writing plays. You will need to write until your fingers are stained blue from your ink. You must write until your pen becomes an indention into your fingers. "

"Yes, Momma." I took my plate to the sink, washed it, and put it away. She was still talking when I left the room and went into the den where Daddy kept his secret. It was a pistol I was sure that he planned to use in his suicide on the day her ranting finally drove him mad.

I had found it two years before, and thought it to be my savior whenever I would run my fingers over its plastic handle and cool trigger. I wondered what would happen to me if I went through with my plans. I walked back to the kitchen in a daze, realizing that I didn't care about the consequences. I'd get out of this just as I got out of everything else. I'd smile the charming smile that some other woman had taught me, cry the tears that I didn't feel, and lie through my teeth.

The surprise on her face stayed there long after the boom rocked the gun from my hand and the life from her body. Daddy ran downstairs and stood stunned as I convinced him that it was an accident. "I was just showing Momma a scene for a play, Daddy ... and I didn't know it was loaded, Daddy! Oh, God, my life is over!"

My father grabbed the gun from my hand, throwing it on the counter as I began shouting orders to him that he was more than willing to follow. Danny Samson had lost his only son, and now his only wife. I knew that he wouldn't be able to stand losing his only remaining daughter, too.

So, my father followed my orders. He moved with a precision that surprised me. Getting a knife from the drawer, cutting through skin and bone to make the pieces of her smaller, and creating a casket from the trash bags we kept under the sink for yard debris.

Daddy worked as a dead man would, or at least like one who was in shock. We really did dump her in the lake over at Camper's Park, but I didn't kiss her goodbye. A prisoner doesn't kiss their jailer, after all.

Too bad the gunshot caught the attention of the neighbors. I sighed, entwining my fingers to form the people and the steeple once more. The noise brought forth phone calls to the police. In fact, so many were made that two units were sitting in the driveway when Daddy and I got home. They were sorry to disturb us, of course, but they wanted to take a look around since so many people had called them.

Seeing the blood on the floor and the gun on the counter, they led Danny Samson away. I burst into the tears that were expected of me. Sorry, Daddy. You were always too much of a sheep willing to follow what other people told you to do, even your own kid. I kept the people locked inside the church of my own making as I folded my palms together and crushed them with a smile. Just like the people damned in that stupid rhyme.

You'll be lost forever in the world of my own making.

Learning to Pray

Debrin Case

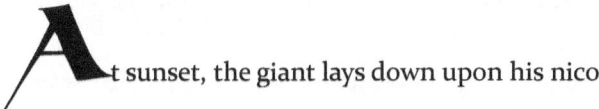

t sunset, the giant lays down upon his nicotine stained couch, pops a Kool out of his pack and into his mouth, lighting it with the same burnished chrome Zippo that had accompanied him through Vietnam and watches the evening news.

Like a metronome his arm moved with rhythm as he would inhale the cigarette deeply, and upon his exhale the lit cigarette would find its way to the awaiting (freshly cleaned) green glass ashtray that was held aloft upon a gilded cherub ashtray stand (that was as immaculate as the day it had been purchased from some trailer trash garage sale my mother had found somewhere in El Toro, California). After the first 6 or 7 drags, the giant that I was to refer to as Daddy, would then make a grab for the fresh cup of coffee my mother would usually have ready for him by then.

If the cup was waiting where he was expecting it (while reaching outward and upward over his right shoulder for the expected cup) and grabbing it correctly by the handle, the maneuver would go quite smoothly.

More often than not my mother's nervousness at making sure everything was perfect before He (the aforementioned Giant) would arrive home; caused her to have worked herself into quite a tizzy and was already tripping all over herself in order to make everything perfect in this little perfect world... a perfect little universe ruled over by a giant, whom (if I hadn't mentioned before) I had been told to call Daddy.

Now granted, he did look an awful lot like me, but much larger. Kind of like a blonde haired Santa without the beard, or the bottle of Coca Cola. No matter how my elder brother had tried to convince me that this giant was indeed my long lost father (I had misplaced him quite some time ago) I knew it wasn't so. After all if this giant happened to be my father, why I'd know it. There is just something special that lets you know those things. A deep gut reaction, it's a feeling. It's a feeling any six year old ought to be able to experience for themselves, after all I should know, I was six.

My elder brother Johnny (who now prefers to go by the name John, as if it's more dignified and less uncommon of a name or something), lovingly tried to convince me that this giant was in fact our dad... it was a pointless effort on his part.

"Geesh Donnie, Can't you tell that it's the same guy as in the pictures. The same ones we looked at over and over again? Do I need to pull out the photo album again? Dad and I even have the same name, which is why I'm a Jr. and you're not."

"Johnny is such a common name, and how do I know those pictures aren't faked?" I asked him bluntly.

We had recently watched an episode of some PBS documentary about faked UFO pictures and I was thoroughly convinced that if Aliens from outer space could fake their own photos so we wouldn't believe they were real (when in fact they were, and I already knew it, I was six; and as I said before where you are six you just know about the rightness of things), then I wouldn't put it past giants to be able to create fake photos as well as alter the memories of my beloved and yet somewhat addlebrained mother and brother. It was tough being the smartest one in this little bunch of bananas but someone needed to take care of them (after all, there were giants about).

"I was there, I remember it...heck Donnie, you were there too."

"If I was there, then why don't I remember it?"

"Maybe because you were a baby," He said exasperatedly.

"I went to Uncle Mack's funeral when I was 8 months old and I remember the whole thing, I even remember the song they sang and how Grandma cried and cried over the loss of her son."

"You don't remember anything," Johnny screeched," You just remember the story Grandma McGee told you over every plate of biscuits and bacon you ever got out of her. Hell, even I remember the funeral and I was still back in Hawaii with Dad, eating pizza and burgers every night. I even had my first taste of beer too."

"Who had their first taste of beer?" My mother quizzed as she peered in at us from the hallway between my bedroom door and the bathroom.

"He's lying mom," I said quickly in order to save my brother the wrath of having tried alcohol at the age of nine, and inadvertently saving the giant's behind as well (though entirely unintentionally on my part). "He was only trying to impress me with being older than me."

"Well drinking beer is nothing to be joking around about," she fussed at him as she fiddled with the worn out doorknob that led into the bathroom, "especially at your age."

With her last word, she slammed the door behind herself to find a Calgon moment in the afternoon.

"So what did it taste like?" I asked with an excited whisper.

"Kind of like cold piss."

"Ewwwwwww..... What's that taste like?"

"How should I know?" and he wandered to his bedroom, got out his banana board and headed outside to pretend he was some kind of Z-boy, there on the torn up asphalt in front of our house.

"There's no way that giant is my Dad." I muttered to myself as I carefully removed all of my toys from the toy chest and laid them out inside the closet, closed the closet door behind me and climbed into my toy chest while pulling the lid closed as well," After all he's a smoker. My daddy would never smoke."

Each night the Giant came home from this thing they called work, he would head towards the bathroom, strip to a white t-shirt and a pair of shorts and plop himself on the couch with relish as he waited for the T.V. to warm up. As he did so and the anchorwoman came into view he would grin slightly and give the room a quick sweep with his eyes before he would allow his smile to become wolfish with hunger.

The cigarette dangling in his lips at times would quiver when the buxom blonde news anchoress came on screen, as her colors shifted from a fuchsia to a more human skin tone. If mom was out of the room it would seem as if his cheeks were flushed with excitement, and if mom was in the room he made sure not to pay the T.V. any attention whatsoever as he attempted to make small talk with either myself or my brother if we happened to be in the room, or grab the Louis Lamour novel conveniently laying on the coffee table for occasions such as these.

More often than not, Dad got to ogle his T.V. Land girlfriend... and so did I, she was a knockout.

As we awaited the giant's coffee, often the camera angle hit the screen just right and we would get to see the top of her bosom in a way that is now elegantly done only on Spanish speaking T.V. channels these days, and when these rare occurrences happened, the giant could not contain his glee. It was as if his team had scored a goal, or a run or whatever damn sports analogy you may infer from this reference, because by golly, that is exactly what it sounded like.

This often would cause my mother to run into the living room from the dining room entryway that adjoined the kitchen, in order to find what all the commotion had been about. After all, excitement was such a rare commodity to be found here in Happy-Land that sometimes those oddball sorts of things were all that was needed to keep one away from the cloudy mindless fog that happened to be our existence.

"Oh I thought I saw someone I knew in that last segment," he would mutter as he took another drag off the Kool he dangled artfully between his lips.

At which point she'd turn around back to the kitchen, he'd give me a wink and a grin and I'd reciprocate to the best of my ability and waited with him for yet another glorious camera shot that was bound to happen before the evening news was completed.

It was during these moments of shared lechery, that I could almost look past his gigantic form and see my father nestled deep inside of him, just waiting to get to know me. This vision would usually pass between puffs on his cigarette, and as quickly as the bond had been formed it would dissipate in the whisper of smoke exhaled from his nostrils and gathering about his head.

At promptly 6:31PM every night, dinner was laid out on the table and the television was turned off, no matter what happened to be on at the time. Though other people we knew had started getting Beta Max recorders and VCRs in our neighborhood, my father couldn't abide such technological fads, and as such we often missed great moments in television history as I discovered from my classmates the following day in school.

During mealtime, he would leave his most recently burning cigarette still alight in the ashtray while he hurried through his evening meal so he could return to his reclining position on the kelly green corduroy couch. Often times finishing his meal with enough time to return to the still smoldering butt of his cigarette that had become a tower of ash in his absence, and still he managed to suck out at least two more drags off the impotent little thing before snubbing it out and lighting up a fresh one.

I had never seen the giant try to light and inhale logging chains, nor even the sorts used to walk a dog. But the man could go through a number of those cylinders in an evening of relaxation in that living room where I grew up on Fenwick drive.

This was normal, this was every single night. This was life in the Case household.

A frantic mother, a brother doing homework in his bedroom, myself sprawled in front of the T.V. and a giant who desperately needed to have a

218

chimney installed in order to maintain the amount of smoke he bellowed from his lungs.

Together, we watched Jack Tripper stumble over himself through another zany misadventure involving scantily clad girls, or reruns of I Love Lucy or the occasional hardnosed western with all the grit and sawdust that Hollywood could muster.

Together we cried over fictional characters that were at best two dimensional, together we discussed matters that didn't truly matter that much in the great scheme of things. Simple family style arguments, and moments of sheer affection as I remember those days when I would be carried to bed while half asleep by the Giant who I was often reminded to call Daddy.

It was one of those nights, one of those times when my eyes were still fuzzy as I fought off sleep while that giant (who may, or may not have been my Daddy) tucked me into bed. It was on that night I asked him a direct question, and I never forgot his answer.

"Why do you smoke?"

He paused for a moment and looked me deep in the eye and said softly," It's the only way I have left to pray."

"Dad, prayer is easy, all you have to do is kneel besides your bed and talk with your hands folded upwards like this, I usually do it every night before mama puts me to bed."

He smiled kind of sharply at me, "Well Donnie, It's been a long time since my mama tucked me into bed. She stopped doing that with me back when I was about four. I had so many other brothers and sisters that needed her attention far more than I did. Oh I tried it by myself, but it just wasn't the same. If it weren't for reading a Man Called Horse, I don't know if I would have ever been able to pray again."

"But it's killing you, Smoking is bad for you." I said very quietly.

"Yes son, it is... but that is why it's a sacrifice. Sacrifice and prayer go hand in hand. Now enough chatter, time for you to get some sleep."

"I don't understand; how can hurting yourself be a good thing?"

"Even Atlas needed a break from holding up the world, Donnie; some believe he even shrugs now and again." He spoke as he wandered out of my room and headed back to the living room to catch the remaining moments of Johnny Carson's monolog (of which I could hear only as a white noise wave of canned laughter and a sharp voice full of intoned wit, without really hearing any sort of detail).

As I lay there in my bedroom that night, I knew the Giant that could very well be my father (if only he would stop smoking) could be saved from his silliness. I knew beyond a shadow of doubt that anyone could pray in the same way that I did it every night. If it weren't as easy as tying a shoelace, or zipping up a pair of corduroy pants then I would never have been able to do it. I knew it for what it was... an excuse, an excuse to shut me up and allow him to continue with his filthy habit.

My crusade to rescue the Giant from himself began the next day, and it lasted for six years.

Six years of no smoking signs placed in his freestanding ashtray. Six years of free literature I would find for the Giant at the public library about the dangers of smoking, artfully laid out for him to read on the coffee table (replacing his trusty Louis Lamour book's position in easy reach of a needed excuse), or in the toilet paper roll holder in the bathroom. Six years of exploding cigarette loads, or snow storm loads, or stink loads or whatever other kind of cigarette ruining device I could find at the local joke shop.

Six year of asking the giant to stop smoking, six years of almost getting him angry at me over my incessant pleas to have him quit smoking forever.

Six years of wasted pleas falling on deaf ears.

Six years of ravaged forests to make pamphlets that were never read.

Six years of a man that knew how to laugh at a practical joke, and since cigarettes were far cheaper in those days, he considered it far more of an entertaining inconvenience rather than some kind of punishable offense. I often wondered if he took some kind of glee in trying to figure out just how we were going to try and spoil his smoking experience that week. We became our own little T.V. sit-com, and it would have been a Neilson success if it would have been given a pilot and a test audience.

My drive to help the Giant to stop smoking transferred over to my mother and brother, as they too worked with me in my nefariously devious schemes to stop him from smoking. Even with all of our great minds working together, we still couldn't prevent nor persuade the giant from inhaling one cigarette after another.

"Dad," My brother would plead with disgust in his voice," Don't you know you are killing yourself every time you have one of those things?"

"Rest assured, Johnny, the cigarettes aren't killing me." He said with a calmness that is rather chilling when I think back upon it now.

Though steam engines would have been put to shame by the amount of exhaust he could exhale in a single day, the giant was quite correct, the cigarettes weren't killing him, but his secrets were.

Giants always have secrets.

The infamous Giant in Jack and the Beanstalk was full of secrets. Mysteries beyond compare, deep magical occult mysteries that were beyond any understanding of mortal men... or boys, like Jack, could even comprehend.

But that didn't mean we couldn't figure those things out. After all, the amazing things in those stories about giants or dragons are never so much about the creature, but the people who conquered or defeated them after discovering their weakness or having their hand lead by something far more powerful than themselves.

Jack may have not been bigger, or faster, or richer or more powerful than his giant. In fact he was a poor little bumpkin from the edge of nowhere. Penniless and virtually starving to death, but he had one thing the giant did not, and that was the wits to figure out how to "Liberate" the giant's wealth and good fortune for the betterment of the world... or at least for his poor old mother, himself and more than likely the local economy.

Like all who grow from childhood into becoming something else, the secrets begin early on in their life, and progressively become deeper and more complex as time winds its way through their existence. From the beginning all the way to the end, a life becomes littered with secrets and moments of reflection (as well as regression) never quite knowing if you did the right thing... never quite knowing if you did the wrong thing. With each regression is produced a progression of girth, a spurt of height or a composite of fat that could form about the child, either gradually taking them into sane adulthood or more than likely reshaping them into the composite creature that their minds believed would be the best form for them in order that they may be able to take on the world.

The Giant had secrets that stretched out for miles in all directions, they started in cotton picking fields when he was 7 and only grew thicker along the road that lead him to becoming a Marine, they carried him through the discovery of his being infected with Agent Orange Disease and through his numerous indiscretions and habits he had formed in order to deal with his impending demise.

Through it all, the Giant had deluded himself into believing that he deserved to be the Giant he had become, and though I knew none of those secrets at that time, I knew that there were secrets and I wanted to help him set those little sorrows free. There was a chance ... a slim fraction of a chance(that I had learned about from all the fairytales and bible stories that I had been exposed to in my life already) that perhaps he didn't have to be a giant any longer.

Even a giant could be saved.

Two years before the Giant fell to the earth and became a mountain (as all giants do according to traditional legends about such things) he toppled to the ground in what was a precursor to the adventure that my family was about to embark on together.

I watched his metronomic flicking of ashes that evening; instead of paying attention to Mr. Roarke, I watched the Giant, he looked different that night. I can't tell you that his skin looked paler or jaundiced, or if his eyes were droopy or twitchy, or if the way he smoked his way through another pack of Kools was somehow slower or faster than before, I could only say things were just a little off in some indefinable way.

When the 9:15 pm commercial break came on, my father rose from the couch (as he had always done) to go make his official nightly deposit in the throne room and with a paperback book in hand, took three steps away from the couch and fell over in such an odd manner, it reminded me of the slow motion replay camera work used during football games.

As he fell his eyes rolled back into his head, and I saw my mother screaming and running forward to catch him. Though what good would it do for a 98 lb. woman to try to catch a 300 lb. man I will never know, but she stretched out her arms as if to cradle him from a fall as the tears streamed down her face while screaming no almost as slowly as the giant fell to the ground. With a shudder the whole house shook, and even the windows rattled slightly when he finally collapsed upon the beige carpeted floors.

As he lay on the ground, the cigarette in his left hand smoldered at the scotch-guarded carpet, which though my mother ignored in her attempts to revive the Giant I quickly pulled it from his hand and stubbed out the very first cigarette I ever touched.

She pleaded with God as she repeatedly slapped and beat upon the Giant,

"Jesus, don't take him away (whack). God don't let him die (smack)... He's too young to leave me now (Slap)... I can't raise a young boy by myself (Pow). We'll go back to church (Thump) we'll tithe regularly (Wham) my youngest son will become your servant (Ka-Blammo)"

The giant's eyes rolled forward, he coughed and asked, "Why is everyone staring down at me?"

With tears of joy my mother helped the giant back to the couch, and convinced the giant he needed to see a doctor right away.

The Giant, my Mother and I were in the emergency room of Baylor hospital for the rest of the night, while we waited for blood tests to come back from the lab and for my brother to join up with us after completing his shift at the local Whataburger.

When the doctor finally arrived with the results from the various tests they had performed, the giant sent us all out of the room. Not even allowing my mother to remain behind; though she tried valiantly to stand up for her rights as the wife of the giant to know what was going on, he patronized her as if he were her father rather than her husband and explained to her calmly with a smile, "If it is anything you need to worry about, I'll be sure to tell you everything, Honeypie."

We waited in the hall as we heard a muffled argument between the doctor and the giant, if the giant had been in better physical shape my imagination informed me that the he would have performed something rather giantly...or Hulk-like, and thrown the puny doctor out the window or through the door. Instead, the Doctor hurriedly ran out the hospital room door with a huff and sneered at my mother as he sharply spat," That man will not listen to reason. He won't even let me tell you what is going on!"

"What can I do for him?" my mother pleaded.

"Whatever you do, don't let him have another cigarette... not half of one, not even one little drag. No more cigarettes...ever."

The giant checked out of the hospital 5 days later, he had already finished 8 packs of Kools by then. Still smoking, even under the watchful eye of the same Doctor who had forbidden him from doing so. Smiling and laughing and punctuating his illustrious tales with popping motions and wild hand gestures with a burning cigarette in his hands at all times. Times were simpler then, no one dared to dream of a day when smoking wasn't allowed everywhere.

"Mr. Case, I already told you not to smoke another cigarette. Your condition can't handle it any longer."

"What condition is he talking about John?" My mother asked worriedly on one occasion.

"Oh he's just puffing up his degree and trying to show us how much smarter he is than a couple of hicks from Mississippi. I'm fine Honey; I will be out of this bed before you know it and back to work without any more problems."

He would then comfort my mother by pulling her to his chest, all the while giving the evil eye to the Doctor, until the man could do nothing other than leave the room.

"But, Doctor's are supposed to know all about these things, John. What if there is a reason you shouldn't smoke anymore. He told me not to let you smoke anymore." She would sniffle out as the giant would smooth out her hair while she cried against his chest.

"Who are you going to trust, Some Doctor you barely know... or me?"

Of course, the giant didn't get any better.

More Doctor visits equated to more cigarettes smoked. What had once been a pack and a half a day habit quickly became a 3 pack a day habit. One lit after another, sometimes he would be holding onto the burning butt of one cigarette in the left hand, while a freshly lit one rested in his right.

Plumes of smoke following him like fog clung to him in every direction as he rose from his couch to head anywhere in our home. While stains of ashes and new cigarette burn holes found their way to decorate not only his white t-shirt but also the couch, coffee table and even the wall that headed down the hall towards the only bathroom in our home.

After months of tests and consulting with different Doctors, one night, at the family dinner table, the Giant finally explained to us some of what was going on.

"They say I have cancer, I'm going to start radiation next Wednesday," he calmly stated between bites of mashed potatoes and the fried chicken we had picked up earlier at the Churches not far from our home.

I had heard of cancer before, it was one of the main reasons I knew for people not to smoke. Smokers got cancer, and Cancer was bad.... Real bad.

"I mean hell, what's cancer?" he asked us in his quiz show voice he saved for those occasions when he had to mesmerize us all with his wit and wisdom," Why if you look at it from an astrological point of view it's a crab. Now as you all already know I'm a Leo... and that means I'm a lion so therefore we can assume that in a fair fight a lion would beat a crab any ol' day... so we've got nothing else to worry about. End of discussion. Honey, could I get another cup of coffee, please?"

In a daze, my mother grabbed his mug walked into the kitchen calmly and then slammed that mug with all of her might into the wall right behind the coffee pot. It hit a beam that was hidden behind the sheetrock; and though the impact barely made a ding to the paint of the wall, the mug shattered and scattered itself so thoroughly and so loudly it could almost be described as the sounds one would hear after someone fired a mortar on a battlefield.

"She'll be fine," the Giant beamed at us while helping himself to another helping of green beans from the quart sized Styrofoam container that sat upon the dining room table.

Later that night as the giant would light one prayer after another while engrossed in an episode of Quincy; my mother was stretched out on her bedroom floor praying as I had never seen her do before. As I peered through the crack between the door and the doorway, she looked up at the precise moment and begged me to pray with her, to plead with God to save the life of the Giant and to protect our family from impending doom.

As we kneeled over the family bible (the big one that was stored under the coffee table in the living room, the only bible we had owned (up to that time)) my mother's prayers became incessant. Pleading with God promising him my life and service, if He (God) would spare the Giant's life. Though giants as a general rule are rather scary creatures, finding themselves a far better fit in storybooks and movies than they do in most people's lives, but I knew deep in my heart that he was our giant and I also prayed that he would be alright. As she cried, I too cried. I cried out to God on that night and many nights after.

Sometimes we would pray with my Father in the room as he got ready for work, or another Doctor's appointment. On occasion we gathered in my bedroom or even outside in the garden as we plucked weeds that were encroaching on our tomato vines.

She prayed for the Giant to stay alive and for the salvation of his soul if that was not possible in the great scheme of things, while I prayed that the

Giant would become a normal man again, and perhaps have the opportunity to become my Daddy.

Radiation treatment and Chemotherapy in the early 80's was nowhere near the art form it is today, many people often preferred visiting quacks and charlatans, on the off chance that some sort of miracle would fall into their laps; many of them believing that they had better chances at beating cancer with metaphysical methods rather than what had been approved treatment plans by modern western medicine.

However my father trudged through the chemotherapy and the radiation treatments like the soldier he had always been. 25 years of military service kind of helps walk you through many different sorts of battlefields, and the warfare of cancer is no different.

He lost his golden blonde hair, and took to wearing a blue denim cap that proved to fans of Steve Martin and Dan Ackroyd that he too was a "Wild and Crazy Guy." He started losing weight, and the rolls of flab that developed under his neck and arms and waist, became new platforms on which old jokes could be propped up nicely. He fell asleep more often while doing other things, only to awaken with a startled look if you tried to help him rescue his glasses from being crushed, or remove the still burning cigarette from his hand.

In the mornings he would cough up copious amounts of slimy green and brownish phlegm (with a roar that sounded like a dying lion) into the rapidly running sink in the bathroom. Often finding either myself, my brother or my mother waiting for him on the other side of the door when he emerged.

He would twist his scowl into a smile before our eyes had a chance to twinkle, assure us that all was well and hurriedly continue on his way.

In those in-between times when he was either dressing or undressing for the day, I saw the dotted lines and X's that had been drawn over his body with permanent markers by the doctors. It was designed like some kind of pirate's treasure map when viewed in conjunction with the many tattoos that the giant had acquired in his 25 years of active service in the Corp.

When I explained my observation to him, he laughed and said that in some ways it could be just like a treasure map, except there was no gold doubloons nor pieces of eight hiding under those Xs that had been drawn onto his skin, but they were the points where there were fiercely malignant tumors and these were the places that had to be bombarded with radiation.

In spite of all of this, the Giant still smoked.

"If ever a man needed to pray, it would be today." He would say if we questioned him about his continued smoking.

"John, that's not a prayer. If you really want to learn how to pray ... I'll teach you, heck, even Donnie or Johnny could teach you." My mother would beseech, through the billowy clouds of smoke he expunged from his lungs into the room.

"I already know how to pray like a man, Sweetie," He would say with another drag, "I will be just fine."

Every night was still the same as it always had been, with one cigarette being burned after another in a succession of Kool filter kings, an homage to a royal lineage, forgotten to the sands of time.

Whether the Giant's prayers that had been held aloft by plumes of smoke had reached God's nose, or by the frantic petitions screeched out by my mother, myself or the local prayer groups had reached the ears of god; I truly couldn't say. Even the doctors were dumbfounded, for one day he had stage 4 cancer and the next there wasn't a single tumor infesting his body.

They called it remission, we called it a miracle.

Though the Giant still couldn't possibly be my father, I had taken to calling him daddy over the years as they trickled by in some kind of richness enhancing slowdown of time. These moments were often punctuated with what can only be described as moments of nostalgic bliss and rapture. They were peppered with the standard amount of love, and laughter and hugs. Gentle brushings of lips against foreheads, and squeezes of joy. Everything had been left in the hands of various gods. Gods of sacrifice who commanded their followers to forgo forbidden pleasures... gods of sacrifice that required pain to be inflicted upon their followers by their own hand in acts of contrition or atonement.

That last year (before the final fall of the Giant I had known could never be my Father) had remolded him into something far more than the storybook illusion of a man I imagined him to be, and though rationally he was nowhere near what I thought my Father would have been given life in a perfect world (and granted there was never such a thing, even if nostalgia clouds your mind into believing otherwise) I allowed him to fill that void and become my Daddy in that last year that I or anyone else ever had the privilege of knowing him.

227

Still he wielded his smoldering prayer stick fervently, zealously, devotedly smoking it down to its fiberglass filter. Each night returned to the dance it had always been. A cup of coffee in hand, some sit-com on the tube and that ever present package of cellophane wrapped Kool filter kings sitting on the table beside his couch.

Lazily he thumbed through the Sunday television supplement that kind of looked like a cheap magazine one night, on that night... on his final night in our home.

With a smile he asked me to change the channel, and just in time we caught the opening credits of a movie I had often heard described as a short story in a book before, but never seen.

"A Man called Horse" was emblazoned on the old UHF channel, and in silence we all watched a simple man become a warrior and I began to understand what the Giant had been saying without words, all along.

Not all of us watched the whole thing. My Mother and Brother couldn't handle the whole experience, often times dashing out of the room at the most elegantly disturbing moments of the film.

I could only stare at the TV in rapt attention, occasionally moving my eyes away to watch the Giant (whom I had recently begun to call Daddy with an honest intent). Catching glimpses of him mumbling lines from the film, or shedding a tear at moments when he felt great pride in the man who left one noble tribe for another.

When the film finally rolled the credits, he looked over at me and was rather surprised that I finished the entire film with him without budging. In fact we were the only two left in the room.

"I thought you would be the first to leave, Donnie." He spoke calmly as he eyed me while lighting another cigarette.

"I had to understand." It was all I could say, and now that I understood I knew that no matter where along the great timeline of all things that the man I formally thought of as a giant was simply nothing more than a man, the very man who happened to be my Father.

The big riddle of secrets that seem to gather about a person as they grow from nothing more than a speck into something far greater or tragically far less than anyone could truly comprehend. Those secrets build you and shape you, transform you and guide you. In your heart they toil and shape with crushing blows, and silent forgotten woes, turmoil and heartache, it was a sad and lonely keening song that flooded your entire being... it was being alive, and sometimes there was nothing left to do when the gods had taken away everything from you than to just give them a little more, oftentimes of your own flesh in exchange for perhaps a modicum of mercy... that always seemed out of reach, and far too often it was never enough.

With a watery eye he spoke, "I believe you might just understand everything about me now."

I hugged him goodnight and went to bed dreaming of what it truly meant to be human, what it truly meant to be a man.

The next day I was woken by my Aunt, instead of my Mother, and as she prepared a bag for me to take with me over to her house she explained that something had happened during the night and my Father was back in the hospital again and I would be staying with her for a few days because there would be no one here in my home to take care of me.

As underwear and pajamas found their way into the waiting gym bag, I could only see images of the man I knew to be my father standing in front of a tribe of Indian warriors as they pierced his chest with eagle talons and hoisted him into the air onto the great tree in order for him to dance unto the sun. As we loaded her old Ford station wagon with various odds and ends I would need for my stay in her home, I thought of the peace pipe being passed among the elders as they watched many brave men dance suspended from their chests as they prayed for each man in turn. With their prayers carried upwards on ladders of smoke that reached from deep within their individual souls and penetrated the nostrils of the creator itself.

As each man swung from the tree they swayed, and sprawled in a macabre dance that only warriors and holy men could ever understand. Standing there against the great all there ever was, and saying look at me... I am yours ... hear me... feel my pain.

The images in my mind faded as we pulled into Sears and I was fitted for a suit, though my Aunt commented how I would have to get one of the husky sized boy's suits, nothing else was shared with me.

Three days later I was being escorted into the hospital and through trickery mingled with the kindness of my Dad's attending physician, I was allowed to enter the room where my father spent his final days. Normally the hospital would not allow children under the age of thirteen to walk past the elevator doors, much less even see this floor. It was there in this last stolen moment where people were allotted a chance at saying goodbye that I met with my Father, alone.

There were no nurses attending to his respirator, which happened to be snugly taped under his nose, no one making sure that the I.V. needle that protruded from the back of his hand was secure with the severe lash like straps of surgical tape that held it firmly affixed in place. No one was peering up from a note pad and trying to prognosticate in whatever manner they could surmise, how to save this man who had once been a giant from the fate of an inevitable death.

Instead there was only him, and I. The hospital bed, and portable desk that stretched out in front of him with a plethora of goodies that seemed somehow gratuitous and gaudy against the pallor of his skin. There synthetic tubes and wires of multiple gauges and lengths that streamed from diverse machines scattered about the room and connecting with almost every visible portion of his body in one form or another. Unlike the freewheeling giant I had known for many of the past twelve years of my life, this withered titan instead reclined like some sickly demented marionette held in bondage by the devices that were given the laborious task of keeping him alive. Just long enough so he could say goodbye, to no one other than me, and me alone.

"Shouldn't Mom and Johnny be in here too," I asked softly as I listened to the monitor thump out his heartbeats, like a metronome they held a solid rhythm keeping time with the concertina wheezing of the respirator behind him.

"I've already had plenty of time with the both of them; I haven't seen you for days. Come on over and sit beside me, I need to tell you a few things."

My father then proceeded to explain to me the mysteries of the universe as only an ex-marine knew how. Bluntly without many sugary flowers to decorate the cake of what would become my life once the giant was no longer in our kingdom, how I too would have to be strong, how I too may have to do things that didn't seem right or wrong. How I too would gather to myself secrets. Secrets to keep people happy, even more secrets to keep people safe. Secrets that would change me, into whatever it was that one day I would become. Whether that be a man, a sorcerer or even a giant like himself.

As we sat there together I slowly started changing into whatever it was I was intended to become, evolving as I listened to a voice I can only remember as something that may have been. Like all great legends (especially those about giants) many details are lost. It doesn't matter how hard you try to hold onto the minutia that creates all of the many nuances of any frozen moment of time.

I knew this was goodbye, goodbye for possibly and quite potentially forever, though I had faith that there could potentially be more, somewhere deep inside myself told me that this moment... this brief second was all that I would ever have. Never again to be repeated, never again to be felt or savored in quite the same way it was right at that second.

"You're going to die, aren't you?"

"Everything dies, everything is born dying. It is a daily struggle, for life to express itself. Entropy abounds around every corner; death is but a breath away. Whether by accident or by design.... Everything dies. Even Gods have died."

I held tightly to my Giant, my Father, and sobbed and sniffled and snotted my way over what had once been a clean hospital gown. He comforted his youngest boy the best an Ex-marine of 25 years knew how... deeply, by holding me tightly to his chest and crying along with me.

"I knew I would see the day you would become a man," He said as he grasped me, "and like me, it happened before you had half a chance to grow any hair on your balls."

We got to sit together for another 5 minutes in silent acceptance of our fates. His to shuffle off this mortal coil, and me to become the responsible man-child who did atrocious things in order to survive a world gone mad without a giant (much like Atlas)who held the world aloft and in order for us all.

As the realization struck me, the nurse came in to let us know that visiting hours were over and I would have to leave now so my Dad could get some rest. As I made my way out of the room, my father asked me for a favor.

"Donnie, would you help me pray, one last time?"

I paused where I stood and without even looking at him again, I nodded my head once and left the room as quietly as I had arrived.

Three days later I was sitting on a metal lawn chair under a green canopy as I listened to a twenty one gun salute being given by four of the honor guard attending my father's funeral, while the two remaining members of the honor guard folded those stars and stripes and field of blue into the shape of a paper football, and handed it to my mother with silence, respect, gratitude and a sharp salute.

As the madness unfolded in pretty fights, and jealousies and well wishes, covered plates of food and heartfelt hugs and tears, I found my way into the garage and pulled out the pack of Kools I had placed inside the pocket of my new blue blazer made for husky boys that I had worn at the funeral that day.

I fished the burnished chrome Zippo (the same one that had accompanied my father in Vietnam) out of the left front pocket of my matching slacks, and with the first turn of the wheel I lit the cigarette that dangled artfully from my pursed lips.

"Our Father, who art in heaven ..." I began as I inhaled the first of many prayers to come.

www.ingramcontent.com/pod-product-compliance
Lightning Source LLC
Chambersburg PA
CBHW050511260626
47157CB00004B/1280